Kubion turned away and walked back to his car. An idea began to nudge his mind. Snowbound, he thought. Nobody can get in or out of the valley. No contact with the outside except by telephone. Made-to-order kind of situation, by God. How much dough was there around? Might even be as much as thirty or forty thousand in the valley. . . .

It was a wild concept: rip off an entire valley. Wouldn't that be something! But three men couldn't execute a caper like that—or could they? Well, there was probably a way to do it and get away with it, all right. The snowbound business took care of any outside interference; it would be like working in a big sealed room. . . .

But a whole valley, a whole goddamn valley.

Could it be done, with just three men?

SNOWBOUND

by Bill Pronzini

A FAWCETT CREST BOOK

Fawcett Publications, Inc., Greenwich, Connecticut

For BRUNI, who suffered too;

and for CLYDE TAYLOR, who had faith and several good ideas;

and for HENRY MORRISON, Agent 001

SNOWBOUND

THIS BOOK CONTAINS THE COMPLETE TEXT OF THE ORIGINAL HARDCOVER EDITION.

A Fawcett Crest Book reprinted by arrangement with G. P. Putnam's Sons

Library of Congress Catalog Card Number: 73-87200

Printed in the United States of America

First printing: April 1975

1 2 3 4 5 6 7 8 9 10

Book One

Monday, December 17, Through Saturday, December 22

Whenever the door of hell opens,
the voice you hear is your own

—Philip Wylie
Generation of Vipers

One

Mantled with a smooth sheen of snow, decorated with tinsel and giant plastic candy canes and strings of colored lights, the tiny mountain village looked both idyllic and vaguely fraudulent, like a movie set carefully erected for a remake of *White Christmas.* The dark, winter-afternoon sky was pregnant with more snow, and squares of amber shone warmly in most of the frame and false-fronted buildings; despite the energy crisis, the bulbs strung across Sierra Street burned in steady hues. On the steep valley slopes to the west, south and east, the red fir and lodgepole pine forests were shadowed, white-garbed, and as oddly unreal as the village itself.

A car with its headlamps on came down through the long, cliff-walled pass to the north—County Road 235-A, the only road presently open into or out of the valley —and passed the pine board sign reading: HIDDEN VALLEY • POPULATION 74 • ELEVATION 6,033. Just before Garvey's Shell, where the county road became Sierra Street, the car moved slowly beneath the spanning Christmas decorations, past the Valley Café and Hughes' Mercantile and the Valley Inn and Tribucci Bros. Sport Shop.

When it reached the All Faiths Church, at the end of the three-block main street, it turned into the fronting lot and then swung around to the small cottage at the rear: the Reverend Peter Keyes, home from the larger town of Soda Grove, eight miles to the north, where he had relatives.

Diagonally across from the church—beyond the village proper, beyond Alpine Street and the house belonging to retired County Sheriff Lew Coopersmith—was a long, snow-carpeted meadow. In its center a boy and a girl were building a snowman, their breaths making puffs of vapor in the thin, chill air. Traditionally, they used sticks for ears and arms and a carrot for a nose and shiny black stones for vest buttons and eyes and to form a widely smiling mouth. Once they had finished, they stood back several paces and fashioned snowballs and threw them at the man-figure until they succeeded in knocking off its head.

Sierra Street continued on a steady incline for another one hundred and fifty yards and Y-branched then into two narrow roads. The left fork was Macklin Lake Road, which serpentined through the mountains for some fifteen miles and eventually emerged in another adjacent community known as Coldville; deep drifts made it impassable during the winter months. Three miles from the village was the tiny lake which gave the road its name, as well as a large hunting and fishing lodge—closed and deserted now, eight days before Christmas—that catered to spring and summer tourists and to seasonal sportsmen. The right fork, cleared by the town plow after each heavy snowfall, became Mule Deer Lake Road and led to a greater body of water two miles to the southwest, at the rearmost corner of the valley. Near this lake were several summer homes and cabins, as well as three year-round residences.

The third valley road was Lassen Drive. It began in the village, two blocks west of Sierra Street, extended in a gradual curve a mile and a half up the east slope, and then thinned out into a series of hiking paths and nature trails. Hidden Valley's largest home was located on Lassen Drive, a third of the way up the incline; nestled in thick pine, but with a clear view of the village and the southern and western slopes, it was a two-storied rustic with an alpine roof and a jutting, Swiss-style veranda. Matt Hughes, the mayor of Hidden Valley and the owner of Hughes' Mercantile, lived there with his wife, Rebecca.

Five hundred yards above was a small A-frame cabin, also nestled in pine, also with a clear view, also belonging to Matt Hughes. Neither the Hugheses nor any of the other residents of Hidden Valley knew much about the man who had leased the cabin late the previous summer—the man whose name was Zachary Cain. They had no idea where he had come from (other than it might have been San Francisco) or what he did for a living or why he had chosen to reside in this isolated valley high in the northwestern region of California's Sierra Nevada; he offered no information, he was totally reticent and unknowable. All they knew for certain was that he never left the valley, ventured into the village only to buy food and liquor, received a single piece of mail every month and that a cashier's check for three hundred dollars, drawn on a San Francisco bank, which he cashed at the Mercantile. Some said, because of the quantity of liquor he bought and apparently consumed each week, that he was an alcoholic recluse. Others believed he was an asocial and independently well-off eccentric. Still others thought he was in hiding, that maybe he was a fugitive of one type or another, and this had caused some consternation on the part of a small minority of residents; but when Lew Coopersmith, on the urging of Valley Café owner Frank McNeil, checked Cain's name and description through the offices of the county sheriff, he learned enough to be sure that Cain was not wanted by any law enforcement agency—and then dropped the matter, because it would have been an invasion of privacy to pursue it further. As a result, the villagers finally, if somewhat grudgingly, accepted Cain's presence among them and left him for the most part strictly alone.

Which was, of course, exactly the way he wanted it.

He sat now, as he often did, at the table by the cabin's front window, looking down on Hidden Valley. He was a big, dark man with thick-fingered hands that gave the impression of power and, curiously, gentleness. The same odd mixture was in the long, squarish cast of his face and had once been in his bar-browed gray eyes, but the eyes now were haunted, filled with emptiness, like old old houses which had been abandoned by their owners. Brown-black hair grew thickly, almost furlike, on his scalp and arms and hands and fingers, giving him a faintly but not unpleasantly bearish appearance. The image was enhanced by the gray-flecked beard he had grown five months earlier for the simple reason that he no longer cared to continue the daily ritual of shaving. The waxy look of the skin pulled taut across his cheekbones and beneath his eyes added ten false years to his age of thirty-four.

The cabin had two rooms and a bath, with knotty pine walls and thick beams that crisscrossed the high, peaked ceiling. It was furnished spartanly: in the living room, a small stone fireplace, a settee with cushions upholstered in material the color of autumn leaves, a matching chair, a short waist-high pine breakfast counter behind which were cramped kitchen facilities; in the bedroom, visible through an open door on the far side of the room, an unmade bed and a dresser and a curve-backed wicker chair. There were no individual, homelike touches anywhere—no photographs or books or paintings or masculine embellishments of any kind; the cabin was still the same impersonal tourist and hunters' accommodation it had been when he leased it.

On the window table in front of Cain was a bottle of

bonded bourbon, a glass containing three fingers of the liquor, a package of cigarettes, and an overflowing ashtray. The only times he moved were to lift the glass to his mouth or to refill it when it became empty or to light another cigarette. It was very quiet in the cabin, but he could hear the cold clean humming of the wind as it blew across the face of the slope, fluttering snow from the branches of the trees and tugging querulously at the weatherstripping around the glass. And he could hear, too, from time to time, the faint strains of the recorded Christmas carols which constantly emanated from the Mercantile's outside loudspeakers and which, owing to the thinness of the air, were sometimes audible even this far above the village.

As had happened before in the past two weeks, each of them brought forth memory fragments from the bright corners of his mind. . . .

> Oh come all ye faith-ful, joy-ful and tri-um-phant,
> Oh come ye, oh co-o-me ye, to Be-e-eth-le-hem. . . .

. . . Angie singing those words softly, sweetly, as they trimmed the tree the year before, smiling, that question-mark loop of gold hair hanging down over her left eye, her face slightly flushed from the hot-buttered rums they'd drunk earlier, and Lindy tugging at the hem of her dress, dancing up and down, saying, "Mommy, Mommy, let me put the angel on top, let me put the angel on top!" and Steve hanging his stocking on the mantel, very intent, very careful, the top of his small tongue held catlike in the open space between his missing front teeth. . . .

> Si-i-ilent night. Ho-o-ly night.
> All is calm, all is bright.
> Round yon vir-r-gin, Mother and Child. . . .

. . . Angie's voice again, softer, reverent, while all of

them sat in the darkened living room and looked at the winking lights of the tree, the kids drowsy but refusing to give in because they wanted to wait up for Santa Claus, Angie's voice making the words into a lullaby that finally put them both to sleep, and he and Angie carrying them upstairs and putting them to bed and then tiptoeing downstairs again and setting out the presents, filling the stockings, and, when everything was arranged, going up to their own room and lying close, holding each other in the silent, holy night. . . .

Cain got abruptly to his feet, shoving his chair back, and carried his glass away from the window. He stood unsteadily in the center of the room, looking at the fireplace, and it reminded him of the one in the house near San Francisco's Twin Peaks, the house that no longer was. He turned away and went across to the breakfast counter and around it into the kitchen area for a fresh package of cigarettes. Spasmodically, he tore off the cellophane and got one of the cylinders into his mouth and began patting the pockets of his Pendleton shirt. His matches were on the table. He went over there again, sat down, lit the cigarette, drained the bourbon from his glass; then he stared again into the valley, refusing to hear the faint carols now, concentrating on what he saw spread out before him.

White world, soft world, clean world; snow had a way of hiding the ugliness and disguising the tawdry trappings of humanity, of creating the kind of beauty a whore creates with makeup and the right kind of lighting. Here, in this idyllic, fanciful little valley, you could almost believe again in Christmas and God and Peace on Earth, Goodwill to Men; you could almost believe life had meaning and was worth living, and that there was hope and joy and justice in the world. But it was all illusion, it was all a lie. There was no God and there was no peace, and there was no justice; there was nothing to believe in, there was nothing left at all.

Cain picked up the bourbon bottle and poured himself another drink.

SACRAMENTO

The three of them went in for the ripoff at two thirty, exactly half an hour before the scheduled arrival of the armored car.

The place was called Greenfront—one of those cash-and-carry super-department stores where you can buy anything from groceries to complete home furnishings—and it was located on the northern outskirts of Sacramento. A former employee had dropped word in the right places in L.A., eight weeks before, that he was willing to sell a detailed package on the complex. Kubion had picked up on it immediately; he was a planner, an organizer—between jobs and looking for something ripe and solid—and on paper the job looked pretty good. He gave the guy an initial finder's fee of five hundred, told him there'd be another two thousand if a score developed, thought things over for a while and figured a three-man team, and went to talk to Brodie. He'd worked with Brodie before, and he was sharp and dependable and had a multitude of talents, like being a good wheel man and having contacts that could supply you with most anything short of a tank; Brodie was looking, too, and said he liked the sound of it so far, count him in. They talked over who to get for the third man. Both of them wanted Chadwick; but Chadwick was unavailable, and so were two others they tried, and finally they had to settle for Loxner. Loxner was big and bluff and slow-witted and knew how to take orders well enough, but the thing about him, like the thing about a lot of strong arms in the business, he was tough only when things were moving smoothly and he was behind the gun. If there was any kind of tight, the word was he went to mush inside and maybe you couldn't depend on him to do anything except crap his shorts. Still, he'd been around a long time and had only taken one fall, and that said something for him right there. So they talked to him, and he was free and hungry, and that made the team complete.

That Monday the three of them had driven up to Sacramento to look things over. A single surveillance of the afternoon ritual with the armored car, using binoculars from a copse of trees to the rear, convinced them that the job was not only workable, it was a goddamn wonder somebody hadn't ripped the place off long before this. Kubion evolved a full-scale plan right away, but they hadn't wanted to use it if there was an alternative method; the financing would be heavy and would cut deeply into the take. They visited the store several times, individually and in pairs, and they camped in the trees for three successive Monday afternoons. But they couldn't find another way to do it that was as clean and sure as the original. They even considered hitting the armored car instead, but that was a dangerous and by no means simple or guaranteed proposition—particularly since the car operated strictly within residential and business districts. And there wouldn't be any more money in the store by doing it that way, since the car delivered each payload to one bank or another after making a pickup.

For reasons known only to its management, the armored car company didn't necessarily use the same guards on the same run each Monday. And, conversely, their signal for admittance to Greenfront never varied: one long, two short, one long on the bell beside the rear entrance door. These two facts, discovered during surveillance, convinced the three of them finally to take Greenfront according to Kubion's initial plan. With the method of operation settled, they agreed to pool their slim cash reserves in order to eliminate outside financing and an even larger slice off the top, and went to work setting it up.

Brodie knew something about photography and spent two days outside the company's offices in downtown Sacramento, taking unobtrusive color photographs of the guards and of the type of armored car used by the firm. When the pictures were developed and blown up, Kubion took the ones of the cars to a mechanic Brodie knew in San Francisco, and the mechanic thought it over and decided he could make a dummy, for around eight thousand, that would pass any but the closest inspection. Then Kubion went to L.A. with the photos of the guards, to a costumers again supplied by Brodie, and put out another two thousand on three duplicate guard uniforms, three sets of simple theatrical disguises, and six money sacks of the type utilized by the armored car concern. Brodie handled the weaponry, through a safe gunsmith in Sacramento; he bought three .38 caliber Colt New Police revolvers, the same model carried by the guards, and a Smith & Wesson Model 39 automatic, .38 caliber, as a backup. On each of the subsequent three Mondays, Brodie followed the car which serviced Greenfront—one stop each week, using different rented vehicles on each occasion, to avoid the possibility of detection; by this means, he learned that the stop just prior to Greenfront was a place called Saddleman's Supermarket, two miles from the department store complex.

The former Greenfront employee had supplied a detailed map of the office as part of his finder's package, and the three of them went over it several times to be sure they knew exactly what to expect once they were inside. The rear entrance, through which the armored car guards were admitted to the building, opened on a set of stairs. At the top was a second door, also kept locked, and beyond there was the office: windowed cubicle occupied by the store manager, six desks manned by the general staff. One door leading down into the store proper, to the far left as you entered from the rear. Safe in the same wall as that door, vault type, to which both the manager and the chief accountant had the combination. Thick plate-glass window beginning waist-high in the fronting wall, which looked down on the aisles and departments and check-out counters on the main floor. Seven employees, plus two armed uniformed security officers—one of those the one who came downstairs to admit the armored car personnel. Two other guns in the building, one each to two additional security cops stationed on the main floor. No alarm system of any kind.

There was no problem in any of that, no problem at all once they got inside. The only sweat was the dummy armored car. They would have to drive it to Greenfront, leave it in plain sight in front of the door for the estimated fifteen minutes it would take them to complete the job, and then drive it away again afterward; but that couldn't be helped, and the score was plenty large enough to warrant the risk.

With Greenfront being open twelve full hours on both Saturday and Sunday and with the armored car coming only once a week, they figured that between a hundred and a hundred and twenty thousand would be awaiting transfer on this Monday afternoon. There might have been more money in the safe the following Monday, Christmas Eve, but it wouldn't be a great deal more; and on Christmas Eve there was always a traffic problem—last-minute shoppers, the big rush—which meant increased police patrols. And according to the finder's package, Greenfront sometimes put on extra security guards just before Christmas. This Monday, then, was the best time for the hit.

Brodie found a garage for rent on a short-term lease, in an industrial area four blocks from Greenfront, and that minimized somewhat the risk with the dummy car; he wore one of the theatrical disguises while visiting the realtor and paid the deposit in cash. Also, as a final precaution, Loxner arranged for a safe place to ground, in an isolated section of the Sierra called Hidden Valley. It was there they figured to make the split and to spend a week or so letting things cool down before they separated.

The week before, Kubion and Brodie had driven up to this Hidden Valley and established residence—two San Francisco businessmen on a combination vacation and work conference, they said—so that they would not be complete strangers when they came back after the job; and when they came back, Loxner would keep out of sight: still two men, not three, to ensure further that none of the locals would tie them in with Greenfront. Brodie and Kubion returned to Sacramento on Friday, and the mechanic delivered the dummy car inside a storage van late Saturday night, directly to the rented garage. There had been nothing to do then but wait for Monday afternoon. . . .

They left the garage at two twenty-five, with Brodie driving and Kubion beside him and Loxner in back. Each of them wore one of the disguises: false mustaches and sideburns and eyebrows, putty noses, cotton wadding to fatten cheeks and distort the shape of the mouth. They saw no police units in the four blocks to Greenfront. Fifty yards beyond the office entrance at the rear was the loading dock, with a couple of semis drawn up to it and warehousemen pushing dollies back and forth on the ramp; none of the men glanced at the armored car as it pulled up and parked.

Brodie went around and opened the rear doors, and Loxner came out with the empty money sacks. The two of them stepped up to the door, while Kubion stood watching by the right rear fender. Loxner pressed the bell, one long and two short and one long, and they stood there under the dark afternoon sky, waiting for the security cop to come down.

It took him two minutes, twenty or thirty seconds longer than usual because they weren't expecting the armored car for another half hour. He opened the peephole in the door and stared out through the thick glass covering it and saw the car and the three uniformed men—everything exactly as it was supposed to be. Satisfied, he worked the locks and swung the door open and said, "You guys are pretty early, aren't you?"

"There's a fire over on Kingridge," Brodie told him. "Big warehouse right across the street from Saddleman's. They've got the streets blocked off, hoses and pumpers everywhere, and we can't get in. So the company told us we might as well go ahead with our other rounds."

"Fires in the middle of December," the guard said, and shook his head. "Well, everything's just about ready upstairs, but you might have to wait five or ten minutes."

"Sure, we expected that."

The guard stepped aside to let Brodie and Loxner enter. When they were past him, he turned and started to close the door—and Brodie's left hand slapped across his mouth, jerking his head back; the swiftly drawn revolver jabbed him sharply in the small of the back. Softly, Brodie said, "You make a funny move or say anything above a whisper when I take my hand away, and I'll kill you first thing. Believe it."

The guard stood motionless, his eyes wide and abruptly terrified; he had a wife and three kids, and he was no hero.

Kubion glanced out at the loading dock and saw that no one on the ramp was looking in his direction. The area was otherwise deserted. He drew his own gun and shut the door, leaving it unlocked. "All right," he said to the guard, "who opens the door up there? You or the other guy in the office?"

Brodie took his hand away, increasing the pressure of the Colt. The guard's throat worked three times before he found words, thickly hushed. "My partner. I tell him it's okay and he opens up."

"That better be right," Kubion said. "If it isn't, you're a dead man."

"It's right."

"Fine. Now when we go into the office, you keep your mouth shut. Don't do or say anything. We'll take it from there."

Convulsively, the guard nodded. Kubion pushed him over to the stairs, and they went up single file. At the top, the guard called out, "Okay, Ben," and there was the scrape of a key in the lock. The heavy steel-ribbed door opened, and the other security cop stood before them with his hands in plain sight. Kubion shoved the first one into the office, moving to one side so that Brodie and Loxner could enter, covering the startled second guard.

"Everybody just sit tight," Kubion said sharply. "No panic, no screams, no heroics."

"It's a holdup, my God!" somebody said, and one of the two women employees gasped—but the two guards just stood there staring at Kubion's gun. Brodie fanned immediately to the left and watched the rigid office staff sitting at their desks; none of them made further sounds. Loxner was at the open door to the manager's cubicle, eyes and gun on the fat, white-faced man who had gotten to his feet within.

For a long moment the office was a fixed tableau fashioned of fear and disbelief. Then Kubion—smiling, thinking that they were going to get it done well within their allotted fifteen minutes—gestured to the manager and said, "Come out here and open the safe. Quick, no arguments." Obediently, woodenly, the fat man stepped out of his cubicle and started across the office.

And that was when the whole thing went suddenly and completely sour. . . .

Two

It began to snow again just after Lew Coopersmith left his house and walked over to Sierra Street.

He pulled the collar of his mackinaw high on the back of his neck, moving more quickly under the thickening flakes. Like most residents of Hidden Valley, he did not particularly mind the snow, but then neither did he relish walking or driving in it, especially when the snowfall had been as heavy as it had this winter.

Lean and tall and durable, like the lodgepole pines on the valley's eastern slopes, he was sixty-six years old, felt forty-six, and surprised his wife, Ellen, every now and then by knocking on the door of her room just after bedtime and asking her if she felt like having a go. There were squint lines at the corners of his alert green eyes and faint creases paralleling a stubby nose, but his narrow face was otherwise unlined. His hair, covered now by a woolen cap, was a dusty gray and showed no signs of thinning. Only the liver spots on the backs of his hands and fingers hinted of his age.

For twenty-two years, up to his retirement four years

before, he had served as county sheriff. Police work had been his entire life—he had been a highway patrolman in Truckee and Sacramento and then a county deputy for eleven years before finally being elected sheriff—but he had always looked forward with a kind of eagerness to what were euphemistically termed his Leisure Years. And yet retirement had developed into something of a hollow reward. Shortly after he finished his final term, he and Ellen had moved from the county seat to Hidden Valley —an area both of them had decided upon sometime earlier—and almost immediately he had felt a sense of impotence, of uselessness. He found himself constantly wondering how his former deputy and the new county sheriff, Ed Patterson, was handling things and took to driving over to the county seat periodically and stopping in to talk about this and that, strictly social, Ed, you understand. Even after four years, he still dropped in on Patterson now and then, as he had done when Frank McNeil and some of the others had gotten their backs up about Zachary Cain, the loner type who had moved into the valley the previous summer.

The trouble was, he didn't know what to do with himself. There was always plenty to do when you were an officer of the law, dozens of things to occupy your time, some excitement to life; but in Hidden Valley, what the hell was there? Reading and smoking your pipe in front of the fireplace and puttering in the basement workshop and watching television and bulling with the locals and the seasonal tourists at the Valley Inn and driving up to Soda Grove occasionally to take in a movie—weekend and evening pastimes, shallow pursuits void of significance or commitment. He felt severed from the ebb and flow of life, put out to pasture. Good Lord, sixty-six wasn't *old,* not when you felt forty-six and your mind was just as sharp as ever and you had always been a doer, a man involved, a man empowered. His retirement very definitely had been premature, but the decision could not be unmade and he would have to go on making the best of it, just as he had done for the past four years.

When he reached Sierra, Coopersmith turned right off Shasta Street and went into Tribucci Bros. Sport Shop. In season, the Tribuccis dispensed large quantities of bait, outdoor wear, licenses, and fishing and hunting accessories to visiting sportsmen; now, in winter, the bulk of their business was in winter sports equipment (on a limited local basis), as well as in tobacco products, newspapers, magazines, and paperback books.

The younger of the two brothers who operated the store, John Tribucci, was alone behind the counter at the far end. In his middle thirties, he had a strong, athletic body and shaggy black hair and warm brown eyes under slightly canted lids; he also had a ready smile and a large amount of infectious energy. When he wasn't tending the shop, he was usually skiing or ice skating or tramping around the woods in a pair of snowshoes or fly fishing for trout or, when he could find the time, backpacking into the higher wilderness elevations of the southern Sierra: Owens Lake and Mount Baxter and the John Muir Wilderness. In an age of electronic depersonalization and ecological apathy and teeming cities and developments which had begun to spread over the land like malignant fungi, Coopersmith thought that any man who took pains to maintain his own identity, who loved and thrived on nature in all her majesty, was worthy of admiration and respect; he accorded both to John Tribucci.

Coopersmith asked, after they had exchanged greetings, "How's Ann today, Johnny?"

"Fat and impatient, same as ever," Tribucci said, and grinned. His wife was eight and a half months pregnant with their first child—a major event in their lives after eleven years of nonconception. "Make you a bet she gives birth on Christmas Day."

"As much as you want a son for Christmas? No way."

Coopersmith winked at him. "Give us a can of Raleigh and a couple packages of pipe cleaners, would you, Johnny?"

"Coming up." Tribucci took the items from the shelf behind the counter, dropped them into a plastic sack, and made change from the five Coopersmith handed him. He said then, "Snowing again, I see. If it keeps up like this, we're liable to have a slide to contend with."

"Think so?" Coopersmith asked, interested.

"Well, the last time we had this much snow—back in sixty-one—there was a small one that blocked part of the pass road; those cliffs will only hold so much before some section or other weakens and gives way. Took the county road crews four days to clear through, the longest we've ever been snowbound."

"Seems I recall, now that you mention it. Nice prospect."

"Inconvenient, all right, but there's nothing you can do to stop an avalanche if one decides to happen. With less snow, though, we should make it through okay."

"Ah, the joys of mountain living," Coopersmith said dryly. He picked up the plastic sack. "See you later, Johnny."

Tribucci laughed. "*Ciao*. Give my best to Ellen."

"Will do."

Coopersmith went out and walked farther north on Sierra, crossing Mooc Street. The snow, slanting down off the western slope on the cold wind, clung icily to his mackinaw and trousers. Except for two cars and a delivery van parked against the two-foot windows along each curb, packed by the village's single snowplow, the street and sidewalks were empty. But he saw three customers inside the Mercantile as he passed: Webb Edwards, Hidden Valley's only physician—a quiet, elderly man given to wearing Western-style string ties; Sally Chilton, Edwards' part-time nurse; and Verne Mullins, another retiree in his sixties who had spent forty-five years with the

Southern Pacific Railroad. The store was the largest in the village and supplied groceries and hardware items and drug sundries; it also housed the Hidden Valley Post Office. Holly wreaths and sprigs of mistletoe decorated both halves of the front doors, and a huge, flat cardboard Santa Claus and two cardboard reindeer had been erected in one of the long facing windows.

Between Lassen Drive and Eldorado Street, diagonally across from Garvey's Shell, the windows of the Valley Café cast scintillas of bright light into the dark afternoon. Within the glow, the flakes of falling snow were like particles of white glitter. Coopersmith paused under the jutting front eaves of the building, brushed his clothing and stamped clinging snow from his booted feet, and then pushed the door open and went inside.

The interior was a single elongated room, with yellow plastic-covered booths and vinyl-topped tables along the left wall and a long lunch counter fronted by plastic stools along the right. In the center of the wall above the counter was a huge, varnished, bark-rimmed plaque, cut from a giant sequoia, on which was lettered the menu in neat white printing. The glaring fluorescent tubes overhead gave the café a sterile, slightly self-conscious appearance.

None of the booths was occupied, and only two of the stools; sitting side by side midway along the counter were Greg Novak, a long-haired, brittle-featured youth in his early twenties who worked for Joe Garvey and who also operated the village snowplow, and Walt Halliday, owner of the Valley Inn—plump, mild-eyed, wearing black-rimmed glasses which gave him a falsely studious look. Behind the counter were Frank McNeil and his sixteen-year-old son, Larry; the youth, recruited to help out during Soda Grove High School's Christmas vacation, as he had been during each summer vacation the past few years, was washing dishes in a stainless-steel sink at the far end, and McNeil stood talking to Novak and Halliday.

Dressed all in white, like a hospital orderly, the café owner was a ruddy complexioned man in his mid-forties, with a blunt face and bristle-cut red hair. In addition, he possessed a sordid sense of humor and a complaining attitude: Coopersmith did not much care for him. But his food was good, his coffee even better than Ellen's, and he was therefore tolerable for short periods of time.

The three men glanced up as Coopersmith entered and called out greetings. He lifted his hand in acknowledgment, slid onto a stool three away from Halliday. "Coffee, Frank," he said.

"Sure thing." McNeil drew a mug from the urn on the back counter, set it before Coopersmith, put a spoon beside it, and immediately went back to stand in front of Novak and Halliday.

"As I was saying," he said to them, "Christmas shopping is a pain in the ass."

"Well, I don't know about that," Halliday said. "I kind of get a boot out of it. How come you're so down on Christmas, Frank?"

"It's all a bunch of commercialized bullshit, that's why."

"Listen to Scrooge here."

Novak said, "So what did you find for your wife in Soda Grove, Mr. Halliday?"

"One of those clock radios, the kind that comes on automatically like an alarm in the mornings and plays music instead of ringing a bell in your ear."

"Sounds like a nice gift."

"She'll like it, I think."

"You'd probably of done better to get the same thing I'm giving my old lady," McNeil said.

"What would that be?"

Without bothering to lower his voice in deference to the presence of his son, McNeil answered, "Well, I'll tell you. It's maybe six, seven inches long and what you call durable, guaranteed not to wear out if you treat it with care. You can use it any time of the year, and the old lady appreciates it more than anything else you can give her. And the best thing about it, it doesn't cost you a cent."

"That's what *you* think," Halliday said, smiling.

"Only one problem with a gift like that, though."

"What's that?"

"I ain't figured out how the hell I'm going to wrap it."

The three men burst out laughing, and Coopersmith sipped his coffee and wondered what had happened to the spirit of Christmas. When he had been young, Yuletide was a time of innocent joy and genuine religious feelings. Now it was as if Christmas had evolved, in no more than half a century, into a kind of wearisome though bearable space-age anachronism: people going through the motions because it was what was expected of them, worshiping mechanically and superficially if they worshiped at all, no longer caring, no longer seeming to understand what it was all about. And so there were dirty jokes and scatological remarks told in all manner of company, and everybody laughed and pretty much agreed that it was just a bunch of commercialized bullshit, can't wait until it's over for another year; it made you feel angry and sad and a little ashamed.

McNeil came down to stand in front of Coopersmith, still chuckling, his face red and damp in the too-warm air circulating through the café's suspended unit heater. "Need a warm-up, Lew?"

"No, I don't think so. Thanks."

McNeil leaned forward, eyes bright, eyes leering. "Say, Lew, you hear this one? I like to bust a gut laughing first time I heard it, and same goes for Greg and Walt there. There's this eight-year-old kid, see, and he wakes up about 2 A.M. Christmas morning. So he goes downstairs to see if Santa Claus has come yet, and sure as hell old Santa is there. But what he's doing, see—"

Coopersmith got abruptly to his feet, put a quarter on

the counter, and went out wordlessly into the falling snow.

McNeil blinked after him for a moment and then turned to look imploringly at Novak and Halliday. He said, "Now what in Christ's name is the matter with *him?*"

SACRAMENTO

Somebody knocked on the door, the one connecting the office and the interior of the store below.

The fat manager stopped moving, his head turned toward Kubion; the tableau froze again, thick and strained with suddenly heightened tension. There was a second knock, and Kubion thought: If we don't open up, whoever it is is going to figure something's wrong. He gestured to Brodie, who was nearest the door.

The guard who had let them in downstairs said in a liquid whisper, "It's locked, I've got the key."

Brodie stopped, half turning, and Kubion said to the guard, "Get the hell over there, then; watch where you put your hands. When you get the door open, stand back out of the way."

The guard crossed the office, wetting his lips nervously, taking the key from the pocket of his trousers. Brodie stepped back three paces, up against the wall beyond the door. A third knock sounded, insistent now, and then ceased as the guard fitted his key into the lock. A moment later he pulled the door inward, stepping back away from it.

"What took you so long?" a voice said in mild reproof from the landing outside.

The guard shook his head, not speaking.

A shabbily-dressed, frightened-looking woman came first into the office, clutching a handbag in both hands;

behind her was another uniformed security officer, one of the two normally stationed on the floor below. He was saying, "Caught this lady here shoplifting in Household Goods. She had—"

When he saw Kubion and Loxner and the guns they were holding, he frowned and stopped speaking. The guard who had opened the door said stupidly, "It's a holdup, Ray," and the floor cop reached automatically and just as stupidly for the gun holstered at his belt.

"Don't do it!" Kubion yelled at him, and Brodie came away from the wall, trying to get around the shabby woman, trying to keep the operation from blowing. But the guard had committed himself; he got the revolver clear and brought it up. The shabby woman began to scream. Brodie knocked her viciously out of the way, and the cop fired once at Loxner, hitting him in the left arm, making it jerk like a puppet's; then he swung the gun toward Brodie.

Kubion shot him in the throat.

Blood gouted from the wound, and he made a liquid dying sound and went stumbling backward into the fronting window; the barrel of his back-flung gun and the rear of his head struck the glass, webbing it with hairline cracks. The shabby woman sprawled against one of the desks, screaming like a loon. The manager was on his hands and knees crawling behind another of the desks, and the other employees had thrown themselves to the floor, hands over their heads, the two women moaning in terror. Like ash-gray sculptures, the two office guards stood motionless. The shrieks of the shabby woman and the echoes of the shots and the sudden startled shouts filtering up from the floor below filled the office with nightmarish sound.

There was no time for the money now, the whole thing was blown; they had no choice except to run. Brodie came over to the rear door immediately, went out onto the landing, but Loxner kept on standing by the cubicle with bright beads of sweat pimpling his face and his eyes glazed and staring at the dark-red stain spreading over his khaki uniform sleeve just below the elbow. Kubion shouted at him, "You stupid bastard, move it, move it!" Loxner's head pulled around, and he made a face like a kid about to cry; but he came shambling forward then, cradling his left arm against his chest. Kubion caught his shoulder and shoved him through the door.

"Stay the fuck in this office, all of you," he yelled. "We'll kill anybody that shows his face!" He backed out and slammed the door, turning, and Brodie and Loxner were already running on the stairs. Kubion pounded down after them. Brodie reached the lower door first and threw it open and the three of them burst outside. Two warehousemen and a truck driver were coming toward them from the loading dock. Brodie fired wide at them, and they reversed direction in a hurry, scattering. Loxner tried to drag open the armored car's front passenger door with his right hand still holding his gun; Kubion elbowed him viciously out of the way, opened the door, pulled him back and crowded him inside while Brodie ran around to the driver's side. There were half a dozen men in the vicinity of the dock now, but they hung back wisely, not attempting to interfere.

The dummy armored car started instantly, and Brodie released the clutch; the tires bit screamingly into the pavement. He took the far corner of the building in a controlled power skid, went through the parking lot at fifty and climbing. At the nearest exit a new Ford had just begun to turn into the lot from the street. Brodie swung the wheel hard right and the armored car's rear end slewed around and made contact with the Ford's left front fender, punching the machine out of the way, spinning it in a half circle. Fighting the wheel, Brodie slid the heavy car sideways again as a Volkswagen swerved to avoid collision. The armored car straightened and began pulling away, made another power skid left at the first intersection, and all the while Kubion sat hunched forward on the seat, saying, "Son of a bitch, son of a bitch, son of a bitch!" in a kind of savage litany.

Three

Smiling with his usual charismatic boyishness, Matt Hughes handed the Reverend Peter Keyes his mail through the gated window of the Post Office enclosure. "Yesterday's attendance in church was very good, Reverend," he said. "Your idea of moving the commencement time up to noon was a good one."

"I expect the fact that this is the Christmas season had more to do with the rise in attendance than the new hour," the Reverend Mr. Keyes said. He was a short, round, benign-featured man, reminiscent of a somewhat scaled-down and clean-shaven Santa Claus: an accurate physical reflection of the inner man and of his spiritual leanings. Hughes thought of him fondly as the antithesis of the fire-and-brimstone mountain preacher of legend and fact. "But in any event, it *was* gratifying. One can only hope this coming Sunday's attendance will be larger still, though I suppose one hundred percent of the able-bodied is too much to hope for."

"Maybe not, Reverend. I'll make a point to remind the good people of the valley as I see each of them this week."

"Thank you, Matthew," the Reverend Mr. Keyes said gravely. He was the only resident of Hidden Valley who called Hughes by his full given name. "Well, I've several things to attend to. I'll see you again tomorrow."

When the Reverend Mr. Keyes had gone, Hughes left the Post Office enclosure and came around the long counter set parallel to the Mercantile's rear wall. The store was empty now, except for his single full-time employee, matronly and white-haired Maude Fredericks, who was stacking canned goods in the grocery section which comprised the northern third of the wide, deep room. The old-fashioned potbellied stove set to the right of the counter glowed dull-red warmth through its isinglass door-window—putting that stove in three years ago had been a very wise idea, he thought; it gave the place a kind of country-general-store flavor that appealed to locals and tourists alike—and the Christmas music added a different but no less pleasant warmth to the surroundings.

Hughes smiled complacently and went to stand by the cardboard Santa Claus in one of the front windows. Outside, the snow swirled and danced in gusts of wind like shifting patterns in a monochromatic kaleidoscope. Mountain winters had always fascinated him—the soft, fat, intricately shaped snowflakes, the trees bending under their heavy white coats, some whiskered with stalactitic icicles like strong old men braced against the winter wind; snow eddies such as those he was watching now, so capricious you felt like laughing in the same way you would at the antics of kittens. As a child, he had used to sit for hours, face pressed to window glass, absorbed in the white splendor without, and when his mother would come in and ask him what he found so intriguing, he would answer her the same way each time, a kind of game they had played: "Snow magic, Mom; snow magic."

At the age of thirty-two, he still retained the aura of that same perpetually enthusiastic little boy. The slope-cornered tan mustache he had worn for two years added a certain maturity to his features—as did the vertical humor lines which extended downward from a Romanesque nose and, like a pair of calipers, partially encircled a wide, mobile mouth; but his bright blue eyes and the supple slimness of his body and the demonstrative way he used his hands when he talked were prominently indicative of bubbling and guileless youth.

Nonetheless, he was unquestionably Hidden Valley's wealthiest and most respected citizen. In addition to owning the Mercantile, which he had inherited from an uncle ten years before, and in addition to having served two successive terms as mayor, he owned a thousand acres of mountain land lucratively leased to a private hunting club, a portfolio of blue-chip stocks, and a high five-figure bank account. He was married to a woman considered by most everyone both intelligent and enviably attractive: an equally substantial form of wealth. If he had been an ambitious man, he might have left Hidden Valley for less secluded surroundings—might have entered successfully into the larger business world or perhaps even into politics. But he was not ambitious, and he derived a great deal of contentment from his position of importance in the valley. To enhance it, he offered unlimited credit to regular customers, maintained a "banking" service for the cashing of personal and business checks, could be counted upon for a loan in any emergency, and regularly contributed money to the All Faiths Church and to civic betterment projects. It was, he sometimes thought, a little like being the benevolent young monarch of a very small, very scenic, and very agreeable kingdom.

Behind him, now, the telephone began ringing distantly in his private office. Without turning from the window, he called, "Maude, would you get that, please?"

"I'm on my way, Matt," she answered. Her footsteps sounded on the wooden flooring, and after a moment the ringing ceased. The loudspeakers began to give out with "Deck the Halls." Maude's voice called above the music, "It's your wife."

Hughes sighed. "Okay, thanks."

He crossed the store and stepped behind the counter again. Small and neat, his office was nestled in the far right-hand corner adjoining the storeroom; it contained a pair of file cabinets, a glass-topped oak desk, and an old-fashioned, black-painted Wells-Fargo safe, bolted to the floor and wall, in which he kept his cash on hand. Entering, closing the door behind him, he cocked a hip against the edge of the desk and picked up the phone receiver and said, "Yes, Rebecca?"

"I just called to tell you we're out of coffee," his wife's voice said. "Would you bring a pound of drip grind home with you tonight?"

"I think you'd better come down and pick it up, dear. I won't be home after closing."

There was a brief silence; then Rebecca said, "Oh?"

"I have to go over to Coldville," he told her. "I was going to call you a little later to let you know."

"Why do you have to go to Coldville?"

"Neal Walker called and asked me to come. He wants to discuss some civic problem or other he's having."

"Mayor to mayor, is that it?"

"Yes."

"I see. And wives aren't allowed?"

"You'd be bored, dear, you know that."

"I suppose I would."

"I'll probably be late. Don't wait up."

"No, I won't," she said, and broke the connection.

Hughes replaced the receiver, sighed again, and then went around the desk and sat down in his leather armchair. He pyramided his fingers under his chin and sat that way for several minutes, lost in thought. Then, abruptly, he straightened, picked up the telephone again, and dialed a Soda Grove number.

A woman's soft young voice said, "Grange Electric, good afternoon."

"Hello, Peggy. Can you talk?"

"Yes. Is something the matter?"

"No, not a thing. I just wanted to talk to you."

"Well, you'll be seeing me in another three hours."

"I know that. I've been thinking about it all day."

She laughed softly. "What were you thinking?"

"You *know* what I was thinking."

"Yes, but tell me anyway."

"I'll tell you when I see you. I'll *show* you."

"Oh, yes, I can imagine you will."

Hughes moistened his lips, and his breathing was thick and rapid. "You know something?" he said. "This conversation is giving me an erection. I never thought a man could get an erection talking to a woman over the telephone."

The girl named Peggy laughed again. "Well, don't lose it, okay? I'll see both of you at six or a little after."

"At six," Hughes said. He waited until she had rung off and then reached out almost reluctantly to recradle the receiver for the second time. Using a handkerchief from the pocket of his gray wool slacks, he wiped away a thin sheen of perspiration which had formed on his forehead; then he stood up and went out again into the front of the store.

Over the loudspeakers, the Mormon Tabernacle Choir was singing about love and faith and the spirit of Christmas.

SACRAMENTO

When they were two blocks from Greenfront and he was certain they had no immediate pursuit, Brodie slowed the armored car to the legal speed limit. Time was a precious commodity, but they couldn't buy any of it if they drew attention to themselves getting the dummy back to the rented garage.

The alley off which the garage was located had both its entrances on parallel industrial streets crowded with trucks and vans. Brodie made the turn onto the nearest of them without seeing any sign of a police car and drove a block and a half to where the alley mouth bisected the block to the left. Kubion, watching the street in a flatly unblinking stare, said, "It looks okay; nobody paying any attention"—and Brodie nodded and made the swing into the narrow opening between two high, blank warehouse walls.

Midway through the block, the alley widened to the right to form a small parking area; it fronted a weathered brick structure which had been independently erected between the rear walls of two warehouses. One-half of the building had a sign on it that said BENSON SOLENOID, MANUFACTURER'S REP. The other half was the garage.

They had left the doors open, and the area was deserted; Brodie drove the armored car inside without slowing. Kubion was out of the passenger side before the car had come to a full stop, closing the two wooden halves of the doors, barring them with a two-by-four set into iron brackets. Turning, he began to strip off his guard uniform, the false mustache and sideburns and bulbous putty nose he had been wearing. Brodie and Loxner, out of the car now, were also shedding their uniforms and disguises—Loxner one-handed, his left arm hanging useless at his side and ribboned with blood. His eyes still had a glazed look, etched with pain, and they wouldn't meet either Kubion's or Brodie's; but he'd kept his mouth shut, and he was functioning all right.

Their regular clothing was in a locked storage box at the upper end of the garage, along with the suitcases in which they had planned to carry the money. Kubion unlocked the box and took out one of the cases. Into it they put the disguises, because they didn't want the cops discovering they had worn them, and the .38 automatic Kubion had had tucked into his belt under the uniform jacket; the uniforms, which were untraceable, were allowed to remain discarded on the oil-splattered floor.

Brodie and Kubion got immediately into slacks, shirts, winter coats; then they transferred the New Police Colts into their coat pockets. Loxner took off his undershirt and tore it into strips with his teeth and his right hand and bound the wound in his arm. He had difficulty getting into his own clothing, but neither Kubion nor Brodie went to help him. With Kubion carrying the suitcase, the two of them moved past the dummy car—it, too, was untraceable, and they had worn gloves from the moment it was delivered to make sure it stayed clean of prints—and crossed to the double doors.

Loxner joined them, struggling into his coat, as Brodie took the bar away and cracked one of the halves. The area was still deserted. Hands resting on their pocketed guns, Kubion and Brodie led the way out and over to where they could look both ways along the alley. Clear. In the distance there was the fluctuating wail of sirens, but the sounds were muted, growing fainter, moving elsewhere.

Slightly more than six minutes had passed since their arrival at the garage.

They went to the right, straight through the block to the next street over. Kubion's car was where he had parked it that morning, a hundred feet from the alley mouth. When they reached the car, Kubion unlocked the doors and put the suitcase on the floor in the back; then he went to the trunk, opened it, removed a folded blanket, closed it again. He gave the blanket to Loxner.

"Lie down on the rear seat with this over you," he said. "Cops will be looking for a car with three men in it, not two."

Loxner still wouldn't meet his eyes. He said, "Right," and stretched out on the seat under the blanket, holding his wounded arm like a woman holding a baby. Brodie took the wheel. Sitting beside him, Kubion opened the glove box and took out the California road map and Sacramento city street map stored within. He folded them open on his lap.

If the job had gone off as planned, they would have taken Interstate Highway 80 straight through to Truckee and then swung north on State Highway 89—the quickest approach to Hidden Valley. But because they were professionals, covering against just such a blown operation as this, they'd also worked out a more circuitous route to minimize the danger of spot checks by the Highway Patrol. There was an entrance to Interstate 80 not far from where they were now, and they could still use that all right; it was only twenty-five minutes since the abortive ripoff, and the cops would need more time than that to organize and set up effective road-blocks. As soon as they reached the Roseville turnoff, eight miles distant, they would cut north on State 65 to Marysville, pick up State 20 to Grass Valley, and then take State 49 through Downieville and Whitewater and, finally, Soda Grove. It would double their time on the road, making the trip to Hidden Valley a minimum of four hours, but it would also put them well clear of the police search and surveillance area.

It took Brodie seven minutes to get them out of the warehouse district, swinging wide of Greenfront, and onto the cloverleaf that fed Interstate 80 eastbound. They saw no police cars until they came out of the cloverleaf and merged with the flow of traffic, and then it was a highway patrol unit traveling westbound with red light and siren, exiting the freeway on the same cloverleaf—alerted but no longer an immediate threat. Kubion had had his gun out and hidden beneath the bottom folds of his coat, but now he slid it back into the pocket. He lit a cigarette and made sucking sounds on the filter, pulling smoke into his lungs.

Brodie accelerated to pass a slow-moving truck. "So far so good," he said, to break the tense silence.

"We're not out of it yet," Kubion said thinly.

"Don't I know it?"

"Hold your speed down, for Christ's sake."

"Take it easy, Earl. You don't have to tell me how to drive."

From the back seat Loxner said, "You got anything in the glove box for this arm? It hurts like hell, and it's still bleeding."

"No," Kubion said.

"The bullet went clean through, but Jesus, it hurts."

"Yeah."

"I never been shot before," Loxner said defensively. "That's why I maybe froze up a little back there. You get shot like that, for the first time, it shakes the crap out of you."

"Yeah, yeah, shut up about it."

"Fucking security cop, fucking cop," Loxner said, and lapsed into silence.

Brodie held the speedometer needle on sixty. "A hundred grand, maybe more, shot straight up the ass. And we're out better than ten on top of it. Now what the hell do we do for a stake?"

"We'll make a score somewhere," Kubion said.

"Sure—but where?"

"You leave that to me. I'll think of something. I'll think of something, all right."

Four

The light began to go out of the somber afternoon sky at four o'clock, dimming rapidly behind a thick curtain of snow, turning the pines and fir trees into wraithlike silhouettes on the steep slopes of Hidden Valley. Distorted by the snowfall, the brightening village lights—the multihued Christmas bulbs strung across Sierra Street—were hazy aureoles that seemed somehow to lack warmth and comfort in the encroaching darkness. And the thin, sharp wind sang lonely and bitter, like something lose in the wilderness and resigned to its fate.

That's me, Rebecca Hughes thought as she sat listening to the wind in the big, empty Lassen Drive house: something lonely and bitter and lost and resigned. A dull candle sitting in the window, waiting for the return of the prodigal. Alas, poor Rebecca, I knew her well. . . .

She reached out in the darkness and located her cigarettes on the coffee table. In the flame of her lighter, the six-foot Christmas tree across the living room looked bleak and forlorn—colored ornaments gleaming blackly, silver tinsel like opalescent worms hanging from the dark branches: a symbol of joy that was completely joyless in the shadowed room. The furnishings, too, seemed strange and unused, as if they were parts of a museum exhibit; she had picked out the decor herself when she and Matt were married seven years before—Pennsylvania Dutch with copper accessories—and she had loved it then, it represented home and happiness then. Now it was meaningless, like the tree, perhaps even like life itself.

Turning slightly to light her cigarette, Rebecca saw her reflection in the hoar-frosted window behind the couch. She paused, staring at herself in the flickering glow. A pretty face once, an animated face, with laughter in the gray eyes and a suggestion of passion in the soft mouth. But in this moment, with her chestnut-colored hair pulled back into a tight chignon at the back of her neck, the face looked severe and weary and deeply lined; in this moment, she was a twenty-eight-year-old woman who was forty years of age.

She moved her gaze from the window, snapping the lighter shut and putting the room in heavy darkness again, thinking: I wonder who she is this time? Not that it matters, but you can't help wondering. Probably not a valley resident; Matt has always been so very careful to preserve his saintly image here. Young, of course. Large breasts, of course, he always did like large breasts, mine never quite appeared to suit him. My God—how insanely ironic if that were the reason behind it all! I'm sorry, Rebecca, your tits are much too small, I'm going to have to find a mistress or two or twenty, you *do* understand, don't you? Yes, certainly I understand, dear; I couldn't possibly expect you to be faithful to me when my boobs are so small, I'm only sorry they didn't grow larger so we could have had a perfectly happy marriage.

Well what difference did it make, really, why he did it? He did it, that was all. Pathetically, in her eyes—like a child who thinks he's being very clever with his mischief; yes, like a child: pleasant, good-hearted, pious, playing an adventurous game and not quite realizing the wrongness of it, not quite realizing his own hypocrisy. When she had found out about the waitress in Soda Grove six years ago and confronted him with the knowledge, he had broken down and cried, head against her bosom, saying, "I don't know why I did it, Becky, it just happened, and I'm sorry, forgive me, I love you," and she had forgiven him, and four months later it had happened again; it had been happening ever since.

This particular little affair had been going on for about a month now. It had started like all the others, with a transparent excuse for not coming home in the evening, and it had progressed like all the others: Matt returning after midnight two and three and four times a week, with perfume lingering on his body and long hairs on his clothes (blond this time), falling into bed exhausted. He had not touched her, of course, since it began; he never touched her, never wanted her, never had anything left for her in any way. It would be like this for a while yet, a few more weeks. Then he would tire of the new girl, or she would tire of him, and the cycle would begin anew: an apology for his neglect, a few less than ardent nights (*she* had always been passionate, that couldn't be the reason for the endless string of mistresses), expensive gifts, a period of attentiveness—and then, just when she would begin to think she had a husband again, he would call her to say that he would not be home until late. . . .

She had not bothered to confront him again after the Soda Grove waitress. He would have told her the same thing he had that first time, and have begged her forgiveness, and have professed his love for her. And the terrible thing was, she knew he *did* love her in some way she could never understand and did not want to lose her. He would never, as a result, leave her for one of the girls with whom he slept. Things would have been so much easier if there had been that possibility, Rebecca often thought; the decision would have been taken out of her hands. But it would never happen, and she had simply been unable to take the initiative herself: Little Orphan Rebecca with no place to go, no particular skills, a little afraid of the big wide world beyond these mountains where she had been born and reared; who could not seem to stop believing in love-conquers-all and happy endings and other fairy tales. So she forgave him tacitly each time and remained with him—enduring, pretending. Withering.

She felt suddenly very cold, as if the wind had managed to get inside the warm house; gooseflesh formed on her bare upper arms, beneath the short sleeves of the blouse she wore. Standing, putting out her cigarette in the cloisonné table tray, she went out of the dark room to the stairs in the main hall. The bedroom she shared with Matt was at the front of the house, directly above the living room. It, too, seemed cold and dismal to Rebecca tonight—and the wide, antique-framed double bed was a kind of index of her melancholy.

She did not turn on the lights. She could see well enough in the dark: walking half-blind through life or half-blind through a familiar house, easy enough to do once you got used to it. Crossing to the walk-in closet, she took out a heavy wool pullover and slipped it over her head. Then she stood for a moment, arms folded across her breasts, hugging herself. What now? she thought. Back downstairs to sit smoking by the window? Television? Soft music? Loud music? Another book? How about a hot bath—or, more appropriately, a cold shower?

She wished she knew how to sublimate. That was what modern women did, wasn't it? They sublimated their frustrations, they developed hobbies or joined committees or became Fem Libbers or played bridge or painted pictures or wrote stories or took jobs or studied astrology or Far East religions—things like that. Well, that was fine for modern women, but what about old-fashioned members of the "weaker sex" like Rebecca Hughes? She wasn't a collector, and she hated card games, and she had no artistic talent of any kind, and the only jobs you could get in an area such as this were prosaic and totally unrewarding, offering no mental commitment whatsoever. There were no committees or clubs in Hidden Valley, you had to go to Soda Grove, and besides, she was neither a joiner nor a mixer, and if that wasn't enough, she was afraid to drive any distance in snow and ice. She had no interest in astrology or Far East religions or any of the other passions of the Aware Woman. It was not that she was apathetic or incapable of individualism; she had always possessed a genuine fondness for literature and read extensively and considered herself well informed and had opinions and believed in certain causes. She belonged to several book clubs and regularly utilized the services of the mobile county lending library when it came through twice a month; she read until her eyes ached and her mind refused to grasp the meaning of words and sentences. And how much reading could you do? Too much —and not enough.

The simple truth was that she did not know how to sublimate; she was not modern, and she was not by any means "liberated." She recalled clearly enough the time she had decided she *was,* two years previously, and her resolution to strike back at Matt in the most fitting manner: by doing exactly what he was doing, sauce for the goose as well as the gander. Why not? she'd thought then. Why couldn't she, too, find solace and fulfill her needs in someone else's bed?

And so she had called Rae Johnson, a girl in Reno whom she had gone to school with, a blackjack dealer in one of the casinos and a self-proclaimed free spirit, and Rae had said, Sure, come on over. Rebecca had told Matt she was going away on a visit for a short while, and he said he thought that was a fine idea, it would do her good —very eager to get rid of her because he was in the middle of one of his affairs then. She took the bus to Reno from Soda Grove, and Rae conducted her on a tour of all the clubs and introduced her to several male friends, sensing that Rebecca had come for a fling without anything having been said about it.

She had liked the man named Doug, she could no longer remember his last name, the moment she'd been introduced to him. Witty, charming, intelligent, easy to talk to, and when he had asked her up to his apartment for a drink, she consented readily enough; she had done a lot of drinking that night—something she seldom did because she was prone to violent and prolonged hangovers—and the liquor and the flashing neon and the bright sophisticated conversation had apparently dissolved all inhibitions, and she had needed desperately to be loved, it had been a long time then as it was a long time now. They sat together on his sofa and drank vodka gimlets, and he kissed her, put his tongue in her mouth, stroked her breasts almost casually—and all at once the euphoria and the anticipation and the passion faded away, and she was completely sober; she was like slick silver ice inside. She broke the kiss, and he looked at her smiling and suggested they go into the bedroom, and she could see the outline of his penis, half-erect, her eyes on him there and nowhere else, and fright spiraled inside her, and she couldn't go through with it, she simply could not go through with it. She pushed away from him, flushed and ashamed, straightening her skirt and blouse, putting on her coat, not looking at him at all then; and even though he did not protest, was in fact nonchalant in his mild defeat, she had had the abased feeling that he was silently laughing at her.

She left Reno the next morning, not explaining to Rae because Rae knew by looking at her what the trouble was, and came back to Hidden Valley filled with the sense of resignation. There had been no more flings. . . .

Aimlessly Rebecca left the bedroom and went downstairs, along the hallway into the bright copper-tone kitchen at the rear of the house. Again, she did not turn on the lights. She rummaged through one of the pine cupboards over the drainboard, looking for the coffee, and then remembered she had used the last of it during the afternoon—that was why she had called Matt, for God's sake. No coffee then, and how about a nice hot cup of tea? Yes, fine, and it did not matter in the least that she hated the taste of the stuff.

She filled a kettle with icy tap water, set it on the stove, and went back to stand in front of the drainboard, waiting in the darkness for the water to heat. As she stood there, she found herself staring through the window over the sink, through the snowy dark and the ghostly pines at the faint haze of light in the cabin five hundred yards farther up the slope. Zachary Cain, reticent recluse, she thought. Never talks to anyone, seldom leaves the cabin. According to Matt, he buys five or six bottles of whiskey a week, which means he sits up there and drinks alone, and I wonder why, I wonder who he is?

When the water finally began to boil, she made the cup of tea and laced it liberally with sugar and carried it into the living room. As she sat again on the couch, she continued to wonder about the man named Zachary Cain—who he was, why he drank so much, what his reason was for coming to a place like Hidden Valley. And, even though it didn't really matter, couldn't really matter, if he too were somehow lonely.

Five

Lying not-quite-drunk in the darkened cabin bedroom, Cain felt a sense of acute loneliness that was for the first time disassociated from Angie and Lindy and Steve.

The day had been another of the bad ones, filled with painful memories of his family that deepened what was an already mordant despair. But with the coming of darkness, those were not the only memories which had plagued him. Inexplicably, he found himself thinking of things he had locked away in a corner of his mind for the past six months.

There was his work, his abandoned profession. He had been an architect—a good one, a dedicated craftsman—and he recalled how it had been and how you could lose yourself in mathematics and blueprints and sheer creativity, and the way you felt when you saw one of your designs taking shape in wood and glass and stone, standing complete, an entity you alone had conceived.

There were the friends with whom he had willfully severed all relations, by disappearing from San Francisco without word shortly after the accident: Don Collins, another senior employee of the architectural firm for which he had worked and his closest friend; Bert Rhymer, whom he had known since their collegiate days at Stanford; Barry Kells, Fred Gaines, Walt Yamaguchi. And all the easy confidences they had exchanged, the interests they had shared, the laughter they had known.

There were the simple pleasures and relaxations, the little things that rounded out and made complete a man's life: the look of San Francisco, the multifaceted jewel of lights that was The City on a warm spring or summer night; drinking ice-chilled beer and fishing languidly for bass beneath the cottonwoods and willows on the narrow waterways of the San Joaquin Delta; sailing on the Bay on bright windy afternoons, venturing under the Golden Gate Bridge and out onto the Pacific beyond Land's End for a glimpse of San Francisco as the seafarers saw it; reading books and viewing old movies on television and listening to the immortal threads of sound woven long ago by Bix and Kid Ory and Satchmo and W. C. Handy. These, yes, and a dozen more.

The memories flooded his mind unbidden, unwanted, and he could not seem to consume enough alcohol to drive them back into that mental corner. The loneliness was born then, selfish pathos, and because he didn't want it and could not reconcile it, he was angry with himself and almost desperately uneasy. The normality of his past life was dead and buried—he too was dead, inside where it counted—and even at Christmas, even if miracles were possible and the effort was worth making, you could not resurrect the dead. But the loneliness persisted, creating a senseless paradox: hollow man who wants and needs to be alone, and is lonely.

Cain lay motionless on the bed, with his face turned toward the closed door—vaguely aware of the thin strip of light filtering in beneath it, aware that he had not shut off the lamps when he'd quit the front room a few minutes earlier. The hell with it, he thought. The hell with the lamps. He moved his head in a quadrant then and stared at the closet door opposite. Inside, the 30.06 Savage was propped against the back wall, fully loaded, where he'd put it when he first came to Hidden Valley. He could not get up and go over there tonight any more than he had been able to do it any of the other nights. He simply did not have the guts to kill himself, the fact of that was inescapable; he had found it out on the evening three days after the accident, when he had left the hotel room in downtown San Francisco, driven out to Oyster Point, got the rifle from the trunk and loaded it and put the muzzle into his mouth, finger stiff on the trigger, and sat there for thirty minutes that way, sweat drenching him, trying to pull that trigger and not being able to do it. It would always be as it had been on that night—but that did not stop him from thinking about it, the single shot that would end all the suffering and allow him the same oblivion which he had through his carelessness inflicted on Angie, on Lindy, on Steve. . . .

"Christ!" Cain said aloud, and reached over to drag the bourbon bottle and an empty glass from the nightstand. He poured the glass half-full, drank all of it in two convulsive swallows, gagged, felt the liquor churning hot and acrid in his stomach.

Lonely. Lonely!

He swung his feet off the bed and went shakily into the bathroom and knelt in front of the toilet and vomited a half dozen times, painfully. When there was nothing left, he stood up and rinsed his mouth from the sink tap, washed his face and neck in the icy mountain water. Then he returned to the bed and sprawled out prone, breathing thickly.

Angie and the kids, gone, gone.

But not architecture, not San Francisco, not Don Collins and Bert Rhymer—not *me*. . . . .

Lonely.
No!
Lonely, lonely, lonely. . . .

Six

In the living room of his brother's Eldorado Street house, John Tribucci sat with his wife, Ann, and played that fine old prospective-parents game known as Choosing a Name for the Baby.

"I still think," Ann said, "that if it's a boy, he should be called John Junior." She was sitting uncomfortably, hugely, on the sofa, one hand resting on the swell of her abdomen; beneath the high elastic waist of the maternity dress she wore even her breasts seemed swollen to twice their normal size. Long-legged and normally slender, she had high cheekbones and rich-toned olive skin and straight, silky black hair parted in the middle—clear testimony to her part-Amerind heritage, her great-grandmother having been a full-blooded Miwoc. Pregnant or not, she was the most beautiful and the most sensual woman Tribucci had ever known.

He said, "One Johnny around the house is plenty. Besides, I refuse to be prematurely referred to as John Tribucci, *Senior.*"

Ann laughed. "Well, then, there's always your father's name."

"Mario? No way."
"Andrew is nice."
"Then we've got Ann and Andy, the Raggedy twins."
"I also like Joseph."
"Joey Tribucci sounds like a Prohibition bootlegger."
She made a face at him. "You come up with the most incredible objections. You're still holding out for Alexander, right?"
"What's wrong with Alexander?"
"It just doesn't sound very masculine to me."
"Alex is one of the most masculine names I can think of."
"Mmm. But there have still got to be better ones."
"I haven't heard any yet."
"Well—the last time you seemed to like Stephen."
"But you weren't exactly overjoyed with it, as I recall."
"It kind of grows on you. I like John Junior better, but I guess I'm willing to compromise—for now, anyway."
"All right, for now it's Stephen. On to girls' names, since the unlikely possibility does exist that I've fathered a female."
"You," Ann said, "can be a damned male chauvinist at times."
"Guilty as charged."
"And balls to you, love. Okay, you didn't like Suzanne or Toni or Francesca, and I don't like Pamela or Jill or Judith. But I've been thinking and I came up with three new ones, all of which are pretty and one of which even you are bound to like. The first is Hannah."
"Somebody's German maid," Tribucci said. Then, when she glared at him: "Just kidding, it's not bad. What's the second?"
"Marika."
"Better, much better. Marika Tribucci. You know, that has a nice ring to it."
"I think so, too. In fact, it's my favorite. But the third is also sweet: Charlene."

Tribucci had been smiling and relaxed in Vince's old naugahyde easy chair; now the smile vanished, and his eyes turned dark and brooding. He got to his feet and walked across to one of the front windows and stood looking out into the darkness.

Behind him Ann said, "Johnny? What's the matter?"

He did not answer, did not turn. Charlene, he was thinking. Charlene Hammond. It had been a long while since he had thought of her and the night on the deserted beach near Santa Cruz. The incident had been in his mind often for the first few months after it happened; but that had been thirteen years ago, when he was serving the last of his four-year Army stint at Fort Ord, and time had dulled it finally and settled it into the dim recesses of his memory. Even so, it had only taken Ann's innocent suggestion just now to bring it all back in sharp, unwelcome focus.

He had met Charlene Hammond in late July of that year, on the boardwalk in Santa Cruz. She'd been blond, vivacious, ripe of body and suggestive in her mannerisms; not particularly bright, but at twenty-two and living on an Army base, you don't really care about a girl's intelligence quotient. They'd had a few dates—dances, shows, summer events—and when they'd known each other for three weeks, she let him make love to her in the back seat of her father's car. He saw her again two evenings later, and that was the night they went to the beach—because the car was awkward and because they were young and there was something exhilarating in the idea of screwing out in the open with the ocean close by and the clear, vast sky overhead. Charlene had chosen the spot, and he'd known she had been there before for the same purpose; she hadn't been a virgin for a long time.

They parked the car on a bluff and descended to a sheltered place under the cliff's overhang where they couldn't be seen from the road above. There they had spread out a blanket and opened cans of beer, made out a little, taking their time, letting the excitement build. Still, neither of them wanted to wait very long, and excitement builds rapidly on a warm, empty night with the sound of the surf murmuring and throbbing in your ears.

They were lying in a tight embrace on the blanket, she naked and he with just his pants and shoes on, when the two motorcycles came roaring down onto the beach.

Startled, they broke apart, and Charlene fumbled for her clothing and made the mistake of standing up to put it on. The moonlight had been bright, and as clearly as he could see the cycles approaching, the two riders could see him and Charlene and Charlene's nakedness. The bikes swerved toward them. He had an instant premonition of danger; he grabbed her arm, tried to pull her away in a run toward the bluff path. But the cycles swung in hard turns, cut them off, forced them back to the overhang.

He saw, as the bikes pulled up in front of them and stopped, that the two riders were young, in their late twenties or early thirties, dressed in black metal-studded denim and heavy boots, one bearded, the other wearing a gold hoop earring. Charlene was crying, terrified; she had most of her clothing on again, but it was much too late—he knew it had been too late from the moment they'd been seen. He tried to talk to the two cyclists, and it was useless; they were either very drunk or flying on drugs. The bearded one told him to move away from Charlene, and he said no, he wasn't going to do that, and the one wearing the earring dropped a hand to his boot and came up with a long, thin-bladed knife.

"Move now, boyfriend," the bearded one said, "or both of you going to get cut. And we don't want to cut nobody, really."

Charlene screamed, clinging to him. The bearded one grabbed her wrist, spun her to him and held her. Instinctively he started to move to help her, but the knife jabbed forward, darting, pushing him back against the dirt and rock of the bluff. Charlene's cries then were near hysterical.

"Soggy seconds for you, man," the bearded one said to the other. "Watch boyfriend here until I'm done." And turned to Charlene and slapped her several times and pulled her over to the blanket and threw her down on it; tore her clothes off again, dragged his own trousers down. She kept on shrieking, and he kept on hitting her, trying to force her legs apart to get himself inside her. The one with the knife divided his attention between them and Tribucci, giggling softly.

He stood it as long as he could, held at bay by the knife and by fear. And then he simply forgot about the knife and forgot about being afraid and waited until the earringed one's attention had drifted once more to the struggle on the blanket, pushed out from the bluff at that moment, and kicked him between the legs with all his strength. The earringed man screamed louder than Charlene, dropped the knife, and bent over double. He kicked him in the face, kicked him in the head once he was down, turned. The bearded one had released Charlene and was trying to stand, trying to pull his pants up from around his ankles. He ran toward him, shouting, "Run, Charlene, run!" and saw her fleeing half-naked toward the path, and reached the bearded one and kicked him three times in the head and upper body and then threw himself on top of the man and hit him with his fists, rolled his face in the sand, hit him and hit him and hit him and hit him—

And stopped suddenly, because he had become aware of the man's blood spattered warm over his hand and forearm. He struggled to his feet, gasping. The bearded cyclist did not move. He turned to look at the other one: not moving either. One or both of them might have been dead, but he did not care one way or the other then; he just did not care. He walked to where the surf frothed whitely over the sand, knelt and washed the blood off himself; then he found his shirt, put it on, and went slowly up the path to the road. Charlene and the car were gone. He walked along the road for a mile or so to where three teen-agers in a raked station wagon responded to his outthrust thumb and gave him a lift down the coast to Fort Ord. He had been very calm the entire time; reaction did not set in until he was in bed in his barracks.

When it did, he could not seem to stop trembling. He lay there the entire night trembling and thinking about what had happened on the beach and asking himself over and over why he had done what he had. He was not heroic or even particularly brave. He had no strong feelings for Charlene. The two riders very likely had had rape and nothing else on their minds. Why, then? Why?

He had had no answer that night, and he had none thirteen years later; he had done it, and that was all.

The next morning he had called Charlene, and she'd asked him briefly if he was all right and how he'd got away and for God's sake he hadn't called the police, had he? Because she didn't want to get involved; if the police came around to her house, her father would throw her out on the street. She did not thank him, and she did not tell him she was sorry for having left him maybe hurt or dying, for not having summoned help. He hadn't seen her or spoken to her again.

For a week he combed every local newspaper he could find, and there was no mention of anyone answering the description of the cyclists having been found dead on the beach or anywhere else near Santa Cruz. So he hadn't killed one or both of them, and that knowledge had taken away some of the haunting immediacy of the incident and he had been able to begin to forget; he'd told no one—not Ann, not Vince, not his parents—about that night, and he never would. . . .

". . . Johnny, what is it? What's come over you?"

Ann had gotten up and crossed to stand beside him, and she was tugging at the sleeve of his shirt. Tribucci blinked and pivoted to her, saw the concern in her eyes—and the dark recollection faded immediately. He smiled and kissed her. "Nothing," he said, "just one of those brooding spells a man gets from time to time. It's finished with, now."

"Well, I hope so."

He put his arm around her and walked her back to the sofa. "I didn't mean to upset you, honey; I'm sorry, I won't let it happen again."

"You had the oddest look on your face," she said. "What could you possibly have begun brooding about when we—"

And the door to the adjoining family room opened, and Vince appeared, sparing him. Heavier and three years older, Vince wore thick glasses owing to a mild case of myopic astigmatism and was just beginning to lose his hair; for the past hour he and his wife, Judy, had been watching television, or what passed for television on a winter night in the Sierra.

"Just saw an early weathercast from Sacramento," he said. "There's a heavy stormfront moving in from the west, coming right at us. We'll likely be hit with one and maybe two blizzards this week."

"Oh fine," Tribucci said. "Great. A few more heavy storms without a long letup, and we'll sure as hell have slides before the end of the winter."

"Yeah, and I'm afraid at least one of them is liable to be major."

"You two sound like prophets of doom," Ann said. "Where's your Christmas spirit? This is supposed to be the jolly season, you know."

"Ho-ho-ho," Vince said, and grinned. "You people decide on names for your offspring yet?"

"We sort of like Stephen if it's a boy."

"And if it's a girl?"

Tribucci looked at Ann. "Henrietta Lou," he said.

She threw a sofa pillow at him.

Seven

Earl Kubion had a savage, pulsing headache when Brodie finally brought them into Hidden Valley at twenty minutes past eight.

They had been on the road for more than five hours, fighting snow and ice from the time they reached Grass Valley, forced to stop in Nevada City to put on chains, forced to drive at a reduced speed over the treacherous state and county roads. And even though they hadn't encountered any roadblocks or spot checks, and the three highway patrol units and two local county cruisers they had seen had paid no attention to them, Kubion sat tense and watchful the entire time, waiting for something that had not happened. Waiting and listening to the monotonous swish of the windshield wipers; listening to the radio newscasts on the robbery: Sacramento police and the highway patrol were making a concentrated search for the three holdup men, one of whom was reportedly wounded in the left arm; the armored car hadn't been found yet; the one security cop was dead and the woman shoplifter had suffered a nervous breakdown; citizens warned to be on the lookout—the same bullshit over and over again.

Waiting and smelling the heavy odor of Loxner's blood from the back seat, nauseating in the warm confines of the car. Waiting and smoking two packs of cigarettes in short, quick inhalations. He felt now as if his nerves were humming like thin wires in a storm, as if he wanted to hit something, hurt somebody; headaches like this affected him the same way each time: making him irrational, poising him on the edge of pointless violence.

Kubion had lived by and with violence for half of his forty-two years, but it had always been rigidly controlled, resorted to only when unavoidably necessary—as in the case of the Greenfront floor cop—and then in a calm, detached way so that he never lost his grip, relied on intellect to bring him through the tight. When he wasn't working, there had been no thoughts of and no inclination toward force and savagery; only soft, big-assed black chicks (he had always had a thing for big-assed black chicks, screw what anybody thought) and the night life in New York and Miami Beach and L.A.—the balling ball money always bought you.

But a little more than a year ago the headaches had started. Any kind of tension brought them on, and any kind of irritation was liable to push him over the brink into impulsive and unreasoning violence. He had broken Tony Filippi's collarbone and fractured his skull with a gun butt after a job in San Diego last spring because Filippi had fouled up his end of it and almost cost them the score; he had seriously beaten one of his women in a Miami hotel three months later because she had tried to play cute-sex when he was laboring over a payroll ripoff—and had been barely able to buy his way out of a threatened assault charge; he had ruptured a kid parking attendant just two months ago in Anaheim because the kid had gotten snotty with him and he had just finished checking out a job which proved unworkable—that, too, costing him money to fix. When he was feeling right, Kubion looked back on these times with disgust and apprehension and promised himself he would never let it happen again; but then he would get uptight about something, and one of the headaches would come on, and all the control would fall away under the black burning pressure of the impulse.

He had gone to two doctors, one in Miami and one in L.A., and submitted to two thorough physical examinations. Neither of the doctors had found anything organically wrong with him. The first one said the headaches were probably caused by nerves and prescribed tranquilizers; Kubion tried them for a while, and they had seemed to be helping, he thought the problem was licked—until the headache in the Miami hotel and the beating he had given the woman there. The second one said severe headaches were sometimes a sign of mental disorder and suggested Kubion ought to consult a psychologist. He hadn't taken that advice; it was garbage for one thing, and he didn't trust shrinks for another. They were nothing but sharks with fancy degrees and fancy two-bit double talk. He remembered the superior, patronizing son of a bitch at the Michigan state prison where he'd done a nickel stretch for armed robbery in the early fifties, his only fall. Penal psychologist, they'd called him, penal meaning prick: probing with endless questions, rapping pure manure about detrimental adolescent environment and sociopathic attitudes and a hint of latent megalomania—leaving Kubion feeling irritated and unsettled each time, alienating him completely. The hell with that crap.

He'd decided finally that he would just have to take care of it on his own—control himself when the headaches came on, work it out the same way he worked out a difficult score. He hadn't been able to do it yet, but he would because he had to in order to keep on working and keep on balling. Things would smooth out all right. Hadn't they always smoothed out for him in the past?

Kubion did not think of any of this as they drove along the snowswept and deserted main street of the village.

There was only the throbbing pain in his head, and the jangling of his nerves, and the bitter frustration of the rip-off that had gone sour in Sacramento, and the overpowering, irrational need to smash something or somebody. He lit another cigarette, staring out through the windshield at the Christmas lights which still burned above the street, the buildings all unlighted save for more Christmas bulbs decorating the façade of the Valley Inn and two squares of yellow which came through its misted front windows. The red and blue and green glow of the bulbs limned his dark face surrealistically—a lean face fashioned of hard, vertical lines that gave it a somehow unfinished appearance, as if it had never been properly planed off and you could, if you looked closely enough, see the marks of a sculptor's chisel. In normal light the darkness of his skin coloring, the sooty black of his hair and eyebrows, the heavy beard shadow combined to create about him a charred look, like a man recently emerged from a coal fire.

Beside him Brodie said the first words any of them had spoken in thirty minutes: "Not even eight thirty and they've rolled up the sidewalks already."

Kubion said nothing, sucking at the filter of his cigarette.

There were rustling sounds in the rear seat, and Loxner said, "Jesus, we finally here?" His voice was thick; Brodie had brought him a pint of gin when they stopped to put on the chains in Nevada City—antiseptic for his arm and anesthesia for the pain, not wanting to chance buying bandages or pharmaceuticals with the word out that one of them was wounded.

"Finally here," Brodie answered.

"All right if I sit up now?"

"Come ahead. There's nobody on the streets."

Loxner sat up, blinking. He was the same age as Kubion, running to fat in the middle from too much ale and food; he had thinning hair the color of tarnished copper and the beginnings of bulldog jowls. "My arm feels kind of numb now," he said. "But I got to get something on it as soon as we get to the cabin, iodine or something. You don't treat a gunshot wound and take care of it, you get infection. Gangrene, maybe."

"Shut up with your whining," Kubion said.

"Hey, I'm not whining. It's just that I—"

"Shut up! I've been smelling your blood for five hours now, and I don't need to listen to you shit at the mouth."

"Take it easy, Earl," Brodie said.

"Stop telling me to take it easy, you son of a bitch!"

Brodie took his foot off the gas and turned his head and looked at Kubion. He was tall, fair-haired, narrow-hipped, and looked like one of those smiling pretty-boy types Kubion had seen around the Miami resort hotels, looking for middle-aged and moneyed pussy; he had violet-blue eyes that were normally soft but which could harden until they resembled chunks of amethyst quartz—and they were like that now. "I'm no son of a bitch," he said slowly, "and I don't like being called one."

"Fuck you, Brodie. You hear that? Fuck you!"

Brodie stared at him a moment longer, his hands tight on the wheel. Then he seemed to shake himself slightly, and his fingers relaxed; he put his foot back on the accelerator and his eyes fully on the road again. They were beyond the village now, at the junction of Macklin Lake Road and Mule Deer Lake Road. Silently he swung the car right, the tire chains making thin crunching sounds on the packed snow which covered the road, and almost immediately they began to wind through thick stands of lodgepole pine. The car's headlights, made furry by the falling snow, tunneled through the darkness.

Kubion said, "Well, Brodie?"

Leaning over the back seat, establishing a small barrier between the two men in front, Loxner said, "You remember if there's bandages and iodine at the cabin, Vic?"

"Yeah, I think so," Brodie answered. "The place is stocked up with everything else."

"We haven't eaten anything since breakfast, you know that? Once I do something about this arm, it's maybe a good idea to put some food on my gut."

"We could all do with a little food. Steaks maybe."

"The hell with it," Kubion said. Ice crackled loudly as he wound down his window and threw the cigarette out; the chill mountain wind blew snow against the side of his face, put an edge on the heater warmth inside the car. "The hell with it, the hell with both of you."

They rode the rest of the way to the Mule Deer Lake cabin in heavy silence.

Eight

Shortly past nine o'clock, in the familiar darkness of a Whitewater motel room, Peggy Tyler sighed and rested her cheek against Matt Hughes' hairless stomach. "Did you like that?" she asked. "Did I please you, Matt?"

"Oh my God!" he said.

Smiling, she moved up into the fold of his right arm. Tawny blond hair, tangled now, flowed over his chest and shoulders; her amber-colored eyes contained an expression, tinged with amusement, that was completely contrary to their normally demure one. Statuesque and heavy-breasted, her body shone like finely veined marble in the darkness.

She was twenty-one years old and had for four years known exactly what she wanted from life. And when the boy she had been dating at age seventeen offered to buy her a new ski sweater if she would take off her clothes and let him play with her, she had known exactly how to go about getting it.

Her goal was twofold: to get as far away from Hidden Valley, California, as it was possible to get; and to marry a man with position, wealth, and a passion for warm places, snowless places where you could lie at the foot of a clear blue ocean in the middle of January and let the sun bake away all the cold, cold memories. But she was not impatient as so many of her school friends had been. She saw no point in leaving immediately, prematurely, after high school graduation for San Francisco or Hollywood or Las Vegas or New York, as some of them had done. Once you were there, you had to play the game because everyone else played it—and all the while some of the excitement and some of the glitter were just around the corner, look but don't touch.

No, that wasn't the way to do it at all. There was a better way, a much better way. It required a large sum of money and a long period of self-sacrifice, but in the meantime you could mature, you could become well read and acquire a certain polish. You put every spare dollar into a special bank account until you had accumulated a minimum of twenty-five thousand dollars, and *then* you left. Then you went to Europe instead of to the mundane cities of America; you went to Paris and Rome and Monte Carlo, and you outfitted yourself in fashionably expensive clothes, and you stayed at the best hotels and frequented only those theaters and restaurants and clubs which catered to the whims of the select; you ingratiated yourself into the lives of the wealthy and the sophisticated, fitting in perfectly because you were perfectly prepared. That was where you would meet the kind of man you wanted, in his milieu, on exactly the right terms. It would not take long, with her looks and her sexual prowess. It would not take long at all.

So she remained in Hidden Valley, living with her mother in the family home on Shasta Street—her father, a county maintenance foreman, having died of a heart attack when she was eleven. She had taken the job with Grange Electric in Soda Grove, and assiduously, she had sought out the right men with whom to sleep—the men with a little money who did not mind making small loans or cash gifts in exchange for the use of her body. Men like Hidden Valley Mayor Matt Hughes.

She had always believed Matt Hughes to be something of a puritan: righteous, religious, happily married, certainly not inclined to extramarital affairs. As a result, and despite the fact that he was the most well-to-do man in the area, she had never really considered him a possible stepping-stone. But then she had gone into the Mercantile one afternoon more than a month ago to buy some groceries for her mother, and he had been there alone; he kept looking at her, she could feel his eyes on her as she moved along the aisles, and when she had gone up to the counter to pay for her purchases, he made overtures that were at once carefully veiled and, to her, altogether obvious.

Concealing her surprise, accepting him immediately because of who and what he was, she had hinted that she found him attractive too, and that she would be willing to see him in more casual surroundings. Nothing more had been said that afternoon, but Peggy knew that she would not have to wait long until Hughes followed through; in point of fact, she was half-expecting his call to her at work the ensuing Monday.

He said then that he was planning to be in Whitewater that evening, would she like to have dinner with him? She pretended to think it over and eventually allowed that she supposed it would be all right. He suggested she meet him, if she didn't mind the short drive, at a place called The Mill—a small restaurant on the outskirts of Whitewater; she said that was fine, and met him that night, and responded to his flattery and to his physical presence just enough to let him know she was definitely interested. After dinner, however, she demurely declined his suggestion that they go somewhere alone; she made it a practice never to seem too eager, which invariably made men like Matt Hughes want her that much more. When he asked if he could see her again, she feigned reluctance and then told him that even though it was probably wrong, dating him when he was a married man and all, she really couldn't bring herself to say no.

They had three other dinner engagements at The Mill before she finally allowed him to kiss her, to fondle her, to maneuver her to the small motel on the outskirts of Whitewater—one which did not ask questions or care to what exact purpose their units' beds were put, this being the middle of the winter off-season. He had been almost laughably excited when she accepted his proposal, as if he were an overeager teen-ager who'd never had a woman before, and she had thought he would probably be totally unsatisfactory as a lover. But he had surprised her in that respect, he was really very accomplished. Sex for Peggy had been a source of intense physical pleasure from the very first, and Matt Hughes was as proficient as any she had gone to bed with in the past four years. It made the arrangement with him all the more satisfying. . . .

They lay without speaking for a time, and the only sound was the penetrating voice of the wind as it whipped through the pine and hemlock outside the motel. Finally, Hughes stirred and rolled onto his side and said, "You're fantastic, Peggy, do you know that?" in a voice still thick with desire.

She smiled again. "Am I, Matt?"

"Yes. Oh yes. Peggy—can I see you again tomorrow night?"

"We still have more of tonight, baby."

"I know, but I want to see you tomorrow too."

"Well, I'm not sure if I can . . ."

"Please? I'll have something for you then."

"Oh?"

"A Christmas present, a very nice Christmas present."

Peggy lifted herself onto one elbow, looking at him closely now in the darkness. "That's sweet of you," she said. "You're awfully sweet, Matt. What is it?"

"That would spoil the surprise."

"Couldn't you give me a hint?"

"Well. . . ." He thought for a moment. "It's something small in size but not in stature."

"Jewelry?" she asked immediately.

"No, not jewelry."

"Something to wear, then?"

"No. No, you can't wear it."

"Matt, don't tease me like this. What is it?"

"I'll give you a broader hint. I'm not very good at buying presents; I mean, I'm always afraid I'll pick out something that won't be quite right. So I don't really buy *anything*, I leave that up to the individual person."

Money, Peggy thought—and said it aloud, "Money?"

Hughes misinterpreted the inflection in her voice. "You're not offended, are you?"

God! "No, I'm not offended, baby. I . . . just didn't expect anything like that. You've been so generous already."

Which was true enough. Peggy had waited until their fourth evening together at the motel before bringing up the subject of money; she had done it very casually and very deftly, as always, saying that her dentist had told her she needed some work on her wisdom teeth but that she really couldn't afford it and she supposed she could endure the minor toothache discomfort a while longer. . . . As she had anticipated, he had been sympathetic and had readily offered to pay for the dental work, a token of his affection for her, wouldn't even think of it as a loan; she had told him she couldn't possibly, and then allowed him to talk her into accepting. And when she said that her dentist would not accept credit from her, that she would need cash, he gave her a hundred dollars that same night and insisted that she tell him when she needed more. She had needed more two weeks later, another hundred dollars, and tonight she had been going to ask him for an additional fifty—proceeding cautiously—and here he was telling her that he was going to make her a cash gift for

Christmas. Wonderfully beneficent, wonderfully pliable Matt Hughes!

He said, "I don't think I've been generous enough. And besides that, I want to do it, I want to give you something nice for Christmas."

"You give me something nice every time we're together," she said, but the words were automatic, disassociated from her thoughts; she wanted to ask him how large the present was going to be—the way he talked, it was a substantial sum—but she did not want to seem overly expectant. Three hundred? Five hundred? Just how generous was he going to be?

"And you to me," he said. "Tomorrow night, then?"

"Yes, Matt. Tomorrow night and any night you want."

He drew her full against him, kissing her eyes as if in gratitude. Excitement stirred in her loins again, as much a result of anticipation of his Christmas gift as in response to his warm and naked masculinity. He clung to her, whispering her name, as she began to stroke him, make him ready again. And while one part of her mind concentrated on their rekindled passion, another part dwelled on the twenty-one thousand dollars she had saved thus far and the concomitant knowledge that if his present was as large as he had led her to believe, if she could prolong the affair with him and he continued to supply her with money, the time when she would finally be able to leave Hidden Valley was very close at hand. Another six or eight months, maybe even less; certainly no later than mid-fall of next year, before her twenty-second birthday, before the cold winter snows came.

Oh yes, long before the snows came. . . .

Nine

Wrapped in mackinaw and muffler and waterproof boots, Lew Coopersmith had just finished shoveling thick powder drifts from his front walk when Frank McNeil came to see him shortly past nine Tuesday morning.

It had stopped snowing sometime during the night, and the air had a crystal quality, clean and sharp like the slender ice daggers which gleamed on the front eaves of the house. A high, thin cloud-cover shielded the winter sun; but visibility was good, and you could see portions of the white-laced peaks marking higher elevations to the east. You could also see the thickening black snowclouds which obscured their crests, and you knew—sourly, in Coopersmith's case—that there would be another heavy snowfall later in the day.

He leaned on the long handle of his shovel as McNeil's ten-year-old Dodge plowed through the snow on Alpine Street and drew up just beyond his front gate—thinking irascibly: Fine, can't think of anyone else I'd rather have come calling this morning. With McNeil, he saw, was the café owner's son; the two of them got out of the car and came over to the gate.

"Morning, Frank, Larry." Coopersmith's voice was blank, without particular interest. "Something I can do for you?"

"I sure as Christ hope so," McNeil said. His eyes shone with dark outrage, and his blunt face was flushed. "Somebody broke into the café last night."

"*What?*"

"That's right. Broke the lock off the rear door and then propped the goddamn door wide open. Storeroom was filled with snow when Larry and me went in to open up a few minutes ago—snow all over everything."

Coopersmith abandoned his careless manner. "What was taken, Frank?"

"Nothing. Not a single thing."

"You positive about that?"

"Hell yes. First thing we did was check the register and my cash box. They hadn't been touched."

"No supplies missing, either?"

"No."

"Vandalism?"

"Just the rear door, that's all."

Coopersmith frowned. "Any idea who could have done it?"

"Damn it, no. It doesn't make a bit of sense."

"You report it yet?"

"I wanted to talk to you first."

In spite of his dislike for McNeil, Coopersmith felt mildly appreciative of the implied confidence. He said crisply, "All right, Frank. Let's go have a look."

He propped his shovel against the cross-slatted fence and went with father and son to the Dodge. McNeil started the car and drove the four blocks to the Valley Café, pulled into the narrow, snowpacked alley that ran behind the building. He parked close to the Café's rear entrance, and Coopersmith got out immediately and went to look at the door.

The lock, old and flimsy, had been cleanly snapped by

means of inserting a crowbar or some similar tool between the door edge and the jamb. There were splinter and gouge marks in the wood there which told him that much. The door was closed now. Coopersmith said, "You wedge it closed from the inside, Frank?"

"No. Latch still holds, even with the busted lock."

Coopersmith opened the door and stepped into the small, somewhat cluttered storeroom. The floor inside was wet, still mounded in places with the snow—melting now—which had blown in during the night. To one side was a half-filled crate of oranges; indicating that, McNeil said, "Crate there was holding the door open."

"That where you usually keep it—by the door?"

McNeil shook his head. "It's supposed to be over there with the other fruits and vegetables."

"Way it seems, then, whoever did it had nothing in mind except letting a lot of snow whip in here."

"Yeah. But what the hell *for?*"

"Could be a practical joke."

"Some joke, if that's it."

"Or it could be somebody wanted to harass you a little."

"Why'd anybody want to harass *me,* for Chrissake?"

"Well—you ruffle any feathers lately?"

"Not me. I get along with everyone, you know that."

Yeah, Coopersmith thought. He moved slowly around the storeroom, found nothing, and pushed open the swing door that led to the front of the café.

Following him, McNeil said, "Like I told you: nothing taken, nothing disturbed."

They went back into the storeroom, and Coopersmith said, "Best thing for you to do is report what happened to the substation in Soda Grove; but if you want, you can tell them not to bother sending a deputy over. Tell them I'll look into it—ask around, see if anybody saw anything last night, and then check in with them later on."

"What about fingerprints, stuff like that?"

"Frank, nothing was stolen, nothing was vandalized. Now I've got a fingerprint kit at the house, and I can get it and come back here and dust the door and the orange crate and everything else in the place, wet as it is. But what's the point? Like as not, whoever did it is a valley resident, and I can't go around taking prints of everybody who lives here. Besides, cold as it was during the night, he was probably wearing gloves anyway."

"I'm supposed to just forget about it, then, is that it? Who's going to pay for the damned lock?"

"I told you I'd look into it," Coopersmith said. "When I find out who did it, he'll pay for the lock or he'll find himself up in front of a county judge."

"He'll go straight to jail, I got anything to say."

Coopersmith pursed his lips. "You want to do it the way I said, or you want to call in a deputy from the substation?"

"Oh, you handle it. I guess you know what you're doing."

"Thanks," Coopersmith said dryly. "You going to open up now?"

"Might as well, I suppose."

"Well, I'll walk home then. Exercise'll do me good."

"You'll be asking around right away, won't you?"

"I will. And if I find out anything, I'll let you know."

Coopersmith started for the door, and McNeil said abruptly, "Listen, Lew, I just thought of something."

"What is it?"

"All of us who live in Hidden Valley, we know one another pretty well, and there's none of us who'd pull a shitty trick like this. But there's one person we don't know nothing about. You understand who I'm talking about, Lew?"

"That Cain fella, I reckon."

"That's right. Maybe you'd better talk to *him* right off; maybe he's the bastard who did this."

"Why should he do it? You have some trouble with him?"

"Not exactly. But it could be he found out I asked you to run that check on him, it could be he's got a hard-on for me over that."

"I ran the check three months ago," Coopersmith reminded him.

"Well, maybe he just found out about it. Anyhow, I don't like that bird; I don't trust him. Living up in the Hughes' cabin all alone, don't talk to nobody, walks around with his nose up like a dog just pissed on his leg. You can't tell what somebody like that will do."

Coopersmith thought about offering further words of reason, decided there was no point in reasoning with a man like McNeil, and said, "I'll see what I can find out." He nodded to the café owner and went out into the valley.

As he walked through the snow to Sierra Street, he realized that there was a certain purposeful spring in his step and that he felt better than he had in weeks. It was, he supposed, damned perverse of a man to feel good as a result of somebody else's troubles, but he could not help himself; if only for a little while, and only on a very small scale, he was involved again, he was useful to others and to himself.

Ten

Kubion spent the morning prowling the large, slant-beam-ceilinged interior of the cabin at Mule Deer Lake: upstairs, downstairs, front and rear, smoking too much, drinking too much coffee. He no longer had the savage headache of the night before, but he felt restless and edgy—an impotent, caged kind of feeling. Two sticks of marijuana hadn't helped either, although the joints he had blown after their arrival last night had dulled his proclivity for violence and allowed him to sleep. That was the problem with pot: sometimes it did for him, and sometimes it didn't. As a result, he didn't use it often, but he liked to keep a supply on hand; liquor soured his belly, and everybody needed some type of high once in a while—ease the pressure, get rid of the down feeling.

Neither Brodie nor Loxner had said anything about the near blowoff in the car coming in, and he hadn't mentioned it either; all of them pretending it hadn't happened. So he'd lucked out of another of those bastard headaches, but unless he could learn to hold himself in check, he couldn't keep lucking out of them indefinitely. He'd wind up killing somebody, sure as hell, and when you killed people without good reason, you were as good as dead yourself. Well, he'd learn; he had to learn, and he would, and that was all there was to it. He just wasn't going to do to himself what all the fuzz in the country hadn't been able to do to him in seventeen years. No way. No frigging *way*.

Kubion came down the side hall from the rear porch into the living room. Loxner was sitting in one of the chairs grouped before a native-stone fireplace. He was his old bluff, stupid self today—pretending, too, that he hadn't let his yellow show through when he'd taken the bullet at Greenfront. His left arm was suspended in a handkerchief sling; he'd found merthiolate and bandages in the bathroom medicine cabinet and had wrapped it up as soon as they'd come in. The bullet had missed bone, exiting cleanly, and he'd be able to use the arm again in a few days, once soreness and stiffness decreased.

In Loxner's right hand was a bottle of Rainier Ale, and he was listening to the table model radio which had originally been in the kitchen—staticky country-and-western music, fading in and out at irregular intervals. The three of them had picked up a newscast on the radio over breakfast, and there were no fresh developments in Sacramento; the cops still hadn't found the dummy car. The news announcer had no further information on the suspected whereabouts of the holdup men, but the implication was that local law enforcement officials figured they were still confined to the immediate Sacramento area. Which was fine, except that it didn't change things much as far as they were concerned. Sure, the odds were good that they could leave today and make it to Vegas or L.A. without trouble and begin looking around for another score, a quick score; but when you're wanted for Murder One, and one of you has a shot-up flipper, and you know how the little unforeseeable things can screw you up—like that security guard coming in at just the wrong time to screw up the Greenfront job—you don't gamble, you don't put your ass on the line.

Kubion wandered around the room and then stopped short near one of the front windows. Damn it, this aimless pacing back and forth wasn't doing him any good. What he needed was to get out for a while: cold air, a sense of movement and activity. He went upstairs and got his coat off the floor in his room, where he'd thrown it last night. When he came down again, Brodie was standing with a paring knife in one hand and a potato in the other, talking to Loxner.

"You going out, Earl?" he asked as Kubion walked across to the door.

"That's what it looks like, right?"

"For a walk, or into the village, or what?"

"Why?"

"Well, if you're going into the village, I could use a couple of cans of tomato sauce. I want to make Veal Milanese for supper tonight."

Tomato sauce, Kubion thought, Jesus Christ. Brodie had this thing for cooking—*culinary art,* he called it—and he was always making crap like Veal Milanese and baked stuffed chicken and pineapple glazed ham. He said it was a hobby with him—he'd gotten interested from his mother, who'd won some kind of national prize once. Some hobby for a man; it was more the kind of hobby you'd expect a fag to have; and Kubion wasn't all that sure about Brodie. Vic had a reputation as a stud, Mr. Supercock, but with that pretty-boy face of his and this *culinary art* business, maybe underneath his hard professionalism he was Mr. Superqueer instead; you never knew these days who was taking it up the ass and who wasn't.

"All right?" Brodie said.

"Yeah, all right," Kubion said, and went out into the chill, rarefied air. When he got to the enclosed garage tacked onto the lakeward side of the cabin, he saw that snow had piled up in two-foot drifts against the doors.

Shit. He stood staring at it for a moment and then lifted his eyes and looked down a long, gradual slope and across a white meadow at the frozen, snow-coated surface of Mule Deer Lake. Pines and taller firs crowded in close to the southern and western shores, but congregated along the eastern shore, where a row of white-fingered piers reached out into the water, were several other cabins and houses and summer lodges. Most of them were unoccupied now, abandoned-looking beneath canvases of snow.

Some bitching country, he thought. The exact center of nowhere. How anyone could live in a place like this the year round was beyond him. Nothing but snow and ice and bitter wind and maybe an influx of stupid fishermen and hunters in season—no action, nothing to do, a goddamn prison with trees and rocks and snow for bars.

He turned and went into the woodshed—looks like an out-house, he thought, *some* bitching place—which was situated at the rear of the property. The cabin, a double-tiered A-frame fashioned of bark-stripped redwood siding, sat on a projection of granite at the long slope's upper edge. Flanked by trees to the north and east, through which its private and currently snowpacked access lane wound upward from Mule Deer Lake Road, it was completely isolated; the nearest dwelling was a fifth of a mile away. The cabin belonged to a man named Brendikian, a long-retired bunco gambler who had amassed a small fortune during and after the Second World War with trimmed and shaded cards and suction-bevel missout dice; then he had gone into score financing and safe housing for the independents working outside the Circle. This was just one of several secluded safe houses he had bought and on which he paid taxes through dummy California and Nevada corporations—totally untraceable should one of them be knocked over. Loxner had once done a job of some sort for Brendikian and had

had no difficulty arranging for the cabin's use at three bills a week.

Kubion found a curve-bladed snow shovel in the woodshed, came back, and cleared the area in front of the doors. Then he threw the shovel to one side and pulled the two halves open. Even though the car had been sheltered overnight, there was a thin film of ice on the windows; the garage felt like the interior of a frozen-food locker. He scraped away the ice, got the car started and out of the garage, and went down to Mule Deer Lake Road.

The village plow had been along there earlier in the morning, clearing it and pushing the snow into windrows at the shoulders; the pavement was slick with ice in parts, and Kubion drove slowly into the village. On Sierra Street, he parked in front of Tribucci Bros. Sport Shop, wedging his car against the long snow mound at the curbing. Music drifted down to him as he stepped out. The hicks always went in for Christmas in a big way—carols and trees and decorations and stockings on the mantel and sleigh rides, all the horse-shit. And this was a hick village if ever there was one. Populated by a bunch of half-witted Eskimos in wooden igloos. Christ!

He went into the shop, and a four-eyed balding guy was behind the counter, wearing a shirt with the name Vince stitched over the left-hand pocket. This Vince smiled at Kubion—friendly, vacuous, sure enough a damned Eskimo. Kubion smiled back at him, playing the game, and bought three packages of cigarettes. Vince wished him a Merry Christmas as he turned to leave, and Kubion said, "Sure, Merry Christmas," thinking it was anything but, after the bust in Sacramento.

Outside again, he walked toward the overloud singing. Tomato sauce and Veal Milanese, you'd think everything was beautiful and they were having a big celebration. Still—what the hell. You had to eat, and there was no point in creating a hassle with Brodie; let him make his Veal Milanese, let him make anything he wanted as long as he didn't try to make *him*.

Smiling faintly, Kubion entered the Mercantile. The store was fairly crowded, noisy, and smelled of wool and dampness and pitch pine burning in the potbellied stove. Kubion had seen most of the people there at one time or another during the previous week, though he did not know or care to know any of their names. But Pat Garvey was the dumpy blond woman being waited on by Maude Fredericks, and the three men grouped around the potbelly rapping about a forthcoming blizzard were Joe Garvey—big, work-roughened, with fierce black eyes and a sprinkling of pockmarks on his flushed cheeks; stooped and fox-faced Sid Markham, who operated a fix-it shop from his Mule Deer Lake home; and Walt Halliday. Matt Hughes stood inside the Post Office enclosure, sorting the mail which had just come in from Soda Grove.

Kubion went to stand near the front counter, close to the trio by the stove. They stopped talking about the weather and were silent for a moment; then Halliday said, "Either of you been over to see McNeil this morning?"

"Yeah, a little while ago," Garvey said. "The way he's yelling, everybody in the county knows the café was broken into last night."

"Funny damned thing: nothing stolen, nothing damaged."

"Don't make much sense, I'll grant."

"Lew Coopersmith find out anything yet, you know?"

"Talked to him just before I came in here," Markham said. "He hadn't learned a thing then."

"He been to see that Zachary Cain?" Garvey asked. "McNeil seems to think Cain might have done it."

"Didn't say if he had or not. But you ask me, Cain didn't have nothing to do with it. Sure, he keeps full to himself, but that don't make him a criminal. And keeping his own counsel is more than you can say for that fart

McNeil, always running off at the mouth the way he does."

"I don't know," Halliday said. "It doesn't seem natural for a man to live all alone like that, never saying a word to anybody. You—"

He broke off as the door opened and a bearded, faintly bearish man came inside. He moved up to the counter, bloodshot eyes fixed directly in front of him, and stood next to Kubion; the three men at the stove watched him, silent again. This must be Cain, Kubion thought—they act like the poor bastard had leprosy. What a bunch of silly turds. If I were in his shoes, I wouldn't stop with breaking into their café; I'd burn the whole village to the ground, do them all a favor.

Pat Garvey finished with her purchases, detoured around Cain, and tugged at her husband's sleeve. "Sure, all right," Garvey said, nodded to Halliday and Markham, and followed his wife out of the store. Maude Fredericks came down to where Kubion was standing, asked him if she could be of service; he told her he wanted two cans of tomato sauce, and she smiled as if he'd ordered a side of beef and fifty pounds of canned goods and went over to the grocery section.

The door opened again, and Verne Mullins came in briskly. He raised a hand to the three men around the stove, went directly to the Post Office enclosure, and said loudly, "Morning, Matt." He was fat and had a huge red-veined nose and the bright, darting eyes of a bird; a bluff, somewhat testy exterior masked a soft Irish heart. Like Lew Coopersmith, he did not look his age: sixty-nine, come February.

Hughes turned, smiling. "Morning, Verne."

"Any mail for me?"

"Couple of things. Wait—here you go."

Mullins took the envelopes and shuffled through them; then he held one up—thin and brown, with the words "Southern Pacific Retirement Bueau" in the upper left-hand corner—and said, "About time they decided to send my check along. Man works forty-five years for the same company, never late and never sick a day of it, and then when he retires, he's got to fight for the damned money he paid into the retirement fund all along."

Hughes winked at him. "That's big business for you."

"Now ain't that the truth?" Mullins said. "Bank open this morning, Matt? Figure I better cash this right off, so it doesn't bounce on me."

"Bank's always open for you, Verne."

Hughes came out of the enclosure and over to the counter. Mullins tore open the envelope, took the check out, endorsed it, and handed it across. "Put it mostly in twenties if you can," he said. "Got to send a few off to my grandkids for the holidays."

"Sure thing."

Hughes took the check into his office, closed the door. Maude Fredericks said to Kubion, "Will there be anything else, sir?"

"What?"

"I have your tomato sauce. Was there something else?"

"No," Kubion said. "No, that's it."

He gave her a dollar bill, and she rang up the purchase on the old-fashioned, crank-type register. She handed him his change, put the two cans into a paper sack. Hughes came out of his office with a sheaf of bills in his hand and counted them out to Verne Mullins—four hundred and fifty dollars. Mullins tucked them into a worn leather billfold, said, "Thanks, Matt, you're a good lad," and started for the door.

Hughes called after him. "Don't forget church on Sunday, Verne."

"Now would a good Irish Protestant like me be forgetting church on the Sunday before Christmas? I'll be there, don't you worry; somebody's got to put a dime in the collection plate."

Hughes laughed, and Mullins went out as Maude Fredericks said to Cain, "Yes, please?"

"Bottle of Old Grandad." Cain said.

Kubion picked up his paper sack and left the store. Bank, he was thinking. Safe in that office. Four hundred and fifty dollars without even looking at the check first. If this Hughes operates a kind of unofficial banking service, if he regularly cashes checks for people who live here, how much does he keep on hand?

Hell, Kubion told himself then, you're starting to think like a punk. A hick village like this, for Christ's sake, the amount in that safe *has* to be penny-ante. We need a score, sure, but something big, something damned big now. And you don't crap on safe ground to begin with, especially not with the kind of heat we're carrying. Forget it.

He went up the snow-tracked sidewalk to his car.

Eleven

When the telephone rang at four o'clock, Rebecca knew immediately that it was Matt and that he was calling to tell her he wouldn't be home again that night. She put her book aside and stared across the living room to where the unit sat on a pigskin-topped table. Ring. Silence. Ring. Silence. Ring. I won't answer it, she thought—and then stood up slowly and walked over to the table and picked up the hand-set.

"Yes, Matt," she said.

"Hello, dear. How did you know it was me?"

"I'm psychic, how else?"

He laughed softly. "I just called to tell you I won't be home again until late tonight. Neal Walker wants me to go to the City Council meeting in Coldville, and I—"

"All right," she said.

"I'll try not to be too late."

"All right."

"Rebecca—is something the matter?"

"Now what could possibly be the matter?"

"Well, you sound tired. Are you feeling well?"

"Lovely," she said. "Have a nice time, won't you?"

"Yes. Don't wait up."

"I wouldn't think of it. Good-bye, Matt."

Rebecca put the receiver down without waiting to hear if he had anything further to say. She stood there stiffly, thinking: How many times have we played that same little scene? Fifty, a hundred? And such trite dialogue, like something written by a third-rate playwright. Rebecca Hughes: character in a pointless drama. Reciting her lines, going through the motions, while the unseen audience watches in boredom and suppresses snickers because the entire episode is so totally and ridiculously conventional.

She went to the main hall and along it into the kitchen. Earlier in the day she had gone down to the Mercantile to get coffee, and she had had the percolator on ever since she returned; she poured another cup—did that make ten for the day, or was it fifteen?—and stood drinking it by the table. Through the window over the sink, she could see white-flecked darkness: snowing again, a whipping veil of snow. Beginnings of a heavy storm. She could remember a time when she relished one of these mountain winter blizzards—curled up with Matt on the rug in front of the fireplace, insulated against the turbulence without, drinking hot eggnog and perhaps making a little love in the cracking glow of the fir-log fire. Soft, shared warmth and soft, shared love.

And wasn't that, too, as trite as the rest of it?

I don't want to be alone tonight, she thought. I don't think I can stand being alone again tonight. But where could she go? The Valley Inn? No, there would be friendly, probing questions as to Matt's whereabouts, and she would have to repeat his lie and then listen to them talk about what a fine, upstanding man he was, and all in all it would be worse than being alone. Ann Tribucci? Ann was her closest friend in the valley, though Rebecca had at no time been able to talk to her about personal matters; she had wanted to often enough, to purge herself woman to woman, but she could never quite manage the courage. Tonight would be no different. If anything, seeing Ann tonight would make things worse: the previous weekend, she and Johnny had moved temporarily from their home near Mule Deer Lake to Vince and Judy Tribucci's house —Ann hadn't wanted to be alone out there with the baby coming—and Rebecca would have to face all four of them; she would have to witness the solicitous way Johnny looked at his wife and the happiness that was theirs with the baby due so soon now. . . .

Abruptly, Rebecca wondered if things might have been different if she and Matt had had a child. Well no, probably not, and anyway, the question was academic. He had told her during their brief engagement that he was sterile —their childless marriage was in no way responsible for his infidelity, either—and she had said then that it didn't matter, they had each other and that was enough. There had been some talk at that time of adopting a baby later on, but neither of them had mentioned it again in the seven years they had been man and wife.

Her eyes strayed to the window again, and she could just make out the familiar, iridescent glow of light in the cabin above. And she found herself wondering about Zachary Cain again, wondering as she had on the previous night if he too was lonely. Would he welcome some company on this stormy night, the same as she? Would he be receptive to a visit from a young-old and cuckolded wife?

Oh, stop it, she told herself. The only thing you'd accomplish by going up there is to make a fool of yourself; remember Reno, remember that, and it doesn't matter that it's not the same thing. There's nothing up there for you, nothing at all.

Rebecca finished the last of her coffee, put the cup down, and went back into the living room. She was cold again—odd how she couldn't seem to keep warm lately. Picking up her book, she climbed the stairs and ran a hot bath and undressed and slipped into the tub. The steaming water helped a little; she could feel herself beginning to relax.

The book she was reading was one of those sex-and-big business best sellers—not really absorbing, just something to read—and she opened it again as she lay soaking. After two pages, she came to another in a long series of boudoir scenes; but this one, as coldly clinical in detail as all the others, had a curiously and intense erotic effect on her. Her nipples grew erect beneath the warm bathwater; her hips moved featheringly against the smooth porcelain; her thighs opened and closed in a gentle, involuntary rhythm. God, it had been such a long time now! Dry-throated, she closed the book sharply and put it aside, shutting her eyes, willing her body still. After a time the sexual need began to ebb—but she was cold again, even in the warm bath she was cold again. . . .

Half an hour later, fully dressed, she sat with a tasteless sandwich—she could not recall the last time she had taken a genuine pleasure in the consumption of food—and a cup of coffee at the kitchen table. Seven o'clock now. Blizzard flinging snow at the window, wailing emptily. It was going to be such a long, long night—

—and I don't want to be alone, she thought.

The window seemed suddenly to develop a magnetic pull for her eyes. After a moment she stood from the table and went there and saw again the diffused yellow light in the cabin. She looked at it for a full minute, and then she thought: Well, I *could* go up there, I could go up and talk to him for a while; there's nothing wrong in that. Just two people, landlord and tenant, talking together on a stormy, lonely winter night. And she *was* curious about him, there was that too.

She kept on standing there, thinking about it—and then she walked into the hall, to where the coat closet was located near the Dutch-doored front entrance. You'd better not do it, she told herself—and knew that she was going to do it anyway. She opened the closet and put on fur-lined snow parka and fur-lined ski boots (presents from Matt in one of his contrite and attentive moments); then she tied a scarf tightly around her head, put the parka's hood over it, drew on a pair of wool mittens. And went out into the blizzard before she could change her mind.

The tails of her parka and the flared legs of her slacks slapped and ballooned in the chill white wind as she crossed the front yard to Lassen Drive. She started up the road, struggling through the dry shoulder drifts. The cold numbed her lips and her cheeks; the night and the snow pressed down on her, sealing her in a thrumming vacuum. Finally, she reached the cabin and stepped off the road, bracing herself against the heaving wind, moving toward the dull warm light in the facing window.

As she drew opposite, she could see beyond the ice-frosted glass, and Cain was there, sitting here in the window. He was smoking, looking down at the table: remote, grim-visaged in his thick grayish beard. Rebecca stopped abruptly, and she was less sure of herself now, less convinced that coming here was a good idea. What did she know about Zachary Cain, after all? He was a complete stranger, she hadn't spoken twenty words to him since he'd arrived in Hidden Valley; what could she say to him tonight, where would she begin? She thought of retracing her steps to the road, leaving as quickly as she had come. But she did not move. Home to the big, empty house had no appeal; being alone tonight disturbed her more than the unknown qualities of Zachary Cain.

The wind slackened and began to gust, and the cold penetrated her clothing to chill her skin. Through the hazy window, she saw Cain rub one hand over his face and through his unkempt hair—a tired, despondent gesture that cemented her resolve. She moved forward again to the front door.

Rebecca knocked loudly several times. When there was

no immediate response, she thought he hadn't heard above the sound of the storm and reached up to knock again. And the door opened with a jerky suddenness, and Cain stood holding it against the force of the wind, peering out at her with red-flecked eyes. There was a surprise in his gaze, but it dulled and faded almost instantly. She saw pain there, too, and what might have been irritation. He did not look drunk, but it was evident that he had been drinking.

She tried a tentative smile and felt the tightness of it on her mouth. He did not return it—except for his eyes, his face was totally impassive—and the doubts began to wash over Rebecca again. Her mind seemed to have gone blank; she could not think of anything to say. She had a foolish impulse to turn and run away into the snow-riddled night.

Cain said finally, "Yes, what is it, Mrs. Hughes?"

She found words then and pushed them out diffidently. "May I come inside? It's terribly cold out here."

He hesitated, and then shrugged and moved aside so that she could step in past him. The cabin was warm, fire in the hearth; but it smelled of liquor and stale cigarette smoke, and when he closed the door, cutting off the scream of the wind, it seemed too quiet. She was conscious of the snow that had blown into the room, that still fell fluttering from her parka; she wanted to say something apologetic about it, but the only words that came to her were acutely inane: *I'm getting snow all over your floor.*

Cain was standing with his back to the door, watching her, waiting silently for her to tell him why she was there. Instead, Rebecca said, "Quite a storm, isn't it?" and those words seemed just as inane as the other, unspoken ones. She began to feel awkward and incredibly silly.

He said, "Yes, I suppose it is."

"Well—I hope I'm not intruding. I mean, you're not . . . busy or anything, are you?"

"As a matter of fact, I was."

"Oh. Oh, I see. I'm sorry, I didn't know. . . ."

"It doesn't matter. What did you want to see me about?"

"Nothing in particular. I just . . . I thought you might like to have some company tonight."

His barlike eyebrows lifted slightly. "Oh? Why?"

"I don't know, I just thought you might. I'm alone too this evening, you see, my husband is . . . away, and it seemed like a good idea to—" She broke off, realizing how wrong that sounded; she looked away from him and then said almost desperately, "I was feeling lonely, and I wanted someone to talk to."

"Why me, Mrs. Hughes?"

"I had the idea you might be lonesome too, that's all."

Something flickered in the depths of his eyes. "I'm not lonesome," he said harshly. "I live the way I do by choice."

"Does that mean you don't like people?"

"I prefer my own company."

"Would it be prying if I asked why?"

"Yes, it would."

"Well I'm sorry."

"Do you make a habit of calling on men you hardly know when your husband is away and you're feeling lonely?"

"Of course not. . . ."

"What would he say if he knew you'd come here tonight?"

Rebecca felt her cheeks begin to flush. "What are you getting at? Do you think I came for some . . . special reason?"

"Did you?"

"No. I told you, I only wanted some companionship."

"You won't find it here, in any variety."

"So you're inviting me to leave."

"To put it bluntly, yes."

Bitter, defensive anger welled inside her; words tumbled out unchecked, mirroring her thoughts. "Oh, we can *really* put it bluntly if you like. We can say, 'You're a bitch, Mrs. Hughes, I don't want anything to do with you, Mrs. Hughes, find someone else to go to bed with, Mrs. Hughes.' That's what you're thinking, isn't it?"

Cain seemed to wince slightly. His voice a little softer, he said, "There's no need to—"

"Of course, how thoughtless of me to bring it out into the open like that. Well, I'll just be going. Thank you so much for your time, Mr. Cain. It's been very pleasant; it isn't every day I get to feel like a cheap whore."

She moved gropingly to the door, fumbled at the latch, and got it open. The sudden gust of wind and snow was like a slap. She ran out and across the yard and down the road: staggering and reeling in a surrealistic coalescence of white and black, the sound of it now raging in her ears like mocking, hysterical laughter.

When she reached the house, an interminable time later, she was asthmatically breathless and trembling uncontrollably. Inside, she stripped off parka and scarf and mittens and boots and flung them into the closet; ran upstairs and into the bedroom. Slacks and sweater and undergarments were icy-damp against her skin, and she shed them urgently and located the warmest nightgown she owned—a heavy flannel—and put that on and got into bed. The shaking refused to abate; her teeth chattered, her body crawled with chills. She tried to smoke a cigarette, could not get it lighted, and finally thew it to the floor, burrowing deeper under the blankets. Cold, cold, trembling, cold. . . .

And after a while, when it became unbearable, she turned her face into the pillow and slid one hand down beneath the covers and pulled the hem of her gown up over her hips; parted her thighs and began to massage herself harshly with her fingertips—a kind of rhythmic self-flagellation. In less than a minute, she climaxed; and her body, at last, was still.

Rebecca rolled onto her side, drew her knees up to her breasts, and willed herself into a sleep fraught with dismal dreams.

Twelve

The blizzard continued to gather strength as the night progressed, dumping huge quantities of snow on Hidden Valley and on the high, steep cliffs through which County Road 235-A passed down into the valley. The last two cars to traverse the road—crawling ten minutes apart shortly before 1 A.M., like yellow-eyed animals in the storm—belonged to Matt Hughes and Peggy Tyler, returning from the Whitewater motel. Both sets of tire tracks were obliterated almost immediately.

More hours passed, and still the blizzard remained relentless. Drifts built higher and higher along the cornice at the near, lee side of the western cliff crown, while the screaming wind dislodged other snow from unsheltered places and hurled it downward into the pass in lacy white spumes. Long since rendered impassable, 235-A had a covering of more than eighteen inches by five o'clock.

At five thirty the blow reached its ultimate savagery. The scattered lodgepole pines clinging to the top of the western cliff were bowed double like genuflecting pilgrims, and the swollen cornice collected ever-greater amounts of heavy snow. It went on that way for a time—and then, just before dawn, the low-hanging clouds that sailed continually eastward on the high-altitude currents began to develop fragmentation lines, like amoebas about to reproduce. The snowfall decreased steadily until it was a thin, fluttering curtain. Gray light filtered into the sky, lengthening visibility, giving substance to the bloated shadows along the crown of the western wall.

The blizzard was over; but the destruction it had fomented was only just beginning.

First there was a rumbling—a low-pitched, throat-clearing sound. The overburdened cornice shuddered, shaking whiteness as if a buried giant had awakened and were trying to rise; slender vanguards spilled free in frothy cascades. The rumbling grew louder, and louder still.

And the entire cornice gave way.

Billowing snowclouds choked the air like white smoke, and a massive tidal wave of snow and ice and rock flooded downward with a thunderous, vibratory roar that was as loud as a bomb blast in the early-morning stillness. Granite outcroppings were ripped loose as though they were no more than chunks of soft shale; trees were buried, uprooted, or snapped like matchsticks and carried along. And in a matter of seconds, the plunging mass filled a section of the pass the way a child would fill an excavation in the sand. . . .

Lew Coopersmith sat bolt upright in bed. The deafening noise rattled the bedroom windows, reverberated through the big, shadowed room. He struggled out from beneath the bedclothes and moved in sleep-drugged motions to the window; but from the vantage point he could see nothing to explain the sudden explosion of sound, now lessening into small, receding echoes.

The door connecting his bedroom with that of his wife's burst open, and Ellen rushed in. Her round, handsome face pale and frightened, silver hair braided into a long queue down her back, dressed in an ankle-length white nightdress, she was a ghostly figure in the semi-darkness. "Dear heaven, Lew," she said, "what is it, what *is* it?"

Cleared now of all vestiges of sleep, Coopersmith's mind began to function normally, and he remembered what John Tribucci had told him in the Sport Shop Monday afternoon. He turned fully from the window. "I think," he said grimly, "that we've just had an avalanche."

John Tribucci knew instantly that they had just had an avalanche.

An early riser by nature, he was in the bathroom shaving when it happened. The magnitude of the noise startled him, caused him to cut his cheek. He put down his razor, tore off a strip of toilet paper, and blotted perfunctorily at the thin ribbon of blood. He could hear Ann's voice calling to him from the spare bedroom adjacent, the voices of his brother and his brother's wife in their room down the hall.

Ann was sitting up in bed when he came hurrying in. He sat beside her, took one of her hands. "You all right, honey?"

"Yes. But you've cut yourself. . . ."

"Just a nick. I'll live."

"It was a slide in the pass, wasn't it?'

"I'm afraid so."

"It sounded like a bad one."

He nodded. "I just didn't think it'd happen this soon, before Christmas, before the baby came."

"You'd better go have a look."

"Will you be okay?"

"I'll be fine. Our child is kicking the devil out of me, but I don't think he's ready to put in an appearance yet."

Tribucci kissed her, went out into the hall, and met Vince on the stairs. Neither of them said anything as they hurried down and out into the cold, gray morning.

In the first moment of wakening, Cain thought it was an earthquake.

He had been born in San Francisco, and natives of that city are sometimes consciously, always subconsciously aware of the network of faults on which they live and of what happens when the pressure in those faults become too great and the earth begins to shift as if in orgasmic release. The deep guttural rumbling, the rattling, skittering vibration of windows and boards and bed which pulled him up out of sleep were sensations not new to him. Immediately, fuzzily, he thought: Quake, big one, Christ it's finally happening—and flung the covers away from his body and rolled out of bed. He was without equilibrium and fell jarringly to his knees. Pain burst through his left kneecap, and the sharpness of it flooded his mind with abrupt reality.

He struggled to his feet and felt sweat icing on him in the cold room. The cabin was no longer trembling, and the sudden roar had given way to a strained quiet. He thought then, sluggishly: *What the hell?* and walked naked into the front room. Leaning against the windowsill, he peered beyond crystallike glass.

Lights on all over the village below. Sky clearing, lightening, and a gentle snowfall now; the storm was finished. To the north there was a sifting cumulus of what appeared to be snow, like a white dust cloud settling. It meant nothing to him.

He turned away from the window. His head had commenced to throb with hangover, and he felt vaguely nauseated; he was shivering from the cold. Maybe something blew up, he thought, but it was a dull speculation. He did not really care what it had been; it was over now, it was unimportant, it could have no bearing on his existence.

Cain went back to bed and lay waiting for the sleep he knew would not come again.

Matt Hughes said, "I'd better get down there. If that slide is as bad as it sounded, I'll be needed in more ways than one." He crossed to the bedroom closet, shedding his pajamas, and began to dress quickly.

Rebecca drew the blankets tightly against her throat and did not look at her husband. The sheets were sleep-warm, but she was still touched by the same cold as on the night before. The masculine odor of Matt's body and the faint lingering perfume he had brought home with him were vaguely repellent in her nostrils.

The sound of the avalanche and the spasming of the house had startled her badily at first; but once she had known what it was, once Matt had jumped up and run to the windows and begun shouting about a pass-cliff slide, the apprehension had left her, and she was calm. He hadn't seen that, though; with maddening condescension he had told her not to be frightened, that everything would be all right—as if *she* were the intrinsic child and not he.

He said now, as he buttoned one of his soft-wool shirts, "John and Vince Tribucci were right, after all. But there's nothing we could have done; you can't control nature or counteract the will of God."

I wish you'd stop talking about God, Rebecca thought. You're always talking about God, you make such a mockery of religion. But she did not say anything.

Hughes put on his mackinaw and stepped around the foot of the bed to kiss her absently on the forehead. "Depending on how bad it is, I'll come back home or call you from the Mercantile. Either way, I'll let you know soon."

It had not even occurred to him, she knew, to ask her along—or to question why she was not eager of her own volition to accompany him. She said, "All right."

When he was gone, Rebecca lay thinking about the

slide to keep from dwelling on last night's experience with Zachary Cain—and on what she had done in this same bed after returning from the cabin. If the pass had been blocked, it meant they were now snowbound for, probably, several days. Was that bad or good? A little of both, she supposed. Nobody could come into Hidden Valley, which meant no mail and no fresh supplies: a minor inconvenience. And nobody could leave the valley, another inconvenience for most, particularly since this was the Christmas season. It also meant that Matt could not meet his current mistress and that he would therefore be forced to spend tonight and the next few nights with his wife. Forced, that was the key word; forced. Still, it was what she wanted—wasn't it?

I don't know, she thought then. I don't know *what* I want anymore.

And got up listlessly to face another day.

Peggy Tyler's mother—a faded prototype of her daughter—came running upstairs and opened the door to Peggy's room without knocking. She was fully dressed and had been in the kitchen making coffee. "It must have been a slide," she said breathlessly. "It must have been a terrible slide in the pass, I don't know what else it could have been."

"I guess that's what it was," Peggy said. She was normally a heavy sleeper, and while she had been awakened by the roaring and the quaking, her mind was still wrapped in lanquid dreams of a warm sun and a warm sea. Her body ached pleasantly; there was a gentle soreness in her loins, and her breasts and nipples tingled from the remembered manipulations of Matt Hughes' hands and lips. The fucking had been very good last night: some of the best she'd ever had. Of course, the reason for that was Matt's magnificent Christmas present, which he had presented to her with a kind of shy expectation, as if he had been afraid she would not be pleased, the moment they had entered the motel room.

One thousand dollars—cash.

Dollar sign-one-zero-zero-zero.

After a gift like that, the fucking just *had* to be very good.

Her mother said, "Thank the Lord it didn't happen earlier. You didn't get home until after one; suppose it had happened while you were driving through the pass? You might have been killed!"

"It didn't happen while I was driving through the pass."

"It might have. Where were you so late again?"

"I told you before, Mother," Peggy said. "I've joined a group in Soda Grove that's putting on a Christmas pageant, and there's a lot of work to be done."

Mrs. Tyler sighed. "We might be snowbound; there certainly is the chance of it. You won't be able to go to work today or maybe for the rest of the week."

How awful, Peggy thought. She said, "I have some sick leave coming. Look, Mother, let's not get into a panic, okay? If we're snowbound, then we're snowbound. It's no big thing."

"Well, we'd better go see, we'd better go find out right away. Get dressed now, don't dawdle." Mrs. Tyler went out of the room and closed the door behind her.

Peggy had no desire to leave the warmth of her bed; but if she didn't, her mother would come back up and there would be an argument, and she felt too good today to want to argue about anything. Oh hell, she might as well get up then, and anyway, the time was not far off when she could spend whole days in bed if she felt like it—not far off at all, now.

Leisurely, she swung the covers back and stood up and padded across to where her purse sat on the dresser. She took out the sheaf of fifty-dollar bills Matt Hughes had given her and stroked the money with one finger, smiling;

then, reluctantly, she tucked it away again in the compartment where she kept her bankbook and began to dress. When she went downstairs to join her mother a few minutes later, she still wore the same smile.

In the cabin at Mule Deer Lake, Kubion and Brodie and Loxner slept unaware of what had happened at the entrance to Hidden Valley; the thunderburst of the avalanche, diminished by the distance, had not disturbed them.

Loxner and Brodie were quiet in their beds, sleeping soundly. Kubion dreamed of spiders—black, cold, feathery-soft; crawling over him with mouths gaping in wet red hunger—and trembled and trembled and trembled.

The Tribucci brothers and Walt Halliday were the first Hidden Valley residents to reach the slide. They met on Sierra Street where it narrowed into County 235-A, and from there they could see it clearly through a light sifting of snow. Solemnly, wordlessly, the three men tramped up the sharp incline of the roadway and stopped when they could go no further, staring at the solid blockage rising up into the gray morning sky.

Sheer slabs of granite and splintered trees with branches and strips of bark torn away, protruded from the irregular surfaces like shattered bones. The western cliff face seemed steeper than it had been, scarred with an inverted fanshell chute that shone blackly against the dove-colored surroundings. In the stillness you could hear the mounded snow and ice and rock settling with a soft rumbling sound, like a thin echo of the slide itself.

Halliday said, his voice subdued, "Bad. Jesus, about as bad as it could be."

Both Tribuccis nodded gravely; there did not seem to be anything else to say.

Several other Hidden Valley residents began to arrive, among them Lew Coopersmith and Frank McNeil and

Mayor Matt Hughes. They, too, were quietly stunned by what they saw.

Hughes said finally, "My God, do you suppose anybody was in the pass when it happened?"

"Not likely," Vince Tribucci answered. "What with the amount of snow dropped by the blizzard last night, I doubt if the road was passable even before the slide. If it had to happen, this was probably the best time for it."

Hughes blew on chilled hands; in his haste he had forgotten his gloves. "I'd better get on the phone to the county seat and let them know about this and ask them to get men and equipment out as quickly as possible." He turned and hurried back to where he had left his car.

Frank McNeil turned to John Tribucci. "How long you figure it'll take to clear through?"

"From the way it looks, I'd guess at least a week. But if we keep getting heavy snows, it could take two or more."

McNeil pursed his lips sourly. "Merry Christmas," he said, "and a Happy goddamn New Year."

Thirteen

By nine o'clock the clouds had thinned and scattered to the east, and the whitish eye of a pale winter sun dominated a widening swath of sky. There was no wind, and the thin air had lost most of its chill. On the inner valley slopes and in parts of the valley itself, some of the deep powder drifts created by the night's storm began to slowly melt, forming little cascades in intricate, interconnecting patterns. Ice unprotected by pockets of shadow crackled intermittently in the warming day; the snow on the village streets commenced liquefying into slush.

Kubion started in from the Mule Deer Lake cabin just before noon, handling the car cautiously, squinting through the streaked windshield. The glare of sun on snow hurt his eyes and intensified the dull ache in his temples. He felt lousy today, badly strung out. Not much sleep last night, that was one of the things responsible—and that dream he'd had, the spiders crawling over him with their red gaping mouths. Jesus! He loathed spiders; they were the one thing which terrified him. He'd never had a nightmare like that before, and it worried him; it was as disquieting as the recurring headaches and his irrational inclination to violence.

The headaches were another source of his uptight feeling. The dull pain in his temples and forehead hadn't developed into one so far, but he knew it could happen easily enough, he knew he could lose control again. He could feel the impulsive need to destroy lying just below the surface of his emotions, like something ineffectually chained in a dark cave, waiting for the opportunity to break free and come screaming into the light.

And there was the need to get out of this frigging wilderness, to get back to civilization, where they could set up another score; the attendant frustration of knowing they couldn't chance it the way things were. According to the morning radio reports, the Sacramento cops had finally found the rented garage and the dummy armored car; there would be no lessening of the heat for some time yet.

Kubion drove down onto Sierra Street and noticed that there was more activity in the village than usual—that two people were walking up the middle of the road toward the pass. Then he became aware of the huge mound of snow and rock and splintered trees which blocked the valley entrance in a long downward fan. What the hell? he thought.

He kept on past the Mercantile—he had come in for a few minor supplies, to get out of the cabin again for a while—and pulled the car into the Shell station and parked it on the apron. He went up the rest of the way on foot, stopping next to the man and woman he had seen trudging along the road: a couple of senior citizens in plaid mackinaws and woolen hats. "What happened here?" he asked them. "Avalanche, is that what it is?"

Lew Coopersmith looked at him, frowned slightly, and then seemed to place him. "That's what it is," he said at length.

"When did it happen?"

"Just at dawn. Woke up the whole village."

"Yeah, I can imagine."

"If you and your friend planned on leaving before Christmas, I'm afraid you won't be able to do it. According to estimates, we'll be snowbound at least a week and maybe more."

"You mean nobody can get in or out of the valley?"

"Not unless they use snowmobiles around and through ten or fifteen miles of heavy timber. The pass is blocked solid."

Some country, all right, Kubion thought: the frozen bunghole of creation. Well, what difference did it make? If anything, it was a favorable occurrence; for the next week or so they would be cut off completely from all the fuzz on the outside.

But he said, playing it cautious, "My friend's wife is going to scream like a wounded eagle. She was expecting us for the holidays, back in San Francisco. We were leaving Saturday."

Ellen Coopersmith said, "Oh, that's too bad."

"Yeah."

"Phone lines are open," Coopersmith told him, "so it isn't like we were completely isolated. Your friend will be able to call his wife and tell her the circumstances."

"He'll want to do that, okay. Thanks."

Coopersmith nodded. "Sorry about the inconvenience, but it's just one of those things that happens. Nothing you can do."

"I guess not," Kubion said. He turned away and walked back to his car and sat unmoving behind the wheel staring up at the slide. An idea began to nudge his mind. Snowbound, he thought. Nobody can get in or out of the valley. No contact with the outside except by telephone. Made-to-order kind of situation, by God. And he remembered the check Matt Hughes had cashed for the old man in the Mercantile the previous afternoon:

unofficial bank and how much *was* there in that office safe? Ten thousand? Maybe not even that much, and then again maybe more—maybe a lot more. How many people in Hidden Valley? Seventy-five or so, wasn't it? Hicks; but hicks sometimes had plenty of money, you were always hearing about some old fart who kept his life's savings in a fruit jar because he didn't trust banks. Might even be as much as thirty or forty thousand in the valley. . . .

Abruptly, Kubion shook himself. Christ! He was thinking like a punk again, there was no score for them here, how could there be? *They* were trapped along with the rest of the damned people, and there was the safe house to think of. The hicks knew him and Brodie by sight, if not Loxner, and realistically there just didn't figure to be nearly enough in it in the first place. Even if there was a hundred grand in cash and jewelry in Hidden Valley, it wouldn't be worth it. Still, it was a wild concept: rip off an entire valley. Wouldn't that be the cat's nuts! But three men couldn't execute a caper like that—or could they? Well there was probably a way to do it and get away with it, all right; the snowbound business took care of any outside interference, it would be like working in a big sealed room. . . . Oh shit, it was crazy and stupid to even consider it. They needed a job like Greenfront should have been: safe, clean, big take, no loose ends, no people who knew what they really looked like and could identify them afterward.

But a whole valley, a whole goddamn valley.

Could it be done, with just three men?

Kubion lit a cigarette and sat drumming his fingers on the hard plastic of the steering wheel. Come on, come on, he thought, it's a pipe dream. And then: Okay, so it's a pipe dream, so actually doing it is all the way out. The thing is, can it be done on paper? Is it workable at all?

He sucked at his cigarette. Well, why not find out? He was uptight, wasn't he? The waiting—at least another ten days of it for sure now—and the worrying about those bastard headaches and that dream about the spiders: all of it pressing in on him, flooding his mind. What he needed was to focus his thoughts on something else, something that would keep him from blowing off, and there was nothing better for that than the working out of a challenging score—even an imaginary one.

Kubion started the car and drove back along Sierra Street and parked across from the Mercantile; got out and slogged through the liquidy snow to enter the store. Except for the white-haired old lady who had waited on him the day before, the place appeared empty. Recorded Christmas music still blared away from the wall loudspeakers: some clown singing about a winter wonderland. Yeah.

Maude Fredericks said when he reached the counter, "Isn't it terrible about the slide? Such a thing to happen just before Christmas."

"Sure," Kubion said. "Terrible. Tell me, you have a detail map of this area?"

Her brow wrinkled quizzically. "Well, we have a specially printed tourist brochure that includes a comprehensive Hidden Valley map. We also have a county topographical map."

"Fine. I'll take both," Kubion said, thinking: And wouldn't you crap your drawers, lady, if you had any idea what I want them for. . . .

Fourteen

Cain spent most of that day snowshoe walking among the lodgepole pine on the upper east slope, where the stillness was almost breathless and the air was thick with the cold, fresh, sweet scent of the mountain forest in winter.

He knew these woods well, the series of hiking paths which crosshatched them, because he had spent a considerable amount of time exploring the area during the summer and fall months. When he was having a particularly bad day and the weather permitted, he had found that taking long walks served as an effective tranquilizer. Alone deep in the forest, you were mostly able to shut off your thoughts and to allow only your senses to govern; and, too, you made yourself physically tired, a weariness that acted like a supplemental narcotic to the liquor.

But on this day, as on the previous two, the forest did nothing to erase the continuing feeling of loneliness which had come over him on Monday night—which lingered like a sudden bright and maddening stain on the fabric of his mind; if anything, the absolute solitude of the surroundings increased it. He felt confused, restless, irritable.

And to make it worse, now the damned people in this valley were starting to bother him.

Two unwanted and unexpected visitors yesterday. First that old man, the retired county sheriff named Coopersmith: pleasant, apologetic, asking politely if he knew anything about a door having been jimmied open at the Valley Café. It hadn't been the indirect implication that he was a malicious vandal which had caused him to snap angrily at Coopersmith; it had been the visit itself, the intrusion on his aloneness. The same was true of Rebecca Hughes' appearance last night. Perhaps she *had* come simply because she was lonely and wanted some innocent companionship, but that had not mattered at the time. He had only wanted to be rid of her; he didn't want conversation, and he particularly didn't want conversation centered on the subject of loneliness; so he had made the obvious insinuations, he had treated her, cruelly, like a tramp.

But this morning when he'd reexamined the incident not long after being awakened by the still-unidentified earthquakelike concussion, he had felt a sense of shame. He'd hurt her, her tears had been genuine when she'd run out, and the last thing he truly cared to do, after what he had done to his own family, was to inflict pain on anyone. Alone and fully sober, he'd thought that he could have got her to leave some other way and was sorry he hadn't. Briefly he'd considered going down to the Hughes' house and apologizing to her, but the embarrassed intimacy of a personal apology was something he simply couldn't face. And if yesterday were any indication, it would become necessary to leave Hidden Valley. There were plenty of similar places in the Sierra; it made no difference at all in which of them he lived just as long as he was left alone.

Cain returned to the cabin in late afternoon—and discovered ten minutes after his arrival, when he went into the kitchen for a fresh package of cigarettes, that the carton there was empty. His mouth twisted ironically; all the walking today, empty walking, and now, because tobacco had become a necessity rather than a habitual indulgence, he would have to walk yet another half mile or so round trip to the Sport Shop.

There was no need for snowshoes on Lassen Drive; he donned only his coat and a muffler before leaving the cabin again. The sun was well hidden now behind the mountain slopes to the west, but the sky in that direction held a faint lavender alpenglow. The temperature had dropped considerably, as it did every day around this time. There was still no wind.

When Cain reached the Hughes' house and drew parallel with the entrance drive—eyes cast down on the icing snow beneath his feet—an awareness touched him and he paused, raising his head, looking into the front yard. Rebecca Hughes had just come out of the house and was moving toward the road.

She saw him at almost the same instant, stopped, and visibly stiffened. One hand came partway up in front of her breasts in a gesture that might have meant anything or nothing. They stood fifty feet apart, motionless, for a long awkward moment. The sense of shame nudged Cain's mind again, and he thought once more of apologizing to her; happenstance had created the situation for it. But he could think of nothing to say; he still did not want a connection of any kind.

She was the first to move. Her hand dropped, and then she turned sharply and went back to the house with quick, jerky steps. At the Dutch-doored front entrance, she fumbled a key out of her purse, got it into the lock, and disappeared inside. The door made a dull slamming sound.

Cain was immediately thankful that there had been no dialogue between them; and yet at the same time he was contrite for not having spoken. More ambivalence—damned ambivalence! With an effort he forced Rebecca Hughes from his mind and continued down Lassen Drive.

He had gone five hundred yards farther, nearing the job in the road which would bring him into the village proper, when he heard the sound of a car approaching. He did not glance up. The sound grew louder, and the car came around the job and pulled abreast of him. It braked to a halt, and the driver's door opened, and Frank McNeil stood up, peering over the roof. His mouth was drawn so thin that it appeared lipless.

"You—Cain!" he shouted.

Cain kept on walking.

"Listen, goddamn it, I'm talking to you!"

He felt the muscles bunch on his neck and across his shoulders, and irritation came thickly into his throat. Finally he stopped and turned and looked at the car, recognizing McNeil vaguely, recalling the man's name. He said, "What do you want?"

"Where you been all day? I been up here three times now."

"What business is it of yours?"

"You think I don't know who's been doing it?" McNeil said in a voice that quivered with outrage. "Two nights in a row now, and you think I don't know it has to be you? Well I know, Cain, and I want you to know I know. I want you to sweat, because as soon as the pass is open, the county deputies will be here to arrest you. I've already called them, and the hell with Lew Coopersmith. You hear me, Cain? You hear me?"

Cain stared at him. "I don't know what you're talking about."

"You know, damn you, and you're going to pay."

The irritation boiled over into anger. Cain took several steps toward the car. McNeil slid back inside, and the door banged shut, and the rear wheels sprayed freezing slush in a long grayish fan as it skidded forward. Well up the road, it swung into the Hughes' driveway, backed and filled, and came down toward Cain at an increased speed. He moved deep onto the shoulder as it passed, but the wheels churned up more slush and flung it at him in an icy spume, spattering his jacket and trousers.

Cain stood trembling, watching the retreating car. Nothing McNeil had said made immediate sense to him; it seemed like gibberish. Then he remembered Coopersmith's visit the day before: somebody breaking into the Valley Café. Two times, McNeil had said. It must have happened again last night, and for some reason McNeil thought he was the one who'd done it. For Christ's sake, why would *he* do anything like that? Why single *him* out for the blame? He'd done nothing to give these people the idea he was that kind of man; he'd never bothered them at all.

And now there would be police, and there would be questions—further intrusion on his privacy—and while they would realize his innocence sooner or later, it might take days before they were convinced. The bastards, the bastards, why couldn't they let him be?

Why couldn't he be left *alone?*

Fifteen

Late Thursday morning Lew Coopersmith sat in front of the quartz-and-granite fireplace in his living room, drinking hot, fresh coffee with John Tribucci.

An hour and a half earlier he had gone to the Mercantile on an errand for Ellen, and Tribucci and Matt Hughes had been discussing slide developments. The latest report from County Maintenance was that a second dozer had been brought in—there was also a rotary snowthrower on hand—and the crews were beginning to make some progress. But at a conservative estimate it would still be the day after Christmas before they had the pass road cleared, weather permitting. Coopersmith and Tribucci had eventually left the store together and then walked up to the slide. You could hear the sound of the machines from there, although the work itself was invisible from within the valley.

After a short time they came back down again, and Coopersmith invited the younger man to the house for coffee since Frank McNeil had decided to keep the Valley Café closed as long as they were snowbound and Walt Halliday did not open the bar in the inn until 4 P.M. Tribucci had readily consented, saying smilingly that as much as he adored his sister-in-law, her coffee was on the same qualitative level as that of an Army mess cook's.

Now Coopersmith began filling one of his blackened Meerschaum pipes from the canister of tobacco on the low table between them. "You think the weather will hold, Johnny?" he asked.

"Hard to say. Forecast is clear for the next couple of days, but we may be in for another storm either Saturday or Sunday. If you want a pessimistic opinion, Lew, it will be two or three days after Christmas before the pass is open again." He paused and frowned into his cup. "I just hope the baby doesn't decide to arrive until New Year's now."

"Even if it does, Ann will be fine. Doc Edwards has delivered dozens of babies in private homes."

"I know, but I'd feel better if she had hospital care when the time comes."

"We'll all feel better once things are back to normal. I don't like being cut off from the outside world for so long a time, even if it isn't total isolation. It makes me feel helpless and vulnerable."

"Vulnerable to what?"

Coopersmith fired his pipe with a kitchen match. When he had it drawing to his satisfaction, he said, "Well I don't know exactly. I guess it's just that I don't have complete control of my own life at the moment. It's like being up in an airplane—you've got to depend on somebody else. And when you're dependent, you're vulnerable. That make any sense to you?"

"I think it does," Tribucci said. "In fact, I suppose in a way that's why I keep worrying about Ann and the baby."

Leaning back in his armchair, Coopersmith sighed and chewed reflectively on the stem of his pipe. At length he asked, "What do you make of the café break-ins, Johnny?"

"I don't know what to make of them. It's a damned

peculiar business, happening two nights in a row like that."

Coopersmith nodded. On the second occasion, as on the first, the rear door had been jimmied and propped open; but the damage had been considerably heavier, owing to the magnitude of Tuesday night's storm: bottles and jars blown off shelves and shattered on the floor, cans and perishables ruinously frozen. Frank McNeil had been livid, far more concerned about his private property than the avalanche which had left the valley snowbound. That was the primary reason he had decided to close the café until after Christmas.

"I talked to most everyone in the valley yesterday and Tuesday," Coopersmith said, "and drew a complete blank. Whoever did it pulled it off clean both times."

"Well, at least it didn't happen again last night."

"That's something, anyway."

Tribucci made a wry mouth. "McNeil says that's because yesterday he told Zachary Cain he knew he was the one responsible and was going to have him arrested as soon as the pass is cleared. Says that put the fear of God into Cain."

"Horse apples," Coopersmith said.

"Yeah. Cain is a funny sort, that's true enough, but he just doesn't strike me as the type to go in for malicious mischief."

"Me neither. He hasn't bothered a soul since he's been here. Besides, the idea that he would do it because McNeil asked me to investigate him when he first came is ridiculous. I told Frank there wasn't any way Cain could have found out about that in the first place, but trying to talk sense to McNeil is like trying to talk sense to a ground squirrel. He'll be lucky if Cain doesn't sue him for slander."

"That's for sure," Tribucci agreed. "Thing is, though, I can't picture anyone else in the valley doing the break-ins either. Not for any reason."

"Same here. But somebody did it, and for some reason." Coopersmith's pipe had gone out, and he relighted it. "Well, whatever the answer, I'll see if I can't ferret it out sooner or later."

The two men had a second cup of coffee and talked briefly of Christmas, of what gifts they had gotten for their wives—Ellen was in the kitchen, out of earshot—and determined they would get together at Vince's house on Christmas Eve for some traditional eggnog and cookies and caroling.

When Tribucci had gone to relieve his brother at the Sport Shop, Coopersmith finished his pipe and brooded mildly over the slide and the café break-ins. He poured himself a third cup of coffee and, tasting it, decided it could use a little sweetening. He stood up and went quietly to the sideboard for the brandy decanter.

Sixteen

Wearing warm old clothes and a pair of fur-lined boots, the Reverend Peter Keyes left his cottage at the rear of the All Faiths Church at one thirty to do his daily shopping.

He was not as deeply concerned about the pass slide as some of the other valley residents, although it *would* prevent him from spending Christmas afternoon and evening with his relatives in Soda Grove. Coming so close to Yuletide, it was of course an unfortunate thing; but no one had been killed or injured, for which thanks could be given, and the Reverend Mr. Keyes was not one to question an act of God in any circumstance. For all the inconvenience to his friends and neighbors and to himself, it was nonetheless the season of joy and charity and great faith: the celebration of the birthday of Jesus Christ.

The Reverend Mr. Keyes walked along the side of the church, beneath the three slender, obelisk-shaped windows and the sharply pitched alpine roof with its squared, four-windowed belfry and tall steeple at the rear: a simple frame church which, he felt, suited perfectly the simple life of those who made the Sierra their home. As he started toward the street, he noticed a medium-sized, unfamiliar man standing at the signboard adjacent to the front walk, reading the arrangement of glassed-in plastic letters which told of the coming Sunday services.

The minister altered his path and approached the stranger—no doubt one of the San Francisco businessmen he had heard were staying at Mule Deer Lake. Perhaps, since the man was reading the signboard, he was thinking of attending services; the prospect, if true, was a pleasing one.

When the newcomer heard the Reverend Mr. Keyes' steps in the snow, he turned. Very dark, he was, almost sooty-looking, with a hard cast to his face and a feral, overbright quality to his eyes. But the minister well knew how deceiving appearances could be, and as he reached the man, he smiled and extended his hand. "Good afternoon. I'm Reverend Peter Keyes, the pastor of All Faiths Church."

"Charley Adams is my name," Kubion said. He took the proffered hand. "Nice to meet you, Reverend."

"I noticed you reading the signboard, Mr. Adams. May I ask if you'll be joining our congregation on Sunday?"

"Well, I just might do that, all right."

"We'll be more than pleased to have you."

"There's only one service, I see."

"Yes—at noon. The village is really too small to make more than one feasible during the winter, although we have two throughout the summer season."

Kubion glanced at the church. "Are the doors open now?"

"Oh, of course. They're seldom locked."

"I'd like to step inside for a minute, if I could."

"Certainly, please do."

Kubion nodded a parting and moved away along the front walk. The Reverend Mr. Keyes watched him climb the five front steps and enter the church and then smiled gently to himself. Appearances were indeed misleading; Charley Adams was an agreeable sort of person—and no doubt a good and devout, if somewhat diffident, Christian.

He thought Kubion had gone into the church to pray.

John Tribucci was alone in the Sport Shop, stocking shelves in the tobacco section, when the dark stranger came in at two o'clock.

"Something I can do for you?" Tribucci asked pleasantly.

"Well, maybe there is," Kubion said. "I was wondering if you've got any snowmobiles in stock."

"Snowmobiles?" Tribucci managed to conceal his surprise. "Why, yes, as a matter of fact we do—just one. It was given to us on consignment by a chain sporting goods outlet in the county seat."

"Be okay if I looked at it?"

"Sure." He led Kubion around to the rear of the store, where the machine sat in the center of a small display of skis, snowshoes, and ice skates. It resembled a two-seat scooter mounted on skis and wide roller treads—black chassis, white cowl, red and white trim. "It's a Harley Davidson, fast and durable. Plenty of features: dual headlights, eighteen-inch molded track, shock-dampened steering, ski-mounted hydraulic shocks. Engine is twenty-three horsepower, good enough for cross-country slogging, and one of the quietest on the market."

"How much gas will it hold?"

"It has a six-gallon tank."

"Okay—what does it sell for?"

"A little better than fifteen hundred, plus tax. That's a good price for the quality, considering what some of the bigger mobiles cost these days."

Kubion frowned. "I didn't know they ran anywhere

near that much," he said. "This the only one in the valley?"

Tribucci said dryly, "You mean, does anybody own an older model they might want to sell for a few hundred?"

"Yeah, I guess that's what I mean."

"I'm afraid not. The only other mobile in Hidden Valley is one my brother owns, and it's a Harley similar to this one—last year's model. He'd be willing to sell it, I think, but I doubt if he'd take less than a thousand."

"Still pretty stiff," Kubion said, and shook his head. Then, in a self-conscious way, he laughed. "You're probably wondering why all the sudden interest in a snowmobile."

"Well—yes," Tribucci admitted. "With the valley being snowbound, it's not exactly the time people think of winter sports."

"Winter sports didn't have anything to do with it; being snowbound is the reason. See, this friend of mine and me—we're staying out at Mule Deer Lake, you probably know that—we're expected back in San Francisco for Christmas. So we got to thinking last night that we could split the cost of a snowmobile and use it to get to one of the towns in the area, where we could rent a car. But we didn't figure the things to be so expensive; we just can't afford that kind of money for something we might not even use again."

Tribucci said, "You could get to Coldville all right in a mobile, swinging east by northeast; it's rough country, fifteen miles of it, but with a map and the mobile's compass and fair weather it could be done safely enough. Still, you'd have to have quite a bit of knowledge of mountain country like this."

"Couldn't we walk out, too, the same way?"

"You could, but I wouldn't advise trying it. That's a hell of a trek on snowshoes—and if a storm hits, you'd freeze to death."

"No shorter way to do it, like going over or around those pass cliffs and then picking up the county road into Soda Grove?"

Tribucci shook his head. "The upper approaches to both cliffs, where the trees thin out, are made up of snow- and ice-covered talus and walls and pinnacles of granite. To the west the terrain drops sharply and there are gullies and declivities filled with drifts of loose snow—you must have noticed coming in how deep and wide the canyon is on the other side of the pass. To the east, you've got a long series of smaller ridges and more deep snow pockets."

Kubion said, "And I guess it would be dangerous to try scrambling over the slide itself?"

"Suicidal is the word. That mass may seem like a solid pack, but it isn't. You couldn't scale this end, and even if you could, your weight on all that imbalanced, down-slanted snow and rock would start a shifting and resettling that'd bury you in seconds. That's why the clearing process is such a slow and methodical one." Tribucci paused. "About the only practical way you could get out of Hidden Valley immediately is by helicopter, assuming the weather holds. But unless your leaving is a definite emergency, I wouldn't count on it. The county only has one chopper, and there are priorities."

"Then I guess we're stuck good and proper, and we'll just have to make the best of it. Sorry to take up your time."

"Not at all."

When Kubion had gone, Tribucci resumed stocking the tobacco shelves. It would have meant a not inconsiderable profit if he'd been able to sell the mobile, and with the baby due so soon, the money would have been more than welcome. But then, he hadn't really expected to make the sale from the first—not under the present circumstances and having correctly assumed the reason for the dark man's sudden interest.

City people, he thought, have the damnedest ideas. . . .

Kubion spent another hour in the village—mainly at the foot of the east slope, beyond Alpine Street, where the telephone and power lines stretched downward into Hidden Valley—and then drove back to Mule Deer Lake. He parked the car in the cabin garage and went inside and directly up to his bedroom.

The dull ache in his temples and forehead was still with him, no better and no worse than it had been the previous day. Last night he had dreamed of spiders again, the same dream, the same ugly black spiders with their redly gaping mouths. But he hadn't thought of these things at all; his mind had been focused for the past twenty-four hours on the theoretical score—attacking it with a vengeance, just as if it were the real thing.

He sat on the rumpled bed and took one of the thin brown marijuana cigarettes from the tin on the nightstand. Leaning back against the headboard, he lit the stick and sucked slowly on it, holding the mawkish smoke deep in his lungs. When the joint was ash against his fingers, he could feel the lift, he could feel his thoughts coming clear and sharp. Then he began putting it all together, everything he had learned from the valley and topographical maps and everything he had found out in the village today.

And he knew it could be done.

The knowledge excited him, stimulated him. It could be done, all right, it actually could be done with just three men. Still a few details to be worked out, still a few angles to consider, but he had the basics completely assembled. It hadn't been much of a problem, not nearly as much a one as he'd first thought; the fact that the valley was snowbound was what made it all so simple.

Kubion lit a second stick of pot and smoked it, working out the details carefully. Time passed—and he had it all then, the entire operation from beginning to end. Nothing left unconsidered, no flaws in the progression. All of it neat, clear, workable.

Darkness settled outside and came into the room in slow, lengthening shadows; and with it came the letdown. The stimulation vanished; an empty flatness replaced it. He became aware of the dull throbbing in his head, and he could feel his nerves pulling taut again. He tried a third stick of grass, but this time it did nothing for him. The sudden downer was heavy and oppressive, and he knew the reason for it; sitting there on the bed, he knew exactly what was the matter.

He'd figured the score, and it could be done, and they couldn't do it.

From the beginning it had been nothing more than a mental exercise, something to occupy his mind for a while. But he couldn't forget it, now that he'd figured it; there would be nothing to do, nothing to focus on, and the pain in his head, and the spiders, the black red hungry spiders, and the blowoff that would surely come, the violence; he couldn't forget the score even though it was useless thinking about it further. Frustration now, and the pain centering behind his eyes, pulsing, pulsing. . . .

Rapping on his door. He jerked slightly, irritably, at the interruption and called out, "What the hell is it?"

"Supper's ready, Earl," Brodie's voice said from outside.

"I don't want any goddamn supper, leave me alone."

Silence. Then, "All right, Earl."

"All right, all right, all *right*."

Kubion stretched out full length on the bed. The room was completely dark now, and cold, and he put one of the blankets over him. It can be done, he thought, we can do it, go over it again and keep going over it, make it even more solid, cancel some of the risks but there are too many of them but the hicks keep money in fruit jars sometimes but they can identify us but a whole valley but this is safe ground but it can be done. . . .

The spiders came.

They came out of the darkness, big ones, big black ones, crawling over the floor and up onto the bed. One of them crept upward along his leg, mouth opened redly, hungry mouth, saliva dripping, he could feel the saliva dripping like hot slime through the blanket and through his clothes and onto his naked flesh. No! but the room was filled with them now, coming for him, one on his arm, one on his chest, one on his neck, black and red and feather-legged with their hungry devouring mouths, get away from me, *get away from me!*

He screamed, and screamed again, and woke up, and came off the bed in a convulsive jump. He stood shivering in the darkness, and the spiders were gone; it had been the dream again and the spiders were gone. Or—were they? What was that, there in the dark corner? Something moving, something crawling. Spider! No, they were gone, mind playing tricks, no spiders here, no spiders, but something was crawling, he could see it crawling there. . . .

He squeezed his eyes shut, nothing there, and slitted them open again, nothing there, nothing there. Think about the score, remember the score that can be done, that we can't do, that can be done. He could not keep his hands quiet; his body was soaked in sweat. The pain in his head was raging now, he could feel himself losing control, his thoughts were wrapped in a gray floating mist and he wanted to smash something, kill something, kill the spiders, the filthy spiders crawling there in the dark corner, and he ran to the corner and killed one spider, and killed a second, and twisted panting toward the bed and suddenly they were all around him, scurrying over the walls and floor and furnishings, they were real and they were after him and all the pain in his head the pain and the spiders coming the red black hungry spiders coming the spiders the—

He stopped shaking.

The pain went away.

The spiders went away.

Just like that, as if a bubble had burst inside him, it all went away, and he was calm again. He stood still for a moment, until his breathing returned to normal, and then bathed sweat from his face and walked slowly to the bed. Sitting on the edge of it, he switched on the lamp and looked around the room.

Good-bye, spiders, he thought, good-bye forever because you're not coming back, I'm not going to let you come back.

And he began to laugh.

He laughed for a long time, tears streaming down his cheeks, drool overflowing the corners of his mouth, stitches in his belly and both sides. Then, just as suddenly, the laughter cut off, and his head came up, and he sat staring straight ahead, lips still stretched in a wetly fixed grin. His eyes were brightly feverish, glowing like round black stones daubed with phosphorescent paint.

He was thinking about the score again, the score, the big big big big score. Oh, there was no question about it now, oh no question; there had never *been* any question.

It could be done—and they were going to do it.

Seventeen

As she stood ladling thick vegetable soup from a tureen into two serving bowls, Rebecca heard Matt come downstairs and then call along the hallway, "Dinner ready yet?"

"Yes," she answered.

"Fine, I'm starved."

He came into the kitchen, showered and shaved and cologned and wearing a clean shirt and slacks. But not for me, she thought; habit, personal hygiene—nothing more. He had been home for a little more than an hour, and the only other words he had spoken to her were "Hello, dear."

He sat at the table, sighed gustily, and said as if to himself, "Soup smells good."

She did not say anything. She placed one of the serving bowls in front of him, and another at her place directly opposite, and laid out a basket of bread and a plate of Cheddar cheese and took a bottle of Mosel from the refrigerator because Matt liked chilled white wine with soup. Then she sat and watched him uncork the bottle and pour their glasses full; and glance at her briefly, almost blankly; and pick up his spoon and begin to eat.

Rebecca despised that look. It was the way he always looked at her during one of his affairs: as if she were not a woman, not even a person, as if she were merely an inanimate object which he owned and could ignore at will. Zachary Cain had seemed to look at her yesterday with that same blank negation, when chance had taken her out of the house—she had been going into the village to visit with Ann Tribucci—at precisely the moment he was passing on the Drive. It might not have been so bad, seeing him again that soon after Tuesday night's humiliation, if he had only paused and then kept on walking down the road, or if, in coming to a standstill, he had said something, anything, to her. But instead, he had looked at her that way, just stood there silently and *looked* at her.

She had wanted to scream at him, just as she sometimes wanted to scream at Matt, that she was a human being with feelings and rights and she deserved to be treated accordingly. I'm *not* a bitch, she had wanted to tell him; I went up to see you for nothing more than a little fellowship, a little kindness. It would have been pointless, however—exactly as it would have been and would be pointless to verbalize her emotions to Matt. And so she hadn't spoken either, had simply turned and fled his gaze like a frightened sparrow.

Tuesday night's misadventure and yesterday's mute confrontation, while essentially immaterial in themselves, had combined with Matt's affairs, his rejection, the emptiness, the emotional need—all of it—to compound and deepen her mental depression. She felt as though she were suffocating. Things could not continue as they had for so long; she could not allow them to continue this way.

Rebecca stared at her soup, at the tissuey pieces of green and yellow and white vegetables floating in it, at the thin sheen of fat-eyes which coated the surface. Her throat closed nauseatingly, and she pushed the plate aside and folded her hands around her wine goblet. Lifting it, holding it without drinking, she watched Matt eat his soup and two slices of bread and a wedge of cheese. He did not once raise his eyes to her.

She waited until he had begun helping himself to a second bowl of soup; then, slowly and deliberately, she said, "Matt, let's go up to bed after supper."

He looked at her then, frowning slightly, poising the ladle over the tureen. "Bed?" he said. "It's only six thirty."

"I want to make love," she said. "It has been more than a month since we made love."

Matt lowered his gaze immediately and went on ladling soup. "That's hardly dinner-table conversation. There's a time and a place, after all. . . ."

"I want to make love tonight, Matt."

"Rebecca, please. I've had a long, hard day, and I'm exhausted."

"Which means you don't want to have sex with me, not after supper and not later this evening."

"I wish you'd stop talking like that," he said. "It isn't like you to be so forward."

"Will you make love to me tonight?"

"Now that's enough."

"Don't you understand what I'm saying? I want you, I need to feel a man inside me again. Damn you, I want to be *fucked!*"

Matt's spoon clattered to the table; his eyes went wide, and his mouth dropped open in a tragicomic caricature of surprise and shock. "Rebecca!"

She stood up and went out of the kitchen, walking slowly. Upstairs in their bedroom, she took off her clothes and stood naked by the bed, listening, looking at the door. Matt did not come. When she was sure that he wouldn't, she got into bed and pulled the covers up to her chin and lay there staring blindly at the ceiling, trying to think, trying to find the strength to make a positive decision because things could not, *they could not,* go on this way.

Eighteen

Brodie was making Spanish omelets, and Loxner was watching him and drinking a bottle of ale, when Kubion came downstairs Friday morning and said he had something important to talk over with them.

They took chairs around the kitchen table. Brodie did not like the way Kubion's eyes looked; they seemed to have tiny burning lights far back in their depths, and it was like seeing a pair of bonfires through the wrong end of a telescope. A sudden uneasiness crept through him.

And Kubion put his hands flat on the table and said, "We've got a new score."

It startled Brodie; it was the last thing he would have expected. He looked at Loxner and then back at Kubion. "I don't follow. Where could you find a score? We haven't been out of this valley since Monday night. Hell, we're snowbound here; nobody can get out."

"Or in," Kubion said, "and that's it, that's the whole thing right there. The valley is snowbound, and the valley is the score. We take it over and we clean it out store by store, house by house. Everything and everybody."

Loxner seemed about to laugh; his mouth curved upward at the corners, but then stayed that way—a rictus. He made no sound. Brodie stared at Kubion for a long moment, said finally, "Earl, you can't be serious. . . ."

"Sure I'm serious, what do you think? It can be done, I've worked it all out and it can be done—no sweat, no sweat at all."

"For *what?*"

"For forty or fifty grand and maybe more, that's for what. The guy that owns the Mercantile runs an unofficial bank: a safe in his office. He cashed a check for one of the other hicks, a couple of days ago, four hundred and fifty dollars without even looking at it first. He's the big man here, it figures they all go to him when they need ready cash; he'll have thousands in there. And these hicks keep money in fruit jars under their beds, they got the family jewels in lockboxes on their dressers—you're always hearing about crap like that."

Brodie and Loxner just stared at him.

Kubion wet his lips; his eyes burned more brightly, now. "Listen," he said, "listen, I know what you're thinking. There's only three of us, right? Seventy-five people in this valley and only three of us. But that's no problem—no problem. We do it on Sunday. Now where do most hicks go on Sunday, where do they always go on the Sunday before Christmas?"

Automatically Loxner said, "Church."

Brodie said, "Oh *Christ*. . . ."

"You see how simple it is? At least fifty or sixty of them are all together in the church: a bunch of sitting ducks. We wait until after the service starts at noon, and then we go in and take them over. We tell them to look around and see who's not there; we make a list of names and addresses. Then we lock the front doors and go round up the rest of them house to house: ring their doorbells, put a gun in their faces; easy. Once we've got everybody penned up in the church—there's no back exit, it's a box—one of us watches the front doors with a rifle just to make sure none of them tries to get out, and the other two rip off the buildings. Ten to twelve hours, and we can strip this valley like a chicken bone."

Brodie started to speak, but Kubion made a silencing gesture with one hand and went on with it.

"Okay, now you're wondering about a getaway with the valley being snowbound. We can't just sit around and wait until the road's open again, right? So what we do, we leave here on snowmobiles—those little motorized scooters that run on skis and treads. The two brothers that operate the Sport Shop have one in stock, brand-new. One of them owns another. That's two, that's all we need."

"Snowmobiles," Loxner said. Without seeming to taste it, he drained the last of his ale.

Kubion was smiling now—an excited, unnatural smile. "One of the brothers told me it could be done; all you need is a compass and a topographical map. I've got maps already, and a route traced out, and the mobiles are equipped with compasses. It's maybe fifteen miles east by northeast to a town called Coldville: four or five hours at the outside. The hicks say the road will be open the day after Christmas; that gives us at least two full days' start if we leave at dawn Monday."

Brodie said, "Goddamn it—"

"How do I figure two full days' minimum?" Kubion said. "Well, we take a hostage or two not long before we go, and we tell the rest that the hostages are dead if anybody even puts his head out while we're still in the valley, and they won't have any way of knowing when we actually do leave. We tell them we're going to take the hostages with us, too; we won't do it, we'll tie them up somewhere or off them, what the hell, but the others will believe what we say. They'll keep right on sitting in the church until somebody comes and lets them out. Another thing we do is cut the telephone lines late tomorrow night; that isolates the valley completely and eliminates any threat of a phone call to the cops if anybody that isn't in the church gets suspicious before we've got them all rounded up. So even if they did get out before the pass is open, what could they do?

"Now: once we reach this Coldville, we buy a used car—they've got a dealership there, it's listed in the phone book, and shagging one is too risky—and then we head for Reno or maybe Tahoe. A little of the blister from Sacramento should be off by next Monday; we play it careful on the road, we're okay. In Reno or Tahoe, we split up and take separate planes south or east or north. We get off the West Coast entirely, relocate somewhere else."

Kubion moistened his smile again. "So there it is—all laid out. Simple, beautiful, a score like nobody ever pulled off before. Well? What do you think?"

"I think you been blowing too much weed," Loxner said, trying to make a joke of it. "Man, that ain't a score, it's like plain fucking suicide."

The smile vanished.

Loxner laughed nervously. "This is *safe* ground, you don't pull a job on safe ground no matter how good it is. Christ, Brendikian would never stand for having this place blown that way. And he's got Circle connections, Earl, you know that."

"The Circle isn't going to pick up on small-time crap like having an independent safe house blown, I don't care what kind of connections Brendikian's got. Screw Brendikian."

"You don't know him, man, he ain't anybody to fool with."

"Screw Brendikian," Kubion said again.

Brodie leaned forward. "Earl, the people here know your face and mine; disguises or masks wouldn't be worth a thing. The cops would have those Identikit drawings on every front page in the country once the ripoff was reported. Our cover identities would be blown, that's one thing. And we've all taken falls; they'd come up with our names sooner or later, they'd have mug shots out in addition to the composites."

"I thought of that, I told you I thought of everything. The hell with it. It's not that hard to build a new cover somewhere. And the FBI's been looking for Ben Hammel for eight years for the bank job he was in on in Texas. He's still walking around."

"I'm not Ben Hammel, and I don't want my ass in that kind of sling. There's a damned good chance the cops would connect us up with Greenfront, too—and the chance we'd run into trouble taking over here and people would get killed. Murder One heat, either way. We wouldn't last a week anywhere in the country."

"Oh, bullshit," Kubion said. "How much play can a thing like this get in Connecticut? In Florida? In goddamn Puerto Rico? A few days and it dies off. Sure, the fuzz keeps right on looking. But you both know how simple it is to change what you look like. You grow a beard for a while; half the men in the nation wear beards these days, and how can some cop identify you when you're wearing a face full of whiskers? You cut your hair or let it grow or dye it another color. You gain weight or you lose weight or you wear padding. You live quiet, don't spread any money around. You know all the tricks as well as I do. And we're split up, that's another thing; three guys in three different parts of the country who don't look anything like the ones who ripped off Hidden Valley, California."

Brodie said, "Damn it, none of it makes *sense*. Even if we could stay on the loose, where are we? Say we could take as much as thirty grand out of here: that's only ten thousand apiece. How long is ten bills going to last each of us? We'd have to look for a new score inside of three months, and with all the heat still on. How many pros are going to want one of us in on a job carrying that kind of blister?"

"So we play it solo for a while. We've all worked solo before. The heat will die, it always dies sooner or later."

"For God's sake, they'd have our *names;* they'd know exactly who did the job. That kind of heat doesn't die."

"Hell no, it don't," Loxner said.

"I'll tell you a way the cops won't get our names at all, a way to come out of it free and clear and to hell with this cabin," Kubion said.

"What way?"

"Set fire to the church or blow it up before we go on the snowmobiles. Don't leave *any* witnesses who can identify us, waste them all."

Loxner gaped at him the way you would at something under a decaying log. Brodie's shoulders jerked involuntarily. "Hey, hey, hey," he said. His voice was incredulous. "What kind of freaky talk is that? Jesus, what do you think we are?"

"Okay, okay, then forget that. But listen—"

"We listened enough already," Loxner said, "I don't want to listen to no more. We don't want no part of what you're laying down here, no part of it."

Brodie said, "Earl, what's got into you? You're all of a sudden after this valley like you got a hard-on for the place, you're acting like a crazy amateur—"

Kubion was on his feet in one swift motion, upsetting his chair. His cheeks had suffused with dark blood, and his eyes were like a pair of live embers. He slapped the table with the flat of one palm, hard enough to topple Loxner's empty ale bottle and send it clattering to the floor. "Call me a crazy amateur, you son of a bitch, call *me* a crazy amateur!"

Loxner and Brodie were standing now as well, backed off a couple of steps, muscles tensed.

"You stupid pricks, can't you see the kind of thing this is? A whole valley, a whole valley, nobody ever did anything like it. Well? Well?"

Watching him, Brodie and Loxner remained silent.

Kubion took a breath, released it sibilantly—and as suddenly as it had come, the rage drained out of his face. "All right," he said, quiet-voiced, "all right then, all right," and turned and walked out of the kitchen.

Very softly Loxner said, "Oh man!" He went to the refrigerator and took out another ale and popped the cap and swallowed half of it without lowering the bottle. Then: "Things are bad enough without shit like that. The last thing we need is shit like that, Vic."

Brodie did not say anything.

"He gave me the creeps with all that crazy talk," Loxner said, "that funny look in his eyes. It was like he's a different person all of a sudden, you know what I mean?"

Brodie's mouth was pinched in at the corners, his eyes grimly reflective. "Yeah," he said slowly. "Yeah, I know what you mean."

Nineteen

Black-edged clouds began to drift over Hidden Valley Friday afternoon, obliterating the pale sun and giving the air a dry, ice-tinged quality; but it did not snow again until very early Saturday morning, and then nothing more than a light dusting which would not interfere with work on the slide. When Matt Hughes came down Lassen Drive a few minutes past 8 A.M., the village seemed bathed in a soft luminosity created by the snow's whiteness reflecting light filtered through the low cloud ceiling. Under normal circumstances, such a view would have pleased him—the serene beauty of a mountain valley, his valley, in literally its best light—but he barely noticed it now; he had too many divergent things preying on his mind.

There was the slide, of course: all the problems it had caused, the extra work it made for him as mayor. There was Peggy Tyler, whom he had seen several times since their lovemaking in Whitewater Tuesday night but whom he had not spoken to for their mutual protection; whose lush and eager body glowed in his memory, exciting him with fresh and consuming desire and filling him with a sense of frustration because he could do nothing about it.

And, finally, there was Rebecca.

Her sudden outburst Thursday evening at dinner had upset him considerably. He loved her deeply, and yet it was a kind of reverent, detached love: the love of an art connoisseur for a masterpiece which he alone possesses. From the moment he had met her, Hughes had never been able to think of her in sexual terms; the act of physically entering her body had never given him pleasure or satisfaction—just as fondling the fragile surfaces of his masterpiece would give the art connoisseur no pleasure and no satisfaction. Sex for Matt Hughes was a savage, primitive urge totally disassociated from love. It was sweating flesh and moaning frenzy and animalistic release with women like Peggy Tyler, women who instilled no reverence in him, women who dazzled his senses and sated completely his carnal hunger.

He wanted only to have Rebecca near him, to know that she was there and that she was his; he wanted only to believe in her and worship her in some of the same way he believed in and worshiped God. He wished desperately that he could explain this to her, but of course he had never tried; she would not have understood. And he lived in constant fear that she would find out about his continual affairs—as she had found out about the Soda Grove waitress several years ago—and that she would, instead of once again forgiving him, decide to leave him. He couldn't bear that. But still he yielded each time the primitive forces inside him demanded it, as if he were two different men, as if he were a kind of sensually emotional schizophrenic.

Did she suspect the current affair with Peggy? Or had her outburst Thursday only been the result of neglect and some of those same base desires which were present in all beings? The latter, of course; he refused to think otherwise. After he had recovered from his initial shock, he had tried to make himself go upstairs and take Rebecca into his arms and make love to her, but he had not been able to do it. He had never been able to correlate the primitive with the reverent; it was one or the other, and he simply could not touch or devote himself to his wife during those times when he was pouring out his lust into the bodies of other females.

The situation had grown worse over the past two days. Rebecca had not spoken a word to him since Thursday, and the atmosphere at home was strained and uncomfortable. The careful juxtaposition of his two lives had been momentarily and maddeningly imbalanced; he needed both Rebecca and Peggy now, he needed the status quo, and he did not have any of them. There had to be an answer, a way to restabilize things, but he had not as yet been able to figure out what it was.

Maude Fredericks had already opened the Mercantile, as she did on most mornings, when Hughes arrived. He went into his office and put through a call to Soda Grove. The slide status, at least, was still quo: progress slow but steady, no fresh slides to complicate matters. He came out into the store again, built a fire in the potbellied stove, and went to work.

The day seemed to drag on interminably. Rebecca and Peggy, Peggy and Rebecca—first one and then the other, endlessly cycling in his thoughts. He found himself wishing Peggy would come in and was both relieved and disappointed when she did not. He thought of calling Rebecca but didn't; there would have been no point in it, there was nothing he could say to her yet. Depression formed inside him like a thick, damp mist.

At four o'clock Hughes stopped trying to find things to do to occupy himself, left Maude to close up, and drove home through the same light, steady snow which had fallen all day. When he entered the house, it seemed filled with a tangible emptiness, and he knew immediately that Rebecca was not there. Gone into the village, he thought;

probably to visit with Ann Tribucci. He listened to the empty silence and felt his depression deepen. In the kitchen he made a light scotch and water and took it into his study and sat tipped back in his leather recliner, sipping the drink and brooding.

And after a time he began to think about Peggy again, about Tuesday night in the Whitewater motel room. His scrotum tightened painfully, and sitting there, he had a full and pulsing erection: the primitive in him screaming for her—now, today, tonight. But there was no way, not until the pass was cleared. Too dangerous for them to meet in Hidden Valley and no place to meet even if they dared to risk it. She couldn't come here to his house, and he couldn't go to hers, and the Mercantile was no good because of its central village location. No other place—

Mule Deer Lake, he thought suddenly. The Taggart cabin.

Hughes leaned forward in the recliner, pulling it into its upright position. The Taggart cabin. Yes—and it wasn't all that dangerous if they were very, very careful. But did they dare? Would Peggy be willing? Some of the depression had evaporated now, and an almost boyish recklessness throbbed inside him. They could get away with it, and he needed her, he *needed* her. Call Peggy, call her right now, take the chance. . . .

Impulsively he stood up and started across the study to the extension phone on his old rolltop desk. And stopped halfway there, touched by abrupt fear. No; it was utter foolishness. They could be seen, they could be recognized, and what then? The affair would become public knowledge, and Rebecca would leave him for certain then; she would have no alternative. Public disgrace, his position in the valley irreparably damaged—he could lose everything that mattered in his life. Besides, it would only be another few days until the pass was open again. They could resume their Whitewater meetings in a week or so, perhaps next Friday or Saturday night. He could wait that long, couldn't he?

He felt the burning, demanding ache in his genitals and was not sure that he could.

Rebecca, he thought with a kind of desperation, if only I could make love to Rebecca tonight. It would solve both his immediate problems; it would make things all right again. But the savagery of his need made it impossible; it was Peggy his body craved, Peggy, Peggy, and he would be completely and unquestionably impotent if he—

Impotent.

Impotence!

That was the answer to his marital dilemma; it had been the answer all along. Of course: impotence, it was so obvious he had never even thought of it before. All he had to do was to tell Rebecca that certainly he wanted to make love to her, but that it was, at the moment, physically impracticable—he had for some time been suffering from sexual incapacity. He had wanted to tell her long before now, he would say, but had been too ashamed to admit it; he was seeing a doctor in Soda Grove, taking hormone treatments to rectify the problem—although to date they had been frustatingly ineffective. She would believe him; there was no reason why she shouldn't believe him. She would be sympathetic and understanding, and there would be no more outbursts, no more periods of uncomfortable silence between them. Then, when the affair with Peggy came to its inevitable conclusion in another few weeks and he was once again able to bring himself to make love to his wife, he would tell Rebecca that the treatments had finally produced positive results. It would be just as simple as that.

Hughes felt immediate relief—one problem taken care of, he was sure of it—but the mitigation was tempered by his urgent desire for Peggy. He thought again of the Taggart cabin, of how easy it would be for them to use it as a meeting place. Nothing *could* go wrong, nothing would go wrong; the gamble was no greater than any of the others he had taken during the past seven years, and in that time no one in Hidden Valley had suspected a thing, they would have no reason to suspect anything now. A cautious hour or two, that was all, and just tonight, never again in the valley. After tonight he would be able to wait until next Friday with no difficulty at all. If he went through with it, there would be no more immediate quandaries with his personal life; he could have Rebecca and Peggy and the status quo, all his again and all tonight.

The recklessness, the excitement swept through him again. Rationalization and his hungry loins had decided the argument: he knew he was going to call Peggy and make the suggestion to her. Quickly, he went to the extension phone—and from there he could look through the study window at the darkened, restlessly clouded sky. It would keep on snowing for some time yet, the night would be very dark. Very dark. He caught up the receiver and then hesitated. What if her mother answered? Disguise his voice, that was it; put his handkerchief over the mouthpiece. He fumbled the folded square of cambric from his back pocket and draped it around the handset, at once realizing that he was being melodramatic and taking a kind of adventurous ebullience in the fact. Then he flipped open the county directory and found the Tylers' number and dialed it rapidly.

Peggy's voice said, "Hello?" on the sixth ring.

Hughes pulled the handkerchief away, releasing the breath he had been holding. "Peggy?"

Pause. "Matt, is that you?"

"Yes. You can talk all right?"

"My mother is over at the Chiltons. But you took a chance, calling like this."

"I know. I had to talk to you."

"That damned slide," she said. "It's going to be such a miserably long time until we can be together again."

"It doesn't have to be," Hughes said fervently. "Peggy, listen, I've just thought of something—a way and a place we can meet."

"You mean *here,* in the valley?"

"Yes. Tonight. I've thought it out, and it's safe as long as we're careful. Do you want to do it?"

"I don't know, Matt. . . ."

"Peggy, I keep thinking about you, I can't get you out of my mind. I have to see you. Please, Peggy."

Pause. "Tell me your idea."

"The Taggart cabin at Mule Deer Lake," Hughes said. "The first one on the eastern shore, the one that sits by itself at the edge of the lake. Well, I've got the keys to it; the Taggarts always leave them with me when they go back to Red Bluff in the fall. We can spend a couple of hours there early tonight, say seven o'clock. And we won't turn on any lights, so that if somebody does pass the cabin, they won't know anybody is inside."

"We couldn't take both our cars."

"No, just mine. You can walk to the stand of trees where Sierra Street forks into the two lake roads, going along the west slope where nobody would see you. I'll pick you up there."

"What if somebody notices your car at the cabin or sees it drive up? The Markhams and the Donnellys live on the eastern shore of the lake."

"Their homes are both well down the shore. It'll be dark at the lake—no moon; the snowing will keep visibility down—and we'll drive to and from the cabin with the headlights off. Somebody would have to be outside and peering along the road in order to see us, and that's hardly likely. The only other occupied place at the lake is the cabin where those two San Francisco businessmen are staying, and it's sheltered from the road by trees. As far as the car goes, I'll park it in the Taggarts' garage; the entrance is open and faces away from the road, and you can't see into it from there."

"Somebody could still notice you leaving the village or returning," Peggy said. "They'd wonder about it."

"If I'm ever asked, I'll say I decided to go for a short drive, just to get some air, and stopped for a while and walked around. That's why we'll meet so early—for that reason, and because of my wife and your mother too. Nobody would question an explanation like that; why should they? It'll look like I'm alone in the car anyway, since you'll be scooted down on the seat. Peggy, I'm desperate to see you, and I'll take the gamble if you will. We'll be very careful; nothing can happen if we're careful."

There was a prolonged silence this time, and Hughes said her name questioningly. Peggy said then, "I really don't think we ought to chance it, but I'm desperate to see you, too. And terribly horny. Are you terribly horny, Matt?"

Hughes had an erection again. "Yes!"

"Then—all right. You'll pick me up at the fork at seven?"

"At seven. I don't want to have to stop but a second, so hurry as fast as you can when you see the car."

"I will."

They said good-byes, and Hughes cradled the handset. He was sweating. He crossed to the lamp table beside his recliner, lifted his drink, drained it, and then looked at his watch: five forty-five. Leaving the study, he went upstairs and took a shower and doused himself liberally with body talc and changed into fresh clothes; came downstairs again and ate a light supper. The kitchen wall clock told him it was six forty when he had finished—time to leave. He would have to stop at the Mercantile to pick up the keys to the Taggart cabin.

Rebecca had still not come home, and he was relieved that she hadn't. He did not want to face her now, with his thoughts and his emotions focused on Peggy Tyler's lush sexuality. She would be home when he got back from the lake at nine or so, and he would tell her then of his contrived impotence. In just a few short hours, he thought as he hurried out of the house, everything would again be exactly as it had always been.

Twenty

Compulsively, Cain put on his coat at six fifty and went out of the cabin and started down into the village.

He walked at a desultory pace, only superficially aware of the cold night and the snow-hazed lights below. His destination was the Valley Inn, and his purpose was to buy himself another bottle of bourbon—he kept telling himself that this was his purpose. There was an unopened quart in the cabin's kitchen that he had purchased in the Mercantile that morning—enough to last him through the long Sunday ahead—but the desolation in him had become so acute the ache was almost physical.

The past two days had been interminable. After returning from the village Wednesday afternoon, where he had learned with indifference of the avalanche and the fact that the valley was snowbound until after Christmas, he had been completely exhausted. Sleep came immediately that night; but it had been restless and shallow, and he had awakened from it gritty-eyed and stiff-muscled and despondent. He'd thought again of Frank McNeil's accusations, and the threat of arrest for something he had not done, and the imminent arrival of probing county police. All right then, he'd decided, let them come and let them ask their questions, and when the episode was concluded, he damned well *would* get out of this Hidden Valley where people persisted in pushing their way into his privacy; he would go somewhere else, he would find a place where the people would leave him utterly alone.

Then he'd thought: But *was* there such a place? Was there anywhere in the world where people would leave you utterly alone? Or would it always be as it had become here: intrusions, invasions, interference? And would the loneliness, the ambivalence continue to plague him wherever he went? It had seemed so simple in the beginning: just go to a small mountain village where no one knew you and no one cared to know you, and live apart, and die by degrees. For six months he had managed to do that, but now it had all started to collapse; it was no longer simple at all.

And tonight, he was going to the inn to buy a bottle he did not need, because he might need it and because it was Saturday night and he was desperately lonely for companionship that he wanted but did not want.

When he reached Sierra Street, he crossed directly toward the inn. Two and a half stories high, and a full block wide, it was the largest building in Hidden Valley. It had a double-balconied, redwood-shingled façade designed to give the impression of comfortable rusticity—alight now with its Christmas decorations—and two separate entrances: one to the small lobby and one to the restaurant-and-lounge that constituted most of its interior at street level. The upper floors were divided into eleven rooms, including the large apartment in which the Hallidays lived.

Cain hesitated in front of the restaurant-and-lounge entrance. Light glowed behind a large frosted window, and there was the sound of soft music and muted conversation from within. Apprehension fluttered in his stomach, but he went woodenly to the door and opened it and stepped inside.

The interior had a low, beamed ceiling and was bisected by square redwood supports. Waist-high partitions, topped with planter boxes of wood ferns, had been erected between the posts. The restaurant area to the right was empty and dark, chairs stacked on tables, closed for the winter season. Only the lounge on the left side was open, dimly lit by two electrically wired wagonwheel chandeliers suspended from the rafters. Eight booths with high, varnished wood backs were set along the partitions; dark leather stools flanked a leather-fronted bar against the far left wall. The rear wall and part of that behind the bar were adorned with deer antlers and glass-eyed deer heads; a glass-fronted case containing two matching and ornate shotguns, replete with boxes of shells; fishing creels and rods and corkboard displays of colored trout flies. Some fifteen people occupied the lounge, most of those in the booths. Only one man—Joe Garvey—sat at the bar, at the upper end, talking with Walt Halliday.

Cain brushed snow from his coat and stamped it softfooted from his boots. Then he walked slowly and directly to the bar, not looking at the people in the booths, and sat on the end stool staring straight ahead. A full minute passed before Halliday came down to him.

"Can I get a bottle off-sale?" Cain asked him.

A frown creased Halliday's plump face; he hesitated. "We don't usually sell off-sale," he said finally.

"I'll pay extra for it."

"No need for that. Okay—what brand?"

"Old Grandad."

"Set you up a drink too?"

"No, I don't . . . yes. Grandad straight up."

"Chaser of some kind?"

"Nothing, just the shot."

Halliday hesitated again, as if he wanted to say something further. Then he shrugged and poured the drink and set the shot glass in front of Cain, took a full bottle from the backbar display, put that down, made change from the twenty Cain slid across the polished surface, and went back to the other end of the plank. When Cain lifted the glass, he was peripherally conscious of Halliday and Garvey looking at him and talking in low voices. He turned slightly on his stool, so that he could see nothing but the rimed front window, and tasted his bourbon. It burned in his mouth, his throat, the hollow of his belly. He put the glass down again and lit a cigarette.

Some of the conversation seemed to have abated behind him, and he sensed that others in the room were also looking at him. He felt conspicuous, like something curious on display. Get out of here, he thought urgently, they don't want you and you don't want them, you don't want any of this; go back to the cabin, be alone.

He swallowed his drink, dropped the cigarette into an ashtray, caught the bottle off the bar with his left hand, and moved hurriedly to the door. Turning out of it, he walked with rapid steps and head down to the corner—and ran into the woman just coming out of Lassen Drive from the west. The left side of his body bumped hard against her and threw her off-balance, so that she seemed about to fall into the packed snow at the curbing. Automatically Cain flung out his right hand and caught her arm, steadying her.

It was Rebecca Hughes.

She stared at him through the lightly falling flakes, and her mouth crooked into a bitter smile. "Well," she said, "we do seem to keep running into each other, don't we, Mr. Cain? Literally, this time." She shrugged off his hand and started away from him.

The shame he had experienced on Wednesday returned all at once, the loneliness made a plaintive cry, and he heard himself say impetuously, "Wait Mrs. Hughes, wait, listen I'm sorry, I'm sorry I ran into you just now and I'm sorry for the way I acted the other night, I had no right to do that."

It stopped her. Slowly, she turned to face him again.

Her features smoothed somewhat, and the bitterness was tempered now with surprise and a wary puzzlement. She did not say anything, looking at him.

The act of speaking seemed to have had a strangely cathartic effect on Cain. He said again, heavy-voiced, "I'm sorry."

Rebecca continued to look at him in steady silence. At length the wariness faded, and she sighed softly and said, "All right. I'm hardly blameless myself for the other night; it was foolish of me to have gone in the first place."

"You only wanted what you said—some simple companionship; I suppose I knew that all along. But it's not the same for me, can you understand that? I don't need it."

"Everyone needs it, Mr. Cain."

"All I need is to be alone—that's all."

Rebecca asked quietly, "Why did you all of a sudden decide to apologize to me? You just . . . looked at me on Wednesday afternoon. You didn't say anything at all then."

"I couldn't."

"Why couldn't you?"

"I don't *want* to talk to anybody."

"You're talking to me now, on your initiative."

"Yes," Cain said. And then, abruptly and without prior thought: "Maybe . . . maybe you do have to have conversations with somebody once in a while, maybe you can't help yourself. It's all a matter of words."

"Words?"

"They pile up inside you," Cain said. He felt vaguely lightheaded, now. "Thousands of words piling up and piling up until there are so many of them you can't hold them in anymore; they just come spilling out."

"I've never thought of it that way before, but yes, I can understand what you mean." She paused. "And I guess the same is true of emotions and needs and frustrations, isn't it? You can't bottle them up forever either; they have to find an outlet of some kind."

"No. No, just words. Too many unspoken words."

Rebecca studied him for a time. "I was on my way home," she said. "Are you going back to the cabin now?"

"Yes."

"We could walk together as far as my house."

No, Cain thought. And said, "All right."

They went across Sierra Street and started up Lassen. In a sporadic way they talked of the slide, only that and nothing of a more personal nature. The spontaneity was gone; the flow of words from within him had ebbed into a trickle of words. Cain felt himself retreating again—wanted it that way, did not want it that way. When they reached the drive of the Hughes' house, he said immediately, awkwardly, "Good night, Mrs. Hughes," waited long enough to glimpse the small, brief smile she gave him and to hear her say, "Good night, Mr. Cain," and then turned away. He sensed, as he continued rapidly along the road, that she was watching him; but he did not look back.

All the way up to the cabin he was aware of the sound of the wind in the surrounding trees—the lonely, lonely sound of the wind. . . .

Twenty-One

Peggy Tyler reached the stand of red fir just above the lake roads fork at ten minutes before seven. Her mother had returned from the Chiltons just after Matt's telephone call, and Peggy had told her she was going for a walk and then to the inn for a while. At six twenty she had left the house, at the western end of Shasta Street, and had turned right instead of left and slipped through the thick growth of trees well to the rear of All Faiths Church, circling toward the fork. She had seen no one, and she was certain no one had seen her.

She positioned herself at the bole of one of the firs nearest Mule Deer Lake Road, shivering slightly inside her fur-trimmed parka, and looked down into the village. Shining hazily through the thin gauze of snow, the lights seemed more remote than they actually were. The streets were typically deserted, and car headlamps were nonexistent.

Now that she was here, waiting in the heavy darkness and the kind of whispering quiet you found only on mountain nights, she was more nervous than she had been earlier. But it was an anticipatory feeling, born not of apprehension but of exhilaration. The past few days had been oh-so-deadly dull, with nothing to do except to watch barely discernible images flickering on the television screen and nowhere to go except out into the very environment she so passionately hated. The prospect of an adventurous balling session in what was literally her own backyard was intoxicating: a lovely and audacious private joke to be played on all the smug little people who lived in this damned valley, one of the few experiences of her life in the Sierra that she would be able to look back on with fondness and pleasure.

Of course, there *was* a certain hazard involved, though not nearly as great for her as for Matt. She didn't give a hair what Hidden Valley thought of her, her mother included, and she didn't give a hair for Matt's saintly reputation; if their affair were discovered, it surely wouldn't have any real effect on her long-range plans. The only consequence of discovery, as far as she was concerned, would be that the goose who laid the golden eggs would be dead: no more generous cash presents like the thousand-dollar Christmas surprise. Still, she wasn't worried. If Matt was willing to chance it—and it wasn't really much of a chance, the way he had outlined it—then she was too. . . .

A pair of lights moving in the village intruded on her thoughts, and she saw that a car had swung onto Sierra Street just beyond the Mercantile. It passed the church, and even though she was unable to distinguish the make, she knew it would be Matt's. Behind the car, the village streets still appeared empty. She swiveled her head to look south along Mule Deer Lake Road; the wall of night there was unbroken.

When the car approached the stand of fir, it slowed almost to a crawl. Peggy waited until it had drawn abreast of her hiding place and then hurried out and opened the door and slipped inside. The dome light did not go on, Matt had done something to the bulb—clever Matt! She curled her body low on the seat, whispering a greeting, as the car picked up speed again.

He reached out a hand and stroked her hair. "Peggy," he said, "Peggy, Peggy."

She smiled and moved over, resting her head on his thigh, the fingers of her right hand stroking over his knee. His breathing came fast and heavy and she sensed the front of his trousers begin to bulge. He said thickly, "There's not a soul on the streets. I made sure of that before I pulled out."

"No one saw me either."

Peggy kept on stroking his leg, higher now, one fingernail moving across the bulge and making him jump convulsively. The area between her own legs had begun to moisten, to pulse demandingly; damn, but she was horny! "Hurry and get to the cabin, Matt. I'm on fire for you."

"I know," he whispered. "I *know*."

It seemed to take a long time for them to reach Mule Deer Lake, a long time before he said, "We're almost there, I'm going to switch off the headlights now."

"Can you see the lake?" she asked as the dashboard went dark.

"Yes. No lights anywhere, except in the cabin where those businessmen are staying. It's just up ahead."

Three additional minutes crept away, and then Peggy felt the car turn and the wheels bounced jarringly; they came to a stop. Hughes said, "We're here."

Peggy sat up, looking through the windshield: a blank wooden wall, the inner wall of the Taggart garage. Hughes had the driver's door open, and she followed him out on that side. They clasped hands and left the garage and went around to the front door of the cabin, on the lake side. The flat, frozen surface of Mule Deer Lake, ridged with snow, stretched out into deep black; the opposite shore was totally obscured by darkness. The only light was a distant glimmer to the north: the businessmen's place. It was so still that Peggy could hear the beating of her heart.

Hughes keyed open the door. "You see?" he said against her ear. "Nothing to worry about, not a thing. Nobody saw us, and nobody can possibly know we're here. . . ."

Kubion knew somebody was there.

He saw the darkly indistinct shape of the car coming without headlights along the lake road, saw it just as he was about to get into his own car parked in front of a two-story, green-shuttered frame house some distance down the shore. Through the thin snowfall he watched it swing off the road at the Taggart cabin and then disappear. Nobody was supposed to be living in that cabin—he'd found out in the village earlier in the day which of the lake dwellings were occupied and which weren't—and he thought: Well now, just what've we got here? Eskimo kids looking for a place to hump?

Smiling fixedly, he slid into the car and started the engine, also leaving his headlamps off, and drove to within fifty yards of the cabin and parked on the side of the road. The building's windows showed no light; whoever it was was probably still in the car. Kubion thought: Fuck her, I did—an old teen-age taunt—and laughed deep in his throat. He sat there for a time: still no lights. Finally he reached for the ignition key, started to turn it; hesitated and released it again. Oh hell, he thought, the more the merrier.

He opened the glove compartment and removed a flashlight and got out of the car. His eyes, wide and unblinking, shone like a cat's in the darkness.

The interior of the cabin was winter-chilled and subterranean black. Hughes closed the door and said softly, "We'll stay here for a minute, until we can see well enough to walk without banging into things."

They stood pressed together, waiting, and eventually Peggy could make out the distorted shapes of furniture, the doors in two walls which would lead to other rooms. Watchfully, they crossed to one of the doors, and Matt widened it and said, "Kitchen," and led her to another. Beyond this one was a short hallway, with a door in each wall; the one on the left opened on the larger of the cabin's two bedrooms.

The bed was queen-sized and unmade, but folded across the foot of the mattress was a thin patchwork quilt; they would need that because of the cold, Peggy thought —later, afterward. They stood by the bed and kissed hungrily, undressing each other in the darkness with fumbling urgency, and then they fell onto the bed, kicking the last of their clothing free, their mouths still melded together. Peggy took hold of his erection in both her hands and heard him moan, and he broke the kiss to whisper feverishly, "Put it in, put it in, I can't wait!," clutching at her breasts as if bracing himself, and she guided him over her and into the waiting wetness of her and he made a jerking, heaving motion as she drew her legs back and said, "Peggy, ah ah ah Peggy!" and came shudderingly.

The rigidity left all his body at once, and he was dead weight on top of her, his face pressed to her neck. Peggy's lips pursed in mild annoyance, but when he raised his head finally to tell her he was sorry, he just couldn't hold himself back, she said, "It's all right, we have plenty of time, baby, we have plenty of time." She held him flaccid inside her, moving her hips, seeking to make him hard again, and when she began to succeed she said smilingly, "That's it, that's my Matt," and he commenced rocking over her and into her, expertly now, and it was the way it had been in Whitewater, it was perfectly synchronized and wildly good, and she could feel the beginnings of her orgasm fluttering and building in her and flung herself upward at him, reaching for it, reaching for it—

—and then a bright white beam sliced away the blackness like a sudden spotlight and pinned their glistening bodies on the bed.

For a single instant they were blindly motionless, still locked together, still one instead of two. Then Hughes made a startled, whimpering sound and rolled away from her, twisting, sitting up. Peggy threw an arm reflexively across her eyes; fright and confusion replaced the passion inside her, dulling her mind, stepping up the staccato pounding of her heart.

A voice—harsh, amused, unfamiliar—said from behind the light, "Well, I'll be damned. It's the banker himself, by Christ, tearing off a nice little piece on the side."

Hughes said in a stark, trapped tone, "Who are you, how did you get in here?"

"You left the front door unlocked. You must have been in some hurry, Banker, some big hurry."

"You have no right to be here, you have no right! What do you want, why did you come in here, put out that light!"

"Hang loose, just keep your head together."

At the periphery of her shielding arm, Peggy numbly saw Matt Hughes swing off the bed, shambling almost drunkenly, ludicrous in his nakedness. His face a matrix of fear, he started toward the white hole in the darkness.

"Stay where you are," Kubion said sharply, "stand right there."

"Put that light out, put it out I tell you!" And Hughes took another step toward the beam.

"Okay, you stupid hick bastard shit."

There was a brief flame, like the flare of a match, to one side of the beam; there was a sudden roaring sound, localized thunder echoing in the confines of the room, and Peggy jerked on the bed as if she had been struck. Then she saw Matt stop moving, and saw part of his face disappear, and saw something red spurting, and saw his hands flick upward, and saw him begin to sag before the hands reached the level of his chest, and saw him fall into a loose wet naked pile on the floor.

"How about you, sweetheart?" Kubion's voice said softly behind the light. "How about you?"

Peggy started to scream.

Twenty-Two

Loxner said, "It's after seven, Vic, he's been gone more than five hours now. Where the hell could he be for five hours? He don't drink, and we got plenty of food right here, and there ain't nothing in the village for him to do and noplace for him to be riding around."

"I know," Brodie said. "I know it."

"Man, I just don't like the way he's acting. Not a word to either of us since all that crap about ripping off the valley yesterday morning, gone most of yesterday afternoon, sitting up in his bedroom all of today until he finally went out. I seen him when he come downstairs, and his eyes were still funny; he was smiling funny, too, showing his teeth. I tell you I don't like it, it's got me all uptight."

They were sitting in the living room, across a coffee table set in front of the fireplace. Up until a few minutes ago they had been playing gin rummy, but neither of them had had their thoughts on the game and they'd given it up finally by tacit consent. Brodie stood now and picked up a blackened poker and stirred the pitch-pine logs burning on the hearth; sparks danced, and the charred wood crackled loudly, like firecrackers going off.

He set the poker down again, turned, and put voice to what had been on his mind for the past hour.

"You ever see anybody freak out, Duff? Like where they come all apart in the head, go crazy, do crazy things?"

Loxner blinked at him, scratching nervously at the bandage on his left arm. The arm was still stiff, and the skin under the bandage itched constantly, but he'd found he could use the limb for normal activity and had taken off the sling that morning. "No," he said, "no, I never seen nothing like that."

"I saw it happen twice, more or less saw it—both while I was doing time. The first guy was a lifer, been in for maybe fifteen years. Happened right out of the blue, one night in the dining hall. He just jumped up and started yelling and foaming at the mouth, got onto the table and ran down it with a fork in either hand and stabbed a con and a screw before they could put him down.

"The second guy was something else again. He'd been a bank teller or an accountant or something on the outside and got caught with his hand in the till; quiet type, mild-mannered, maybe thirty and good-looking. He'd been inside about six months when they switched cells on him, put him right down the block from the one I was in. The two cons in his new cell were hard cases, and on top of that they were fags, buggers. They got to him right away and raped his face and his ass and told him they'd kill him if he didn't cooperate from then on. So he cooperated, and for maybe a couple of months they passed him back and forth like a private whore. He still didn't say much, and he didn't look any different; we thought maybe he'd had some fag in him all along and had gotten to like it. Then the word got around that there was going to be a break, that this guy had masterminded it for himself and the other two. Nobody paid much attention to it; you know how the grapevine's always humming with word of a break. But they did it, they pulled some fancy moves and went over the wall from the roof of the library, where the accountant had been working. Only the next day the screws found the two hard cases lying in a ditch five miles from the prison—with their balls shot off. The guy stayed loose a week before they caught him, and in that week he offed six other fags in two cities, shot all their balls off. He'd freaked out too, is what I'm getting at, but it had all happened inside where you couldn't really see it; and what it did was turn him into a machine with one thought in his head: kill the hard cases and kill as many other fags as he could before they got him. He was like supercrazy—ten times as dangerous as the other one I told you about, because he could still think and plan and nothing mattered to him except one crazy idea."

Loxner said, "Jesus," and wiped his mouth with the back of one hand. "You think something like that's happened to Earl? You think he's really freaked out?"

"Maybe," Brodie said. "And maybe *his* crazy idea is ripping off this valley."

"Jesus," Loxner said again. Sweat had broken out on his forehead, and his hands twitched noticeably.

"It could be he's still okay and it's nothing but the pressure getting to him and he'll snap out of it pretty soon. But if he has freaked, there's no way we can know for sure until maybe it's too late. We can't afford to wait, Duff. There's only one thing we can do; it'll make problems for us in other ways, but it's got to be done."

"You mean—waste him?"

"I mean waste him."

Loxner got to his feet and paced rapidly forth and back in front of the fireplace. "Yeah," he said. "Yeah, yeah, you're right, we can't take no chances, we got to think about our own asses." He came to a standstill. "When do we do it?"

"Tonight. Just as soon as he gets back. I've still got the

extra set of car keys he gave me, and when he's inside here, I'll go out and unlock the trunk and get one of the guns out of the suitcase."

"You going to pull the trigger, then?"

"I'll pull the trigger."

Loxner looked relieved. "What about the body?"

"There's no place to bury it with all the snow. We'll wrap it in a blanket and put it in the garage; it'll keep until we're ready to leave."

"Then what?"

"Put it in the trunk of the car. When we're a few miles away, we'll dump it into a canyon. There're plenty of them in these mountains."

Loxner sat down, got up again almost immediately, and said, "I need a goddamn drink." He went into the kitchen.

Brodie stared into the fire with eyes that were, now, like chunks of amethyst quartz.

Kubion returned to the cabin at eight fifteen.

They heard the sound of the car coming up the access lane, and Loxner wet his lips and looked at Brodie. Brodie said, "Deal the cards"—they were playing gin again—and obediently Loxner dropped his gaze to the deck. He shuffled it awkwardly, dealt ten cards to each of them with diffident flicks of his wrist.

When the front door opened, Brodie did not glance up. But there were no footsteps, no sound of the door closing again. A cold prescience formed inside him, and his head lifted then, and Kubion was standing there smiling a skull grin and holding the .38 backup automatic. His eyes seemed huge, streaked with lines of blood, and neither they nor the lids above them moved. No part of him moved, he did not even seem to be breathing.

Brodie's lips thinned, his body tensed. He thought: Oh fuck yes he's blown out, I should have known it yesterday, I should have killed him yesterday; we waited too long.

Loxner saw the change in Brodie's face and jerked his head around. Color drained out of his cheeks. He struggled to his feet, sweat once more breaking out on him, mouth opening as if he were going to speak, closing, opening again, closing again—all like a huge fish caught on an invisible line.

There was a long moment of silence, heavy and menacing. Snow fluttered across the threshold behind Kubion, like a sifting of white flour; chill, biting air rushing into the room robbed it of warmth, made the flames in the fireplace dance and gutter.

"We're going down to the lake," Kubion said finally. "Got a little something I want you to see."

Brodie forced his voice to remain even. "What's that, Earl?"

"You'll find out when we get there."

"All right—sure. But what's the gun for? There's no need for throwing down on us."

"Isn't there? Well, we'll see about that."

Loxner began thickly, "Look, look now—"

"Shut up, you gutless prick!" Kubion said with sudden viciousness. "I don't want any arguments, get over here and get your coats on, we're going now right now."

Brodie got up immediately and walked with careful strides to the closet; sweating heavily, not looking at Kubion, Loxner followed. They donned coats and gloves, and when they were ready, Kubion gestured outside and trailed them at a measured distance around to where the car waited, engine running and headlights burning, in front of the garage. He said there, "Vic, you take the wheel. Duff, you sit in front with him." He waited until they had complied and then opened the right rear door and slid into the back seat. "Go. I'll tell you where."

Brodie drove down to Mule Deer Lake Road and

turned right and went along the eastern lakeshore. The taut silence was broken only by Loxner's asthmatic breathing. They passed the Taggart cabin and several other winter-abandoned structures; then Kubion said, "That house there on the left—pull up in front."

The house—a two-story frame with green shutters—was set back from the road, inside a diamond-pattern, split-log fence. It was shrouded in darkness. Brodie stopped the car where he had been told, and the three of them got out, Kubion hanging back slightly. They stood at the open front gate.

"Go up there and look inside, both of you," Kubion said. "The door's not locked, and the light switch is on the left."

They stopped through the gate opening and made their way slowly along the ice-slick front path; Kubion again followed at a distance. Brodie climbed the porch steps first, stopped at the door, and Loxner said, "I don't want to do it, I don't want no part of what's in there. . . ."

Not listening to him, Brodie spun the knob and pushed the door inward. There was nothing immediate to see except darkness. He reached inside and felt along the wall and found the switch and snapped it upward; light spilled into the room, forcing the night back into crouching corner shadows.

Loxner said, "Oh *Christ!*"

There were seven people in the room—two men, three women, a boy of nine or ten, and a girl a few years older. All of them were tightly bound hand and foot with heavy-duty clothesline, gagged with torn strips of bedsheeting, lying on the carpeted floor near a tinseled Christmas tree with a nativity scene and several brightly wrapped presents at its cotton-draped base. They were all alive and apparently unharmed. Their eyes blinked against the sudden illumination, wide with terror. Two of the women whimpered; one of the men made a strangulated retching sound.

Cold fury knotted the muscles in Brodie's stomach, and he had difficulty pulling air into lungs. He slammed the door violently, spun around. Kubion had come up the path and was standing at the foot of the porch steps; he held the .38 automatic with deceptive looseness.

"It took me about four hours," he said through his fixed smile. "Duck soup, taking them over, but I had to bring the two from the house down the way to this place and that took a little extra time. Then I shook both houses down. I was just getting ready to start back when I made out this car without lights pulling into the first cabin on the lake, and I went to have a look. You know who it was? The banker, Matt Hughes; he's been getting a little on the side from that blond bitch in there. So I had to bring her over here, too."

He stopped speaking, watching them. Brodie said, "What about Hughes?"

"Well, he gave me a little trouble. You don't have to worry about him anymore, not a bit you don't."

"You killed him, is that it?"

"That's it. I killed him, all right."

Brodie began to rub the palms of his hands along his trouser legs: a gesture of suppressed rage. Loxner said in a kind of whine, "Why? Why all of this?"

"The two of you made it nice and clear yesterday how you felt about ripping off the valley, and I knew I couldn't talk you into it, right? But you didn't know how bad I want this one, I want it like I never wanted any other score, it's the cat's nuts. The only thing is, I don't figure I can make it alone, so I had to force you into it, you see? It's simple."

He paused, and his smile became sly. "Those people inside, I did a little talking to them. I told them all about the ripoff, and that's not all I told them. I told them we were the ones who did the Greenfront job, I told them everything except our names—what do you think of that?"

Loxner had the same look on his face—that of a kid about to cry—that he had had after the security guard shot him at Greenfront. "Crazy cocksucker," he muttered under his breath, "oh you crazy *cock*sucker!"

If Kubion heard him, he gave no indication. The smile still sly, he said, "I know what you're thinking now, both of you, you're thinking you want to put a bullet in me, maybe you've been thinking it ever since yesterday and that's why I took the guns out of the suitcase in the car if you don't already know about that and why I watched you like a goddamn hawk every minute I was at the cabin, I did you know. But suppose you could do it, suppose somehow you're able to jump me, take this gun away, put one in my head? Where would it leave you? These hicks here know who you are but say you had the guts to kill seven people, three women and two kids, say you had the guts, well the rest of the hicks and the cops would figure damned quick who had to've done it and you know what kind of heat you'd have then, right? So you let them live and then you cut and run, use one of the snowmobiles to get out of the valley, but that's the same situation as if we do the job only worse because these Eskimos would be found almost immediately and even if you took the time to bury Hughes' body and cut the telephone lines and put the second snowmobile out of commission, even if you could do all of that without being hassled, you still wouldn't have a clear jump. And you wouldn't have any bread either, that's the important thing, you'd have to knock over a place for ready cash, you'd have to shag a car, you'd be taking risks every time you turned around and all with Murder One heat ready to blow you on your asses at any time."

Kubion paused again and studied them cunningly. Brodie said in a flat, soft voice, "Keep talking, Earl."

"Okay, you're getting it now. You do things my way, you help me make the score, and we come out fine just like I told you yesterday. Bread in our pockets and two full days' jump, time to travel, time and money to get a long way from Hidden Valley before the lid comes off." Kubion used his left hand to take a roll of currency from his coat pocket. "Listen, you think there's no money in this place? Nine hicks out of seventy-five and only two of the occupied buildings so far and I've already picked up fifteen hundred, two bills from the Eskimos that live in this house and eighty from the ones down the way and a hundred and twenty from Banker Hughes' wallet, and that blond bitch, she had a thousand in her purse, just sitting there in her purse all nice and crisp in her *purse* for Christ's sake. Fifteen hundred already and we haven't even started."

He shoved the money back into his coat and made a sweeping gesture with the gun. "So what do you say? I say we go inside the house here and work over the details again, and this time you listen good. I say we do the job tomorrow, just as I told it to you. I say when it's done and we've made the split, we leave on separate snowmobiles and you go your way and I go mine, we're quits. Well? Do we get it on together or what? You tell me, you tell me."

There was a long, brittle silence. Loxner looked at Brodie to keep from looking at Kubion. And Brodie said finally in his flat, soft voice, "You haven't left us any choice, Earl. We do it your way."

Book Two

Sunday, December 23

Oh ye gods! what darkness of night there is in mortal minds!

—Ovid

One

At eleven fifty-five Sunday morning, in the vestry behind the candlelit altar, the Reverend Peter Keyes released the bell rope and ended the resonant summons in the steeple belfry above. Then, opening the vestry door, he stepped out onto the pulpit and went to stand behind the lectern on the far right, to watch the last of the congregation file into All Faiths Church. Opposite him on the pulpit, Maude Fredericks sat waiting at the old wood-pipe organ, a hymnal propped open in front of her.

Seven of the twelve pews on each side of the center aisle were completely full, but the last five on either side were only partially taken. The Reverend Mr. Keyes had entertained little hope for a capacity attendance, but he had expected a larger turnout than this. He scanned the congregation—the women and girls in their warm, brightly colored winter finery (you did not see somber hues in church these days, which was, he thought, as it should be); the men and boys in carefully pressed suits and bright ties, to which they were for the most part unaccustomed—and a small frown tugged at the corners of his mouth. He did not see Matthew Hughes, and Matthew never missed Sunday services, was in fact always one of the first to arrive; very odd indeed that he was not present on this particular Sunday, two days before Christmas. He also did not see the Markhams or the Donnelly family, who rarely failed to attend as well; nor the San Francisco businessman, Charley Adams, to whom he had spoken on Thursday afternoon.

Maude Fredericks turned slightly on the organ bench and glanced at him, and he indicated that she should begin playing; it was just noon. Deep-toned chords, reverent and felicitous, filled the wide interior. The Reverend Mr. Keyes waited, looking out through the open half of the double doors at the empty, snow-dappled walk beyond; the Hugheses and the Markhams and the Connellys did not arrive. Finally, sighing inaudibly, he nodded to this Sunday's usher, Dr. Webb Edwards. The middle-aged physician returned his nod, stepped out to look both ways along Sierra Street, and apparently saw no late arrivals in the vicinity; he came back inside, closed the open door, and took a place in one of the rear pews. The time was twelve five.

When the organ music had crescendoed into silence, the Reverend Mr. Keyes offered a brief invocation; a moment of silent and conjoined prayer followed. Then he led the congregation in the singing of "O Jesus, We Adore Thee" and "Savior, Blessed Saviour" and "Joy to the World." Time: twelve twenty. He arranged his notes on the lectern, cleared his throat, and prepared to deliver his traditional pre-Christmas sermon, the Bible text of which had been taken from the first chapter of the Gospel of St. Luke.

Time: twelve twenty-one.

And the double doors burst apart, the two halves thudding loudly against the interior wall, and three men came quickly inside. Two of them held deer rifles and fanned one to either side along the coat-draped wall. The third, pointing a handgun, stood with his feet braced apart just inside the entrance.

Heads swiveled around; faces blanched with incredulity and nascent fear. Kubion, who had the handgun, called out in a sharp, commanding voice, "All right, everybody just sit still. We don't want to hurt any of you but I'll shoot the first one who makes a move in this direction, let's get that understood right from the start."

The Reverend Mr. Keyes stared at the man he knew as Charley Adams, the man whom he had thought to be a good and devout Christian, stared at the two strangers with the rifles—and he could not believe what he saw or what he had just heard. It simply could not be happening; it was utterly impossible. He felt an unfamiliar but suddenly acute sense of outrage; his round cheeks flamed with it, his fingers gripped the edges of the lectern until the knuckle joints seemed about to pop through the stretched white skin. "How dare you!" he shouted. "How dare you come in here with guns! This is a house of *God!*"

"Calm down, Reverend," Kubion said. He seemed to be smiling. "All of you calm down, keep your heads, and then I'll tell you what it's all about."

The command turned the Reverend Mr. Keyes' outrage to blind fury. He pushed away from the lectern and came down off the pulpit. Lew Coopersmith, sitting in the right front pew, said, "No, Reverend!" but Keyes did not even hear the words. He started into the center aisle, his eyes fixed on Kubion.

"Hold it right there, preacher man."

Reverend Keyes brushed past the arm Coopersmith put out to restrain him and walked slowly and grimly down the aisle. He was not afraid because he knew he would not be harmed, not *here*; his anger was righteous, his position was sacrosanct, and he said, "I won't have guns in my church, I won't have you bringing weapons of destruction in God's house," and Kubion unhesitatingly shot him through the right hand.

The hushed, strained silence dissolved first into the hollow roar of the gunshot and then into terrified screams and cries from women and children, shocked articulations from the men. The Reverend Mr. Keyes had stopped moving. He held his hand up in front of him and stared at the blood beginning to stream from the hole just below the thumb: numbly, not believing what he saw any more than he quite believed, even now, that any of this was actually happening.

"Dear God," he said then, and fainted.

Lew Coopersmith was on his feet and three steps into the center aisle before he realized he had moved at all. Abruptly he stopped and allowed his hands to unknot at his sides, standing rigidly. Others were on their feet now as well, faces stricken—John and Vince Tribucci, Webb Edwards, Verne Mullins—but none of them had moved from their places. The whimperings of the women and children intensified the atmosphere of horror which now pervaded the church.

Kubion said, "When I say something I mean it, you'd all better get that straight right now, the next one that makes a funny move I'll shoot his face off. Okay—one of you's the doctor, which one?"

"Here," Edwards said.

"Get out here and tend to the Reverend."

"I don't have my bag. I'll need—"

"You'll need nothing. Get out here."

Edwards went to where Reverend Keyes lay inert on the floor, knelt beside him, and examined the bullet-torn hand; it was still bleeding heavily. He used his belt as a tourniquet, his handkerchief to swab the wound.

Kubion said, "He got a key on him to the church doors?"

"I don't know," Edwards answered woodenly.

"Well look through his pockets and find out!"

Edwards probed quickly, gently, through the minister's dark-gray suit and discovered a ring of keys. He held them up. Kubion made a tossing motion, and Edwards flipped the key ring underhand, as carefully as he would have thrown a ball to a three-year-old child. Making the catch with his left hand, Kubion turned and pulled the entrance doors nearly closed. He probed at the latch on one with three of the keys, found one that fitted, and then dropped the ring into the pocket of his coat. He faced the congregation again.

"Couple of you pick the Reverend up and put him on one of the benches."

Coopersmith came forward, and Harry Chilton stepped out. With Edwards' help, they lifted Keyes gently and laid him supine in the nearest pew.

"The rest of you men—shut those women and kids up," Kubion said. "I want it quiet in here, I want every one of you to hear what I'm going to say, and I don't want to have to say it more than once, you got that?"

While husbands and parents did what they had been ordered to do, Coopersmith retreated a few steps and glanced over his shoulder to where Ellen was sitting; she was motionless, hands pressed against her white cheeks, her eyes round and glistening wet with tears. He saw Ann Tribucci sitting near Ellen, one arm wrapped in an unconsciously—or perhaps consciously—protective way around the huge convexity that was her unborn child, her other hand holding tightly to one of her husband's. John Tribucci's face, unlike most of the others, was as stiff and empty of expression as a store mannequin's.

Kubion said as the congregation quieted, "That's better. Here it is, then, plain and simple: we're here because we're taking over the valley and everybody in it and once we've got complete control we're going to loot it, building by building. Money and expensive jewelry, that's all we're interested in, and if you people cooperate that's all we'll take, nobody else will get hurt."

He paused to let the concept sink in fully. Then: "All right, now some details. When I'm done talking one of us will come around with a sack and you put your wallets and purses into it and anything else you've got in your pockets, don't hold anything out, turn your pockets. After that's done we'll want a list of names of everybody who lives in the valley that's not here right now, I mean everybody, because we're going to go round them up one by one after we leave here and if we find anybody whose name isn't on the list he's dead. You can forget about the Markhams and the Donnellys and Matt Hughes and Peggy Tyler; we've—"

Agnes Tyler's shrill, near hysterical voice cried, "Peggy? Peggy? Oh my God I should have known something was wrong. I should have known that telephone call last night was a lie!" She was standing, one hand clutching her breast, eyes like a pair of too-ripe grapes pressed into a lump of gray dough. "You've *hurt* her, you've hurt my daughter. . . ."

Kubion looked at her and said, "Somebody shut that bitch the hell up."

Beside her, Verne Mullins took hold of her shoulders and eased her down again. Agnes buried her face in her hands and began moaning softly. Coopersmith said in a carefully expressionless voice, "What do you mean we can forget about those people? What have you done to them?"

Kubion's gaze shifted to him. "Nothing to any of them, old man—except Hughes. We'll bring them in later."

"Except Hughes?"

"He's dead," Kubion said, and the smile transformed on his mouth and made it look like an open wound. His voice was savage with impatience. "I killed him last night and he's dead, you'll all be dead you stupid hicks unless you shut up and listen to me and do what I say I don't want any more questions I don't want any more crap you understand me!"

The aura of horror had reached the point of tangibility now: it could be felt, it could be tasted, it lay like a pall of invisible mist inside the church. No one moved, no one made a sound; even the children and Agnes Tyler were silent. The Reverend Mr. Keyes shot in his own church, the valley about to be taken over and looted, Matt Hughes—their mayor, their friend, their benefactor—inexplicably murdered, all their lives suddenly in the hands of three armed men and one of whom was nothing less than a psychotic: they were literally petrified with fear.

Coopersmith swallowed against the rage and revulsion which burned in his throat, struggling to maintain calm and a clear head, and looked at each of the other two men, the ones with the rifles. Neither of them had made a single motion since their entrance; they were like wooden sentinels. But there was sanity in their faces, and the big heavy one was sweating copiously, and the fair-haired one, despite a guarded, stoic expression, appeared to be tensely uneasy as well. Why were they a part of this? he thought.

Merciful God, why *any* of this?

Kubion was smiling again, and when he spoke his voice was once more controlled, matter-of-fact. "Now like I said, once we have the list of names two of us will go round up the other people and bring them back here, and when everybody is in the church we go to work on the buildings—just two of us, the other one will be out front with a rifle, watching. We figure it'll take us most of today to get the job done, but when we're finished we might not be leaving right away, we might stay one day or two or even three before we go, and the way we'll go is on snowmobiles so don't get the idea we're trapped in the valley until the pass is open. But *you'll* wait until it's cleared, you'll stay in here until the day after Christmas. We'll bring in some food later and some water and you'll be nice and comfortable as long as you don't try any stupid tricks. The important thing for you to remember is that you won't know when we'll be leaving, you won't know when we're gone, and if you try to break down the front doors or knock out a window before the day after Christmas and we're still here, we'll kill everybody we see. Clear? All of that clear?"

Figures in stone.

Kubion said, "Good, we're going to get along fine now; you keep on sitting there like you are now and we're going to get along just fine." He looked at the heavy, dull-faced rifleman and made a gesture with his free hand. Loxner came over and put the weapon down against the wall, moving mechanically, using his left arm as if it were stiff and sore; then he took a folded flour sack from under his coat and walked up the center aisle. Coopersmith watched him as he passed down to the end of the right front pew; his damp face contained what might have been a kind of masked fear of his own.

When Coopersmith faced front again, he saw that the fair-haired rifleman had also set his weapon against the wall and had produced a pencil and a pad of paper. Kubion said, "Names now, everybody not here and where they live in the village." His eyes rested on Coopersmith. "You, old man, start it off. Who's not here?"

Coopersmith hesitated. Then, because there was nothing else he could do, he began in a leaden voice to recite. And all the while he was talking the same cold, voracious thought kept running through his mind: I wish I had my gun now because I would kill you, I think God forgive me I would kill you right where you stand, right here in church, and sleep tonight with a clear conscience. . . .

Two

When Brodie and Loxner had preceded him out of the church and gone halfway along the front walk—holding the rifle barrels down against their legs as he had instructed them to do—Kubion stepped out and shut the doors and locked them. His watch said that it was one fifteen. Very good: fifty-five minutes, five minutes less than he had anticipated. You couldn't do much better than that, bet your ass you couldn't.

He went down the steps and followed Loxner and Brodie to where his car was parked eastward of six others in the fronting lot; the automatic rested in his coat pocket now, his hand lightly gripping the butt. Sierra Street was still deserted, he saw with satisfaction, and there was no sign of activity anywhere else in the village. It had begun to snow thinly from a silky gray sky, but the drifting clouds to the west were black-bordered and pregnant; it would snow much more heavily before long.

Brodie and Loxner stopped beside the car, and Kubion halted ten feet away. "You see?" he said to them. "Easy, easy, no sweat at all."

"Why did you shoot the Reverend?" Brodie asked

tautly. "You didn't have to do any shooting in there; it wasn't necessary."

"Don't tell me what was necessary and what wasn't, I know exactly what I'm doing. You got religion now, maybe?"

Brodie said nothing more. His fingers caressed the stock of the rifle, one of the three taken from the Markham and Donnelly houses; but it, like the one Loxner carried, was empty. Empty! Kubion laughed out loud. They had done the church scene with just his automatic, one loaded gun was going to take over the entire valley, and that was funny when you thought about it, that was a real gutbuster when you thought about it.

For a while yesterday he'd considered wasting Brodie and Loxner and ripping off the valley all by himself. The idea of that appealed to him all right, but he'd finally decided against it. Hicks would be more afraid of three men with guns than one man with a gun, the old psychological advantage—that was one thing; another was that he might need some help in rounding up the rest of the hicks, maybe in other areas too; a third, and this had been the main deciding point, was that he liked the idea of keeping the two of them alive as long as he felt like it, playing with them a little, hamstringing them, using them to prolong the score because the longer it lasted, the sweeter it would be. And there wasn't a shred of doubt that he could handle the two of them—stupid gutless Loxner and culinary fairy Brodie; he could handle anybody and anything, he was like ten feet tall and nobody could touch him with all the power he possessed, the power that had been there all the time if only he'd recognized it for what it was and let it come free.

What it was, this new outlook of his, was like being on a perpetual grass high: you saw everything crystal clear, inside yourself and outside yourself, and you didn't worry about shit like headaches and spiders (*they'd* never come back again; he'd killed every last one of *them*), and you didn't worry about violence either. If you had to do something violent, why then you just did it and it was *all right*; in fact it gave you a kind of release, it made you feel loose again like you felt after you'd popped your cork into one of those big-assed black chicks. So when the impulse came over him, the way it had last night when he'd found Hughes and the blond bitch together, he'd just let it tell him what to do and then followed orders. It had come on again in the church, just a little, but it told him not to kill the Reverend because that might have led to hysteria and the hicks had to be kept docile until the ripoff was completed, so he'd put one through that preacher man's hand. When it came on again, and sooner or later it would, it'd tell him just the right time to waste Brodie and Loxner and he'd do that; and maybe it would tell him to waste all the hicks too and he'd do *that*, a bunch of Eskimos like that were better off dead anyway. Right? Right on.

"Okay," he said, "let's get to work. Put the rifles in the back seat. Duff, the flour sack, too."

Brodie opened the rear door, and they tossed the weapons inside. Loxner laid the sackful of wallets and purses and other items on the floor matting, threw the door closed.

"Now we get those other hicks out of the pickup and into the church," Kubion told them.

They moved out silently, went around the south side of the building and along to the rear wall of the minister's cottage. The battered Ford half-ton belonging to Sid Markham was parked in close to the cottage wall, the glass in its rear window broken out at Kubion's instructions, its bed draped and tied securely with a heavy tarpaulin.

At the Donnelly house last night, with Loxner and Brodie under control, Kubion had first considered what to do about the families of Matt Hughes and Peggy Tyler. Go in and take them over too, bring them out to the lake?

Too much extra hassle, he'd concluded; he had enough hicks under wraps as it was, and he didn't want to risk jeopardizing the operation planned for Sunday. Better to use the telephone and make excuses as to why Hughes and the blonde wouldn't be home that night, didn't really matter what kind of excuses because nobody was going to figure special trouble with the valley snowbound and they would accept anything that sounded halfway reasonable. He had had Brodie ungag Peggy Tyler; but she'd just sat there like a damned dummy, and slapping her hadn't done any good. He'd told Brodie to gag her again anyway and then to untie Martin Donnelly. Donnelly hadn't given any trouble; he had answered all of Kubion's questions about Hughes and Tyler and their people, and agreed to do and say exactly what he was told. So they took him to the Markham house—Kubion had disabled the Donnelly phone—and he called the blonde's mother and told her her daughter wouldn't be home until the next day because Donnelly's wife and both his kids were sick and he had seen Peggy in the village when he'd gone for the doctor and asked her to spend the night; the mother grumbled a little and finally said okay. Then they telephoned Rebecca Hughes, and Donnelly told her Hughes had come out for a visit and that a tree had fallen across the road in the interim, and Hughes was out with Sid Markham trying to do something about it but they didn't know if it could be gotten off the road tonight, don't worry if he doesn't make it home until tomorrow sometime. She didn't question the explanation. And that took care of that.

Later, past midnight, the three of them had driven into the village, and at Kubion's direction Brodie had climbed one of the utility poles beyond Alpine Street and cut the telephone lines. The remainder of the night was spent in the kitchen of the Donnelly house, going over details and then just sitting there and waiting: each of them wide awake and watchful, Kubion not even tired because he had slept most of Saturday morning in preparation for the all-night vigil. After a late, cold breakfast, which Kubion had eaten with relish and Brodie and Loxner had barely touched, they'd loaded the seven captives into the pickup; then, at exactly noon, they had come into the village again—Brodie driving the half-ton, Loxner driving Kubion's car and Kubion in the back. The streets had been completely empty when they reached All Faiths Church. Brodie had pulled the pickup around here to the blind side of the cottage, and Loxner had parked the car in the lot, and then they had met at the steps to begin the takeover.

Now Kubion stood to one side while Brodie and Loxner started untying the tarpaulin. When they had it off he could see the seven people lying just as they had been placed earlier, shivering with cold, their bloodless faces like those in the church: masks of crippling fear. He smiled across at them.

Loxner dropped the tailgate, and he and Brodie dragged the seven from the bed and put them on the snow-covered ground. Kubion took out his heavy, thick-bladed pocketknife and tossed it to Loxner, told him to cut the clothesline bonds and remove the gags. He said when that had been done, "Close it up and toss it back, nice and careful," and Loxner obeyed instantly.

Sid Markham and Martin Donnelly rubbed circulation into their stiffened limbs and then moved to help the women and children; no one looked at Kubion. The little Donnelly girl began to cry, and her mother held her tightly, crooning into her hair. Peggy Tyler sat slump-bodied in the snow, lips moving in a soundless monologue, eyes wide and glistening like bright wet agates. Markham could not seem to get her on her feet, and Kubion finally had Brodie do it—stupid little bitch.

Once all of them were up and walking, he made a motion with his left hand. Brodie and Loxner prodded them down and around to the front entrance, where they stopped and huddled together in a knot. Kubion went up and unlocked the doors, calling out, "Stand back in there, you've got company." Then he looked at the seven hicks —and they mounted the stairs with the resigned, mechanical movements of condemned prisoners climbing a gallows.

Kubion relocked the doors after them, returned the ring of keys to his coat pocket; he could hear but did not pay any attention to voices rumbling within, the thin, sharp cry of a woman. He came down off the steps and told Brodie and Loxner to move over to the car.

When they reached it, he said, "Duff, you'll stay here and start emptying out that sack so we can see what we've got to start with. Vic and I will go after the rest of the hicks. And Duff—if you're gone any of the times we come back, I'll kill Vic first thing and then I'll go inside the church and shoot five of the women. You understand me?"

Loxner looked at a point several feet to the right of Kubion. "Yeah. Yeah, I understand."

"Give me the car keys."

As carefully as Edwards had tossed the keys inside the church, Loxner threw him the leather case containing the car keys; then he opened the door and slid into the front seat. He sat there with his hands splay-fingered on his thighs, staring through the snow-dappled windshield. Kubion said to Brodie, "Put that list of names and addresses on the roof, Vic, and then back off fifteen or twenty steps and keep still like a good boy."

Brodie did as he was told. Kubion lifted the pad, took out the tourist brochure that had the village map on it, and alternately looked at those items and at Brodie standing well out away from the car. Nineteen names, ten houses, maybe seven trips in all; start with the places nearest the church and move outward until he had them all. He picked out their first three stops, tucked the list into his coat, paused, and then called to Brodie, "Okay, Vic, move out, around to the pickup again."

Once Brodie had pivoted, Kubion told Loxner, "Get to work on that sack, Duff, take it out of the back and get to work—come *on*."

A moment later he slammed the car door, thinking, Now then, now then, and hurried, glitter-eyed, after Brodie's retreating back.

Three

Frank McNeil was on his hands and knees in front of his old Magnavox radio-and-record player console, fiddling with the radio dials in an effort to tune in the AFL pro football play-off game, when the doorbell began ringing insistently. He looked up in irritation. "Now who goddamn it is that?"

His son, sitting on the living-room sofa, said, "You want me to answer it, Pa?"

"Well what do *you* think, dummy?"

Larry stood up and went out into the hallway. McNeil heard voices at the front door and paid them no mind. Damn these mountains sometimes; you could seldom get a decent picture on television even in the best of weather, and today the damned *radio* was too badly static-ridden to be intelligible. If he could at least. . . .

Footsteps in the hallway, and Larry's voice—high-pitched, frightened: "Pa? Pa?"

McNeil looked up again and saw the two men standing on either side of the youth; one of them was familiar, the other a complete stranger. And then he became aware of the gun in the hand of the dark familiar one, and his irritation dissolved into disbelief. He jerked awkwardly to his feet, flutter-eyed and gape-mouthed.

"No problems if you keep your cool," Kubion told him, "no problems at all."

McNeil continued to blink at him, almost spastically now. With impossible suddenness there was death in the room, *his* death—he could feel it, he could see it staring at him from the eyes of the dark one with the gun—and he began to shake his head, as if by doing that he could make the men and the gun and the stultifying presence of death vanish.

Kubion said, "Who else is here in the house?"

McNeil kept on shaking his head. His mouth and jaws worked soundlessly, as if in exaggerated pantomime of a man chewing gum; he was incapable of speech.

Larry said, "My mother . . . just my mother."

"Where?"

"In the kitchen."

"Call her in here."

"You . . . listen, you won't hurt her?"

"Now why would I hurt your old lady, get her in here."

"Ma," Larry called; then, louder: "Ma!"

"What is it?" a woman's voice answered.

"Come into the living room."

"Who was that at the door?"

"Ma, come in here, will you!"

Sandy McNeil—a dark-haired, soft-featured, harassed-looking woman wearing an apron over a faded housedress—appeared in the doorway. "What—" she began, and then stopped speaking and stopped walking as she saw the men, the gun Kubion held. Her eyes grew very round, and the intake of her breath was loudly sibilant, like the hiss of valve-bled steam. The dishtowel she had been holding slipped loose and fell unnoticed to the floor.

Larry went to her and put a protective arm around her shoulders, partially shielding her body with his own.

"What are you going to do?" he asked. "What do you want with us?"

Kubion said, "We're going to take you to a party."

"Party?" Sandy McNeil said blankly.

"At the church. A little party at the church."

"I don't understand," she said. "I don't *understand.*"

"You don't have to understand. You just do what I tell you. Let's go."

Larry guided his mother toward the hallway. But McNeil stood frozen in front of the console, eyes glazed with terror; he couldn't move, he could not make himself move.

Kubion looked at him, and then stepped quickly forward and cupped a hand around the back of McNeil's neck and sent him reeling across the room. McNeil made a strangled, bleating sound, caught his balance, and groped sightlessly into the hall—pushing his wife and son out of the way as if they were bundles of sticks. His face was the wet dirty color of slush.

A small stain began to spread on the front of his trousers, and Kubion laughed when he saw it. "Well, if you aren't a pisser," he said. "If you aren't a real pisser." He kept on laughing all the way out to the pickup waiting in the side drive.

Somebody began pounding on the downstairs lobby door just as Walt Halliday and his wife finished making love.

"Oh for goodness sake," Lil Halliday said drowsily. She was a thick-bodied woman with butter-yellow hair and a pleasantly homely face. Lying naked on the rumpled double bed, her husband's balding head pillowed comfortably on her heavy breasts, she looked younger than her forty-two years.

Halliday raised his head and listened to the pounding —louder now, demanding—and finally sat up in annoyance. His nose began to run, and he reached one of the Kleenex off the nightstand and blew into it. He had awakened that morning with a sore throat and the runny nose and a slight fever and knew he was coming down with the flu; instead of getting up and dressing for church, as he might have done, he had decided to stay in bed. Lil, who was not much of a churchgoer and went only when he did—fifteen or twenty Sundays in any year, most of those during the quiet off-season months—had brought him a tray breakfast and had then come back to bed with him. They had dozed for a while, talked for a while, been leisurely in their lovemaking: a good Sunday, a fine Sunday. Until that damned persistent pounding on the door.

Standing, Halliday put on his glasses and pajamas and robe and slid his feet into ankle slippers. "Whoever that is," he said, "is going to get a piece of my mind. There's no need to beat on the door like that."

"I'm just glad they didn't start that racket about five minutes ago," Lil said.

"That's something, anyway," Halliday agreed.

He went to the door and glanced back at his wife, and she was still lying there uncovered; she knew he liked to look at her that way. He gave her a broad wink and left their apartment, which was on the first floor of the inn, at the head of the stairs, and started down to the lobby. He shouted, "I'm coming, stop that hammering!" but the sound continued. It was heavy enough now to rattle the glass in the adjacent window.

More than a little irritated, Halliday unlocked the door and jerked it open and said, "What's the idea of—" The rest of the sentence died when he saw the two men and the automatic one of them was pointing at him.

Kubion said, "Back inside, hurry it up, you kept us waiting too long already."

Halliday did what he was told, rapidly, putting his

hands up over his head. His mind, all at once, was wrapped in dreamlike confusion. "What do . . . what do you want?"

"You'll find that out soon enough. Nothing will happen to you as long as you do what you're told. You've got a wife—where is she?"

"Upstairs. She . . . but she. . . ."

"Take us to her."

"She's in bed, my wife's in bed."

"So what? Come on, get your ass in gear."

Halliday stared at the gun, at the face behind it, and turned instantly to the stairs. As he began to ascend, he could not seem to think of anything except the way Lil had been lying when he'd left her moments ago; and he found himself hoping almost desperately that she had covered herself. Whatever was about to happen, he did not want these two men to see his wife naked. . . .

Je Garvey opened his front door, and one of the two men standing on the porch outside showed him a gun and said, "Back off, we're coming in; do what you're told and you won't get hurt."

Garvey said incredulously, "What the *hell*!" and stayed where he was. The fingers of his right hand still clutched the edge of the door.

"Inside," Kubion said. "Move it."

"Listen, what is this, you can't come around my house waving a gun—"

Kubion kicked the door out of his hand, jarring loose the candle-festooned holly wreath which hung from the outer panel, and crowded forward. But instead of giving ground as he was expected to do, Garvey braced himself in anger and indignation and made a reflexive lunge at the extended automatic. Half turning, pulling the gun in against his body, Kubion blocked the sweeping arm with his shoulder and made a horizontal bar of his left arm and hit the other man across the chest with it. Garvey banged into one of the inside corridor walls, came off it again like a ball bouncing, and Kubion clubbed him full in the face with the barrel of the weapon.

Bawling with pain, broken nose spraying blood, Garvey staggered into the wall a second time and then went down hard to his knees. Kubion took four more steps into the corridor without breaking momentum and swung around in a crouch and said, "Don't do it, Vic."

Brodie was through the doorway, one arm upraised like a bludgeon, moving in a rush. He brought himself up three feet from the muzzle of Kubion's gun and dropped his arm and backed away immediately, around the kneeling figure of Joe Garvey. His face, momentarily savage, became blank again; only his eyes maintained their polished amethyst shine.

Pat Garvey's voice began calling in querulous alarm from somewhere in the house. "Joe? Joe?"

"Stupid, Vic," Kubion said. "Stupid, stupid."

Brodie said, "All right, I lost my head."

"You'll lose it permanently if you do something else that's stupid. I need you to work the rest of the take-over, you're still in for a third of the take, but I'll make you a dead lump of shit if you push me. You'd better have that straight now."

"Okay," Brodie said. "Okay."

Garvey took his hands away from his face and stared at the blood on them, at the blood dripping from his pulped nose to stain the white front of his shirt. Throbbing pain ringing in his ears, nausea in the back of his throat. What's happening here? he thought dazedly. I don't know what's happening here.

His wife came running into the corridor, saw the two men, saw the gun, saw Garvey kneeling on the floor with the bright red fluid all over him. One hand came up to her mouth, and she screamed softly. "Joe, oh my God, Joe!" She started toward him.

Kubion stepped in front of her and caught her arm; she

shrank back away from him, struggling vainly to release the grip, her eyes darting from his face to her husband. "He'll be all right," Kubion told her, "and so will you if you both keep your mouths shut, I mean *shut*, you hear?"

Leave her alone, you filthy son of a bitch! Garvey thought. He tried to put voice to the words, but there was blood in his throat; he began to cough instead.

The blood and the coughing saved his life.

Greg Novak wondered where the hell everybody was.

Sierra Street was deserted all the way up to the slide, and there was no sign of life anywhere else. He hadn't seen a soul since he'd left his parents' home on Modoc Street five minutes before.

For that matter, where were his father and mother? They'd gone to church at a quarter to twelve, and it was three o'clock when he came out of the house for a little fresh air, and they still hadn't returned. He supposed they'd gone to visit somebody, though they didn't usually do that on Sundays. Usually they came straight home and his mother fixed a light lunch and then they played canasta. Church and canasta were both a drag, as far as he was concerned. Sometimes he got pressured into both, because it was easier to give in than to start a hassle; but he'd stayed in bed this morning, and for a change his mother hadn't tried to talk him out. All things considered, his folks were pretty good people, even if they were hung up on religion and canasta.

So where *was* everybody, anyway?

Novak felt as if he were walking in a village that had been abandoned, and the feeling made him oddly uncomfortable. He stopped and turned and looked back down Sierra—and a Ford pickup had swung out of the lane to the north of the church and was coming up toward him. Sid Markham's pickup. The uneasiness left him, and he stood watching the half-ton approach, waiting for it.

When it had come close enough so that the two men in

the cab were visible through the windshield, he realized that neither of them was Sid Markham. He began to frown. The pickup slewed over to him, and the passenger door opened; the guy on that side jumped out with a gun in his hand, vaulted the packed snow at the curbing, and said, "Stand right where you are, kid, don't move a muscle."

Novak did not even breathe.

Emily Bradford was seventy-five years of age, a thin and frail old woman confined by chronic arthritis either to her bed or to a wheelchair for the past eight years. She lived with her daughter and son-in-law, Sharon and Dave Nedlick: six months in the Macklin Lake hunting lodge which the Nedlicks owned and operated, and six months in the two-story frame house on the corner of Alpine and Modoc streets, where she now lay in her upstairs bedroom.

Sharon and Dave had left for church just before noon, and Emily had spent the next hour faithfully reading her buckram-bound Bible. She had long ago learned to live with her invalidism, but she was still bothered by the fact that she could no longer attend church. Reading the Bible for the length of a Sunday service compensated somewhat, although it was simply not the same thing and never would be. At one o'clock she had resumed her current crocheting project, waiting for her family to return home.

It was presently three thirty, and they had still not come back.

When Sharon and Dave planned to be away for any period of time, they always asked one of the neighbors—mostly an obliging Ellen Coopersmith—to stay with her; but Sharon had said this morning that they would return immediately after church, because they were having turkey for Sunday dinner and she wanted to get it into the oven by one thirty, and Emily never minded being alone for an hour or so. Almost four hours was something else entirely, particularly when the prolonged absence had no apparent explanation, and as a result, Emily had fretted herself into a state of acute anxiety. Something was wrong, she felt it in her bones. She could not imagine what it could be, what with the valley being snowbound as it was, but that only made her all the more apprehensive.

She reached out to the telephone on the bedside table, the third time she had done so in the past hour, and lifted the receiver to her ear. There was no dial tone, it was *still* not working, and why did there always have to be problems with the telephone when you needed it most? She dropped the handset back into its cradle, keenly aware of the stillness of the house and the quick beating of her heart. Why didn't Sharon and Dave come home? Why didn't they come home?

Something made a crashing, shattering noise downstairs.

Emily started violently. One of her veined hands flew up to clutch at the high neck of her nightdress, and her eyes widened behind the lenses of her glasses until they were like luminous brown-and-white pellets. She sat tensely, listening.

More sounds came from below, heavy footsteps. Sharon always walked softly, as did her husband, and Emily thought: Somebody else, there's somebody else in the house! Her breath made a rasping sound in her throat, and her heart began to pound now like a fist within her thin breast.

The heavy footfalls were on the stairs now, ascending.

"Who is it?" she cried, but her tremulous voice was a whisper instead of a shout. "Who's out there?"

The bedroom doorknob rattled—and then the door popped open, and she was looking at two men she had never seen before; men with hard, dark faces and the tangible aura of malevolence about them, one of them brandishing a gun—a *gun!* That one came into the bedroom, sweeping it with deranged eyes, looking at Emily as if she were just another of the room's furnishings.

The other one said, "For Christ's sake, they told you in the church she was an invalid. What's the point of coming up here like this?"

"To make sure," Kubion said. And to Emily, "Take it easy, old woman, nothing's going to happen to you."

"We're not taking her out of here, Earl—not her."

"No, she won't be any trouble."

Kubion stepped back into the hall, motioning, and Brodie swung the door shut. Their footsteps retreated along the corridor, on the stairs.

Emily did not hear them for the thunder in her ears, the loud loud thunder of her heart. And then the thunder began to fade—fading, fading, becoming only a stuttering whisper—and her free hand lifted and fumbled at the air as if imploring. A moment later, like an autumn leaf drifting from tree branch to earth, it fluttered slowly back to the bedclothes and lay still.

The house was once more silent, once more empty; but now the silence was sepulchrally hushed, and the emptiness complete.

Four

Restlessly pacing the living room, smoking her fifteenth cigarette of the day, Rebecca was intensely aware of the metronomic ticking of the antique pendulum clock on one wall. Ordinarily she did not even hear the familiar tempo, but today, this afternoon, now, it seemed to have grown in volume with its marking of each passing second, so that it filled the room and hammered at her consciousness and at her nerves in the manner of a steadily dripping faucet.

Twenty till four, the clock hands said.

The cigarette tasted raw and noxious, and she turned to the coffee table and jabbed it out in the cloissoné tray. I can't go on with this passive waiting any longer, she thought. I've got to find out where Matt is and why he hasn't come home.

When Martin Donnelly had telephoned her the previous evening—she'd been in bed at the time, thinking about the curiously intimate encounter with Zachary Cain; that he was a man tortured by a personal crisis greater than her own and that she had selfishly misjudged him—Rebecca had unhesitatingly accepted Donnelly's account of a fallen tree likely stranding Matt overnight at the lake. There was no reason to doubt Martin's word—he was a scrupulously honest man—and no reason to suspect anything wrong.

But when Matt did not return this morning or call as he always did when legitimately or illegitimately detained somewhere, she had experienced a vague presentiment of things being not quite right. There was little to support such a foreboding, other than the fact that a team of men should certainly have been able to clear the road of a down tree by midmorning, but it had nagged at her until, finally, she had gone to the telephone with the intention of calling the Donnelly home. The phone had not been working—lines down someplace probably, it happened occasionally during the winter months—and that, she told herself, was obviously the reason Matt hadn't called. Everything was quite normal, otherwise. After all, what could happen in a snowbound little place like Hidden Valley?

And yet—

At eleven forty, with Matt still not home, Rebecca had briefly considered going to church. But then she thought that Matt would never think of setting foot inside All Faiths Church on Sunday unless he had dressed for the occasion in his best suit and tie and shirt and shoes. Since he hadn't come home to change, it was axiomatic he wouldn't be in church—and was then, supposedly, still out at the lake. Too, formal religious observance had been destroyed for her some time ago by Matt's hypocrisy: seeing him in fervent, righteous prayer on those Sundays when she knew he had lain with another woman the previous night; she continued occasionally to accompnay him when he insisted and for the hollow sake of appearance, but while she still believed in God, actively worshiping Him had been and was impossible. And so she remained in the house, busying herself with prosaic chores, waiting.

One thirty had come. No Matt. She'd tried the phone again, and it was still out of order. Two o'clock. Three.. Three thirty. The premonition of wrongness had steadily amplified until, now, it made further waiting unconscionable. Perhaps it was only a case of too much imagination—the making-mountains-out-of-molehills syndrome—and there was some simple and innocuous reason why Matt hadn't returned; but she had to find out, she had to know.

Rebecca went into the hall and opened the door of the coat closet. Boots, hat, parka, mittens. She would, she thought, go to the Tribuccis first. They would know about the fallen tree business, and if there *was* more to it than that, if they weren't aware of his whereabouts, John or Vince would drive her out to Mule Deer Lake so she could talk to Martin Donnelly. Quickly she buttoned her parka and then opened the front door and hurried outside.

She was halfway across the front yard when Sid Markham's old pickup pulled into the drive and the dark, smiling stranger stepped out to confront her. . . .

Beneath the lean-to which ran the full rear width of his cabin, Cain stood at a round, flat, tablelike stump and used a hatchet to split halved pine logs into kindling. The logs were stacked evenly along the rear wall, several cords of them flecked with icy snow; the area covered by the long, shake roof was otherwise bare. He worked mechanically, breath puffing white and hazy, and the thudding, splintering sounds he made reverberated hollowly in the brittle late-afternoon stillness.

Inside him, with an intensity that had mounted throughout the day, guilt fought with memories and despair grappled with rebirthing personal need.

He had had a recurring dream last night, so sharply vivid that it had half awakened him three or four times and had left him, when dawn finally came and ended all sleep, feeling weak and shaken. In the dream he was walking alone on a huge, sere plain, under a copper-colored sky. Far ahead of him he saw that the withered grass gave way to a stretch of bright green, and he went toward it and recognized as he approached that someone was standing just beyond the separation line between green and brown. The someone was one-half of himself—and he realized that there had only been half of *him* the entire time he'd been on the burned section of prairie, that he had been hopping on one leg instead of walking on two. Frightened, he stared with his single eye as though transfixed by his second eye.

And the other half of him said, with half a mouth, *Why do you keep fighting me? Sooner or later we're going to merge, you know that. We're going to become whole again.*

We can never be whole again, he said.

We can and we will. And when we are, we have to go back—back to architecture, back to San Francisco, back so we can pick up some of the pieces. It has to be that way; you can't run away from me any longer.

You're dead, do you hear me. You're dead!

I'm alive, we're alive. Listen, now, listen.

No.

Question: Would Angie have wanted you to do what you've done to us? Would Lindy and Steve, as young as they were, have wanted it?

That doesn't matter. They're gone, it doesn't matter.

Yes it does, oh yes it does. Question: Why weren't you able to suicide us? Wasn't it because I stopped you? Wasn't it because I, you, we want to go on living, after all?

Enough, I don't want to hear any more.

Question: If you truly wanted to turn us into an alcoholic, moribund vegetable, why did you come to Hidden Valley—why did you choose to live among people—in the first place? Aren't there hundreds of totally seques-

tered areas in this country where you could have become a literal hermit? Didn't I stop you there, too, even though you were stronger then?

Shut up, shut up.

You're not stronger anymore, I'm stronger. The incident with Rebecca Hughes was more than a spilling over of words, it was me taking over at last, it was the beginning of the end of these past six months. You know that, why won't you accept it?

I can't. I won't.

You can and you will. It's inevitable. Come to me now, come to me and we'll be whole again.

No!

He turned and tried to run, but with his single leg he could only hop; and the plain shimmered and suddenly became a quagmire that made accelerated motion impossible. Darkness took away the copper light of the sky, folding around him, and he could feel warm breath against the back of his neck—the other half of him pursuing, unimpeded by the boggy ground, coming closer, touching him then, touching him. . . .

At this exact point he would come out of it—only to sink back into slumber and have it start all over again.

When Cain had gotten up at dawn, and the shaken feeling had passed, he tried not to think about the dream; but it was fixed in his mind, each detail as ineradicable as the stain of loneliness. He dressed and went into the kitchen and fried two eggs, and couldn't eat them; poured bourbon into his coffee, and the smell of it gagged him. It was cold in the cabin, and he made a fire with the last of his kindling. The cold seemed to remain. He sat at the table by the window, chain-smoking, but the sitting began to gnaw at his nerves. Pacing did not help, and he thought of going for a walk and didn't want to do that either.

Sunday, today was Sunday. And on Sundays he and Don Collins would go out to Sharp Park or Harding and play eighteen holes of golf. On Sundays he would watch that intricate war game known as professional football on television. On Sundays he would take Angie and the kids to Golden Gate Park, where they would eat a picnic lunch at Stow Lake and then visit the De Young Museum or the Steinhart Aquarium or the Japanese Tea Garden or the Morrison Planetarium. On Sundays—

Shivering, Cain got a broom from the closet and swept out all the rooms; emptied an overflow of garbage into the can outside; made the bed and straightened the bedroom; washed the bathroom sink and shower stall and walls and floor. In the front room again he put more wood on the fire—and was acutely aware of how incredibly still it could get in there, how sterile and empty the surroundings actually were. He found himself wishing that he had a radio, that he could listen to some music or the news; realized he had not heard a newscast or read a paper in all the months he had been in Hidden Valley; realized he did not know, except for snatches of disinterestedly overheard conversation between valley residents, what was happening anywhere in the world.

I need to talk to someone, he thought, like I talked to Rebecca Hughes last night. I need—*I need. . . .*

He made a sandwich and forced himself to eat it. He could not think of anything else to do after that, and spent five minutes smoking six cigarettes and coughing up as much smoke as he exhaled normally before he remembered that there wasn't any more kindling. He got the hatchet then and came around here to the lean-to and began splitting logs.

There was, now, enough kindling lying in the snow at his feet to last him for weeks.

Cain buried the hatchet blade in the stump, wiped perspiration from his forehead with one gloved hand. Take all this inside, come back and carry in more halved logs to stack by the fireplace; keep busy, keep finding things to do. Stooping, he gathered up an armful of the kindling; straightened again, turned, took two steps—and came to a standstill.

Rebecca Hughes and two men he did not recognize were standing in the falling snow just outside the lean-to.

Cain opened his mouth to speak, closed it when he saw that the darker of the men, positioned well apart, was grinning oddly and holding a gun. The other one had his arms down at his sides, fingers curled in against the palms. As still and pale as a piece of marble statuary, Rebecca looked at Cain with eyes that were wide circles of fear. A feeling of unreality fled through him, as though the three of them had been conjured up from his subconscious—a kind of snow mirage.

"Drop that wood and get over here," Kubion said.

Cain found words, pushed them out. "Who are you? What's going on here?"

"You'll find out soon enough. Now shut up and do what you're told."

"What do you want with me, with Mrs. Hughes?"

"Get the fuck over here, I said!"

Cain sensed, incredulously, that the man would not hesitate to shoot him if he failed to comply; the feeling of unreality modulated into one of surreality. He let the kindling fall out of his arms in automatic reaction, walked forward stiffly and came out from under the roof and stopped again. Kubion's eyes followed him, and when Cain stared into them he saw unmistakable dementia shining there. His stomach contracted, and a brassy taste came into his mouth; he could not seem to think clearly.

"That's better, that's fine," Kubion said. "Now we go for a ride."

He gestured with the gun, and the second man—tight-mouthed, sane-looking—prodded Rebecca's shoulder. She moved forward, paused in front of Cain, and there was bewilderment commingled with fright in her expression; she seemed to have no more idea than he of the two men's motive or intent. Her dread was palpable; he could feel it as he could feel the knife-edge of the wind blowing along the cabin's side wall, and a rush of anger took away some of his own confusion—caring anger, an emotion (like the brassiness in his mouth) he had not experienced in a great long time.

He did not want her to be hurt; he did not want to be hurt himself.

I don't want to die, he thought almost detachedly. It's true, I really *don't* want to die. . . .

"Step out!" Kubion yelled at them. "Move!"

Rebecca edged close to Cain as they trudged forward through the snow. He said in a low voice, "Are you all right? They haven't hurt you?"

"No. No. But God, I—"

"Shut the hell up," from behind them. "I don't want to have to tell anybody again, you understand?"

Cain clamped his teeth together; Rebecca stared straight ahead, walking like a life-size windup toy. They went around to the front and across the yard to where an old Ford pickup was parked nose downhill on Lassen Drive. Brodie half circled it and got into the cab on the driver's side, and Kubion came forward then and said, "Both of you now, woman in the middle."

When Cain had pulled the door open Rebecca climbed awkwardly onto the front seat, drawing up a full twelve inches away from Brodie. The door slapped against Cain's hip as he wedged in after her, then latched under the pressure of Kubion's hand. Kubion swung onto the running board, over into the bed, and his face appeared in the broken-out rear window. He said to Brodie, "Nice and slow, Vic, you know how to do it."

"Yeah," Brodie said, and reached out to switch on the ignition.

Like a child huddling impersonally for warmth and support, Rebecca leaned against Cain with hip and thigh and shoulder and one breast—soft, yielding flesh through the parka she wore and despite the trembling tension in her. It was the first time he had been in physical contact with, conscious of, a woman's body since Angie, and defensively he felt his muscles stiffen.

But he did not withdraw from her as the truck glided forward and down through the empty afternoon.

Five

Coopersmith was one of the first to move when the three gunmen left the church and the key turned in the outside lock. He hurried to where Webb Edwards was bending over the still-unconscious form of the Reverend Mr. Keyes and holding his limp left wrist between thumb and forefinger.

"How is he, Webb?"

"Pulse is holding steady," Edwards answered shortly. "Get me a couple of coats, Lew. Only thing we can do is keep him warm."

At the front wall, Coopersmith dragged two heavy winter coats off the canted wooden pegs. Others were milling about now, as if in a kind of posthypnotic confusion. You could smell the sour odor of fear, Coopersmith thought; and you could feel the ripplings of panic like a dark undercurrent beneath the surface of sound and movement. Voices shrill and questioning assailed his ears as he took the coats to Edwards.

Judy Tribucci: "How can a thing like this happen, how can it happen to *us*. . . ."

Minnie Beckman: "A spawn of the devil, did you see his eyes, those terrible eyes. . . ."

Harry Chilton: "Why are they doing it? Why, for God's sake, why, why. . . ."

Verne Mullins: "Who are they, they're not businessmen, where did the third one come from. . . ."

Maude Fredericks: "Matt can't be dead, he can't be. . . ."

June Novak: "Oh my Lord please don't let Greg be harmed, please. . . ."

Sharon Nedlick: "Dave, Mother's heart won't stand any kind of shock, if they break into the house and try to bring her here even after what we told them. . . ."

Agnes Tyler: "Peggy *has* to be all right, they haven't hurt her, they haven't hurt her. . . ."

Edwards' nurse, Sally Chilton, had joined him at the minister's side. She took one of the coats from Coopersmith, folded it, and carefully pillowed Keyes' head; Edwards covered him with the second and then began unwrapping the blood-soaked handkerchief from his torn right hand, telling Sally to find a clean scarf or something to use as another makeshift bandage.

Coopersmith pivoted away—and Ellen was there, coming into his arms, pressing her wet face against his shoulder. He held her clumsily, felt the tremors fluttering through her body, and had no words to comfort her. Acrimony, helplessness formed an acidulated knot in his chest.

After a moment he lifted her chin with gentle fingers, brushed his lips across her forehead, took her slowly back to where they had been located in the right front pew. Opposite, on the left forward bench, Ann Tribucci was still sitting in the graceless, spread-legged, flat-footed posture of the pregnant woman in her final month; her abdomen, moving with the quickened tempo of her breathing, seemed enormous. Tie pulled loose, shirt unbuttoned at the throat, John Tribucci squatted in front of her.

He was saying, "You're *sure* you're okay, honey?"

"A little queasy, that's all."

"It's not the baby. . . ."

"No. No."

"Do you want to lie down?"

"Not just yet. Johnny—"

"What, honey?"

"If . . . Matt has been killed, do you think Becky—"

Inadequately he said, "Shh, now, try not to worry about Becky or anything else."

"How can I help it? I'm so frightened—for all of us, for the baby. . . ."

Tribucci took her hands in his and held them tightly. "I know," he said, "I know, I know. But nothing will happen to any more of us; we're all going to come out of this just fine."

There's no conviction in his voice, Coopersmith thought—and I don't think I believe it either, not after the things that homicidal lunatic said and has done already. He looked at Ellen and then swiftly averted his gaze again; he did not want her to see on his face what was in his mind. Spontaneously, he went up onto the pulpit and stared at the wooden crucifix on the wall above the prayer cloth-draped altar. The constriction in his chest had tightened, and he realized that he was short of breath. A new apprehension tugged at him. He had had a physical checkup three months before, and Webb Edwards had pronounced his heart as strong as ever; but he was sixty-six years old—*old,* not young—and an old man's heart could give out at any time under stress, wasn't that a medical fact?

Knock it off, he told himself sharply. You're not going to have a stroke. Whatever else will happen today, you're not going to have a stroke.

He kept on standing there, staring at the crucifix. A minute or two passed, and John Tribucci came up beside him. Some of the younger man's control had clearly begun to slip; his normally amiable face was dark-flecked with an admixture of anxiety and savage fury. "Lew," he said in a voice liquid with feeling. "*God,* Lew."

"Easy, son."

Tribucci closed his eyes, released a heavy shuddering breath and opened them again. "I've never hated anybody or anything in my life, but those three men, that maniac. . . ."

Coopersmith knew what he was thinking: exactly the same thing he himself had thought when the dark gunman ordered him to reveal which valley residents were not present inside the church. He did not speak.

"It's so *senseless,*" Tribucci said. "Reverend Keyes wounded and Matt Hughes murdered and maybe others dying, maybe all our lives in jeopardy—for what? For what, Lew? There isn't any money or valuables in Hidden Valley worth stealing."

"Johnny, don't try to find reason in the actions of a madman."

"All three of them can't be crazy."

"No, but it was obvious who's running the whole show. I can't figure why the other two are in it. Maybe for some other cause than what little the valley can be looted for."

"Well alone or not, that psycho has been planning it for days. He came into the Sport Shop on Thursday and asked me a lot of questions about snowmobiles and ways to get out of the valley. I believed the excuse he gave, told him everything he wanted to know. He looked all right then, I didn't suspect anything to be wrong. . . ."

"How could you? How could any of us? We—"

"*Stand back in there, you've got company!*"

The shouted command from outside sliced off conversation, jerked heads around, turned Tribucci and Coopersmith and brought them down off the pulpit. There was the sound of the key in the lock, and then one of the door halves swung open and the Donnelly and Markham families, and Peggy Tyler, filed inside. The door banged shut, and the key scraped again.

Agnes Tyler cried, "Peggy!" and rushed down the center aisle. The blond-haired girl had stopped just inside the entrance and was standing as immobile and expressionless as a mannequin. When her mother reached her and flung arms around her, moaning her name, she blinked several times but did not otherwise move; she seemed only vaguely aware of where she was. Coopersmith saw, as he and Tribucci approached, that the others seemed in better condition and apparently unharmed, although the adults were all haggard and eviscerated and shaking with cold or fear or both. The two Donnelly children clung to each other like waifs lost in the night.

Webb Edwards pushed his way forward and swept each of them with a clinical glance that concluded only Peggy Tyler was in immediate need of medical attention. He stepped to her, disengaged Mrs. Tyler s enfolding arms, and probed the damp ivory face, the vacuous eyes. His mouth thinned; he took one of her lax hands.

"What is it, what's the matter with her?" Agnes Tyler said frantically. "God in heaven, what did they do to you, baby, what did they *do* to you!"

Taking Peggy's other arm, Sally Chilton helped Edwards steer her to one of the rear pews; her mother hovered nearby, hands clenched together at her breast, teeth biting deeply into a tremulous lower lip. The Markhams and Donnellys found benches near the south-side wall heater, and Coopersmith and Tribucci and Harry Chilton brought extra coats for the women and children.

Minutes later, in subdued and exhausted tones, Sid Markham and Martin Donnelly related some of the grim details of their ordeal. When they were finished, Coopersmith said, "So it was just the lunatic at first."

Markham nodded. "I don't think the other two knew

anything about it. He didn't bring them around until he had us all tied up in Martin's living room, and they were shook when they saw us—plenty angry."

"Why did they join in with him, then?"

"They didn't have much choice. For one thing, the crazy had his gun out and they didn't seem to be armed, and he looked like he'd use it on them if they gave him any trouble. For another, he'd told us everything about the three of them except their names—and I guess told them that he had. He sat there grinning after he had us tied and said how he planned to take over the valley and that they're professional thieves and that they tried to rob some place called Greenfront in Sacramento last Monday and killed a security guard and didn't get any money. He said that lake cabin where they've been staying is what he called a safe house." Markham's foxlike face remained desolate, but his words took on a sardonic edge. "We've had criminals hiding out in Hidden Valley off and on for years, seems like. Right under our noses the whole time."

Coopersmith was not surprised that the three men were professionals; despite the madman's actions, they had taken over the church in a phlegmatic, businesslike manner with which he was all too familiar after forty years of law enforcement. But the fact that the Mule Deer Lake cabin had been an established hideout for the criminal element was an unexpected and galling revelation. Right under our noses, he thought. Right under the nose of a retired old fool of a county sheriff named Lew Coopersmith, who kept bemoaning a severed involvement in his profession while God knew how many wanted felons camped with impunity in his backyard and maybe drank Saturday afternoon beer with him in the Valley Inn bar. The knot in his chest tightened again, and he felt now every one of his sixty-six years; he felt incredibly tired and used-up and incompetent.

Tribucci asked, "Do you know about Matt Hughes?"

"He's . . . dead," Donnelly answered, purse-lipped.

"We were hit with that much, but not where or how or why."

Markham and Donnelly exchanged silent glances.

"Have you got any idea how it happened?"

"I guess we do," Donnelly said.

"How, then?"

"Better if we don't talk about it," Markham said.

"We've got to know, Sid."

"There's enough on everybody's mind as it is."

Doris Markham—a thin, shrewish woman whose hands jumped and fluttered as if wired to invisible electrodes—swung around to look at her husband. She said stridulously, "Oh for Lord's *sake*, Sid, what's the use of trying to hide the truth? They'll find it out anyway, sooner or later. Tell them and have done with it."

"Doris—"

"All right then, I will. Matt was killed at the Taggart cabin. He was with Peggy and the crazy found them together and shot Matt and then brought her to Martin's and tied her up with the rest of us. She saw Matt killed; that's why she's the way she is now. There—it's all out in the open."

Audible intakes of breath, murmurs. A gaseous sourness bubbled in Coopersmith's stomach.

Maude Fredericks said, "You can't mean they were—I don't believe it! Matt . . . Matt wouldn't have. . . ."

"Well I couldn't believe it either at first, but it's true. The crazy told us how he found them"—her mouth twisted—"and told us exactly what they'd been doing. He laughed about it. He stood there and laughed—"

"He was lying!" Agnes Tyler, on her feet now, stared at the other woman saucer-eyed. "Not Peggy . . . Peggy's a good girl, Matt was a good man . . . no!"

Doris looked away. Markham started to say something to her, changed his mind, and spread his hands toward Agnes in a gesture of mute deprecation.

"No, no, no, no," she said and began to sob, one hand

fisted against her mouth. The sound of her weeping and the susurration of voices grated corrosively at Coopersmith's nerves; he turned on legs that, always strong, now felt enervated and frail-boned, and returned to the forward pew and sank onto it and stared at his liver-spotted hands.

Matt Hughes: paragon of virtue, energetic and benevolent community leader, the man everyone looked up to and wanted their sons to emulate. Matt Hughes: unfaithful husband, hypocrite—and dead because of it. The Reverend Mr. Keyes was still unconscious, but he would learn the harsh truth about the murdered head of his flock eventually. And so would poor Rebecca. Everything seemed to be crumbling around them on this cataclysmic day—secrets revealed, illusions shattered, beliefs shaken, and no one spared in the least. All for the Greater Good? Could they still believe in that now and in their collective salvation?

Coopersmith looked up again at the crucifix above the altar. And a passage from Proverbs in the Old Testament flickered into his mind: *Be not afraid of sudden fear, neither of the desolation of the wicked, when it cometh. For the LORD shall by thy confidence, and shall keep thy foot from being taken.*

"All right," he murmured aloud. "All right. '

Peggy Tyler lay quiescent on the hard wooden pew bench, tangled blond hair swept away from her face. A small part of her was aware that she was inside the church, that her mother and Dr. Edwards were beside her, but a much larger part was still in the Taggart cabin at Mule Deer Lake. It was as if she were coexisting in two separate realities, two separate time streams. Jumbled voices from both seemed to whisper distantly, hollowly in her ears, images from both were strangely superimposed on one another.

Shivering, she said, "I'm cold, I'm cold."

Mrs. Tyler tucked the heavy fur coat tighter beneath Peggy's chin; then, tears still trickling along her cheeks, she leaned down and said imploringly, "It's not true, is it, baby? You weren't sinning with Matt Hughes, tell me you weren't. . . .'

"Stop it, Agnes," Edwards said. "I told you, she doesn't seem to be able to comprehend anything we say to her. You're not doing either of you any good."

Matt? Peggy thought. Matt—Matt? You killed him! You shot him in the face, his face is gone, oh the blood the blood . . . no, don't touch me! Don't touch me, don't you touch me!

"Mother?" she said.

"I'm here, baby, I'm here." Mrs. Tyler lifted her entreating gaze to Edwards. "Can't you do something for her?"

"If they bring me my bag, I'll give her a sedative. There's nothing else I can do, Agnes, I'm only a village doctor. She needs hospitalization. And, the way it looks, psychiatric care."

"Psychiatric care?"

Edwards said gently, "What she saw last night seems to have had an unbalancing effect on her mind. It may only be temporary, but—"

"I won't listen to that kind of talk. There's nothing wrong with her mind, she didn't see Matt Hughes killed, she wasn't with him at the Taggart cabin or anywhere else."

"Agnes. . . ."

"No. She was captured by those murderers and had a terrible experience and she's in shock, that's all, just simple shock. She'll be fine in a little while—won't you, baby? Won't you?"

He took my money, Peggy thought, he took my thousand dollars. Give it back, it's mine. I earned it, I need it, I almost have enough to leave now. Leave these mountains forever, go to Europe, lie under a hot sun by a bright blue ocean. Warm places, snowless places. Soon. Matt? Soon.

"I'm so cold," she said.

The next two and a half hours passed in grim cycle.

"Stand back in there!" the voice outside would shout, and talk would instantly fade, and eyes would fasten on the entrance; the lock would click, the door would open—

Frank McNeil, sweating, shaking, face and eyes like those of a woman on the brink of hysteria; in sharp contrast, Sandy and Larry McNeil following as if narcotized.

—and the door would close, the lock would click; vocalization and constrained activity would commence again, questions would be asked, questions would be answered; the waiting tension would mount; and then it would all begin anew:

"Stand back in there!"

Walt Halliday, rubber-legged, sniffling and coughing into a mucus-spotted handkerchief; Lil Halliday, lower jaw paroxysmic, hands clasped in front of her as if in prayer.

"Stand back!"

Joe Garvey, face bloody, clothing bloody, staggering slightly but waving away the proffered assistance and attention of Webb Edwards; Pat Garvey, lachrymose and looking as if she were near collapse.

"All right, stand back in there!"

The Stallings family.

"Stand back! '

Bert Younger, Enid Styles, Jerry Cornelius.

"You people stand back in there!"

Greg Novak, more dazed than frightened, immediately enfolded in the tearful embrace of his father and mother. . . .

Through it all John Tribucci was in constant prowling motion, like a panther in a zoo cage. He paced from back to front, from side to side, pausing only to make sure Ann was still all right or to exchange brief dialogue with his brother or Lew Coopersmith or one of the new arrivals. Veins pulsed along his forehead, on one temple; impotent frustration was toxic within him. Trapped, trapped, no way out, nothing any of them could do, no way out—

Abruptly, near the lectern on the left side of the pulpit, he came to a standstill. His head snapped up, and he stared at and mentally beyond the high, wood-raftered ceiling.

The belfry, he thought; the belfry.

And the voice outside shouted, "Stand back in there!"

Six

Waiting beside the Ford half-ton, Brodie watched Kubion lock the last two valley residents—Hughes' wife and the big bearded man—inside the church. His mind was still sharply alert, but physically he had begun to feel the effects of the long sleepless night, the constant tension; his eyes were sandy and his neck ached and fatigue leadened his arms and legs. The chill mountain weather made it worse. The wind was up now, and it kept getting colder, and snow fell in turbulent swirls of fat, dry flakes. Night shadows, thickened by the density of the bloated gray clouds overhead, crept rapidly through the village and across the valley.

Brodie turned his head to look toward the car parked sixty yards distant, and through the snow and the rimed windows Loxner was a blackish outline behind the wheel. He'd been visible there each of the times they'd brought prisoners back here to the church, probably hadn't even got out of the car in all that time; no guts and no brains, Brodie couldn't have asked for any worse an ally. Well, he hadn't expected Loxner to try to take Kubion, had thought that if Duff did anything at all, it would be to run his ass into the woods somewhere and hide. The only way Brodie was going to get out of Hidden Valley alive was to handle Kubion himself.

He'd been in tight situations before, been under the gun before, but making a move against an armed man and making a move against an armed supercrazy and superdeadly psycho were two different things entirely. You just didn't want to gamble, because when you got desperate around a maniac, you got dead—period. So you hung on grimly to your cool, and you waited for a mistake or some other clear-cut opportunity. Only Kubion hadn't made any mistakes—his whip hand had been unbreakable so far—and there just hadn't been any openings. What had seemed like one when Kubion pistol-whipped the pockmarked guy had turned out to be a blind corner instead, and he'd been within a half step, a half second of taking a bullet for his effort. Since then he'd been able to do nothing except to wait and keep on waiting.

And now maybe he had waited too long.

They'd rounded up all the valley people, and Kubion didn't need him or Loxner to loot the village. It could be he intended to let them both keep on living a while longer; but he was totally unpredictable, and there was no way you could second-guess him. If this *was* it, Brodie's only option was that desperate gamble; he wasn't going to die a frozen target, any way but a frozen target. The only other thing he could do was to try to buy himself time, and the way to do that was to remind Kubion of the Mercantile's safe.

When they'd first taken Hughes' wife, Kubion had asked her for the combination; she'd said she didn't have any idea what it was, no one knew it except her husband and he had committed it to memory. Too scared to be lying, even Kubion had seen that. So the safe had to be cracked—and Kubion was no jugger, he didn't know the first thing about busting a box. Brodie did, though. Jugging was a nowhere business these days, owing to modern improvements in safe-and-vault manufacturing: drill- and acetylene-resistant steel alloys and self-contained alarm systems and automatic relocking devices to help guard against lock blowing with nitro or plastic gelatine; but there were still a few old hands around, and Brodie had worked a couple of scores with one of them, Woody Huggins. Kubion was aware of that and had to be aware, too—made aware, convinced—that Brodie could open that box a hell of a lot quicker and surer than he could do it himself. . . .

Kubion returned to the pickup, which straddled the front walk thirty feet from the church entrance, and stopped by the tailgate. He said, "All of them now, all of them, didn't I tell you the way it would be? You should have listened, you and Duff should've listened from the start."

"That's right, Earl," Brodie said, "we should've listened from the start."

"Now the gravy, eh Vic? Now the gravy."

"The safe in the Mercantile first?"

Kubion gave him a sly look. "Could be.'

"I hope it's one I can jug without any sweat."

"Maybe I could jug it myself, you know?"

"Maybe you couldn't, Earl," Brodie said slowly. He watched the automatic the way you would watch a coiled rattlesnake.

"Yeah, maybe not," Kubion agreed, and laughed.

"Do we move out now?"

"How come you're so anxious, Vic, how come?"

"I just want to see how much is in that safe."

The slyness vanished. "Well so do I. Let's get to cracking." He paused, realizing what he'd said, and found it to be funny; his laughter this time was loud and shrill, echoing on the wind. "Pretty good, hey? Let's get to cracking."

Brodie relaxed a little, not much. "Pretty good, Earl," he said.

He watched Kubion go around to the passenger door, open it; they got into the cab simultaneously. So Kubion wasn't worried about Loxner any more than Brodie was counting on him; he was giving them *both* some extra time. Well, screw Loxner, Loxner just didn't figure to matter at all. What mattered was an opening, a mistake. And it would come, he had to keep telling himself that; it would come, it would come.

Brodie started the engine, drove across the front church-yard and onto Sierra Street and up to the Mercantile. They got out of the pickup, climbed over the windrows onto the icy sidewalk. The wind hurled snow in gyrating flurries, moaned in building eaves, rattled boarding and glass, singingly vibrated the string of Christmas lights spanning the street. In its emptiness the village had an almost eerily desolate feel, like an Arctic ghost town.

"Kick the doors open," Kubion said.

Brodie looked at the holly wreath and mistletoe decorating the two glass halves, over at the cardboard Santa Claus and cardboard reindeer in one of the windows. Then he tongued cold-chapped lips and stepped up to the entrance. Raising one foot, he drove it against the lock in the wooden frames where the two leaves joined; the doors held. He kicked again, and a third time, without being able to snap the lock.

Impatiently, Kubion told him to break the pane out of one of the halves.

He did that, and the holly wreath flew inside with splinters of glass and scattered berries and leaves across the floor. He used his foot to punch away the remaining shards, ducked through the open frame and into the semidarkened interior. When he was eight steps across the wooden floor, Kubion came in and said, "Light switches are on the wall over there, behind the counter."

Moving slowly, Brodie passed the potbellied stove and went around and found the metal control case and flipped the row of switches within. Warm yellow illumination flooded the store. Kubion waved him a short way along the aisle between the counter and wall shelves of liquor and other bottled goods; then, without taking eyes off him, he rang up No Sale on the cash register and rifled the drawer. Seventy or eighty dollars, if that much. He wadded the bills into his trouser pocket, made another waving motion, and they went down to where the office was located.

The door was locked, but this one gave and bounced inward the first time Brodie slammed the bottom of his shoe against the wood above the latch. While Kubion stood watching from just outside the doorway, Brodie crossed to the heavy oak desk and put on the lamp there. The glass top held no potential weapon, not even a letter opener, but would Hughes have kept a gun in one of the drawers? Not likely—and Kubion wouldn't let him into the desk anyway. He gave his attention to the safe. A cheesebox, it could be opened in a maximum of thirty minutes; all you had to do with one of these old one-pieces was to knock off the combination dial.

Kubion said, "How long?"

"I'm not sure. I might have to peel it."

"A crate like this?"

"It's more solid than it might look.'

"I don't want any bullshit, Vic."

"No bullshit."

"All right, what you need?"

"Hammer, chisels, pry bar, maybe a high-speed drill."

"Nice and convenient hardware section out front, right?"

Out of the office, around the counter, through the grocery section. "Hold it," Kubion said.

Brodie stopped immediately. "What?"

On top of one of the shelves was a cardboard carton of paper towel rolls; Kubion motioned to it. "Dump out that carton and bring it along."

"What for?'

"So you don't get any ideas, baby."

"I don't know what you mean."

"No? I'll lay it out for you then: I don't want you carrying hammers and chisels and pry bars loose in your hands, I don't want you even touching any of that stuff until we get back into the office, now do what I told you."

A tic fluttered one corner of Brodie's mouth. He turned and took the carton down and emptied the paper towel rolls onto the floor. In the hardware department, Kubion instructed him to put the box down and then turn around and lace his hands behind him. After Brodie complied, he heard tools begin to clatter into the carton, Kubion's voice calling off the name of each. Then: "Okay, that everything you need?"

Brodie considered asking for an awl, because of the tool's thin sharp-pointed blade; telling Kubion he might need it for work on the lock mechanism. But if Kubion saw through the lie, there was just no telling what he'd do; the last thing Brodie could afford now was to antagonize him. And Christ, even if Kubion let him have one, he'd never get close enough to stab him with it; and the round, beveled handles on the things made them too awkward for throwing, overbalanced them.

He said, "That's everything, Earl."

"Turn around and pick up the carton."

Wordlessly, Brodie carried the heavy container back into the office. He set it down in front of the safe, took off his coat and gloves, and knelt beside it. He could feel Kubion's eyes on his back as he began to sort through the jumble of tools, lifting them out of the carton one by one, trying to stall without seeming to do so.

"Vic," Kubion said finally, "Vic baby."

Brodie stopped stalling then and went to work on the safe.

Seven

The moment Rebecca stepped inside the church she knew that Matt was dead.

She felt it like a chill in the strained, hushed atmosphere, and saw it reflected in the staring faces of the people huddled throughout. Everyone who lived in the valley seemed to be there, everyone except Matt, and he was not there because he was dead; he had been killed somehow by the men who had kidnapped her and Zachary Cain and all these others, too. The presentiment of things being wrong, Matt's unsatisfactorily explained absence, had planted the seed in her mind, and it had germinated swiftly with the appearance and actions of the wild-eyed gunman and his demands for information about the Mercantile's safe. A kind of creeping mental numbness—a defensive barrier erected against the sharp stabbing edges of fear—had kept her from dwelling continually on the possibility, but now there could no longer be any resistance because there was no longer any doubt.

Matt was dead.

She stood very still and tried to feel grief, some sense

of personal loss. There was only the terror and a hollow despair. Dreamlike, she watched people converging on her and felt Webb Edwards' hand on her arm and heard him asking if she were all right, if she wanted to sit down; heard other voices murmuring but none of them saying anything about Matt, uneasily avoiding the inevitable, and so she said it for them, she said, "Matt's dead, isn't he?"

Ann Tribucci was at her side now. "Becky, you'd better come and sit down. . . ."

"He's *dead*, isn't he?"

"He . . . yes. Oh Becky—"

Woodenly, "How did it happen?"

"You don't want to know, not now."

"I have to know. I don't know anything about what's going on. Why are we here? Who are those men? How did Matt die?"

In hesitant, succinct words they told her who the men were and what had occurred last night and today. Rebecca was beyond the point of shock; she comprehended the facts, accepted them, abhorred them automatically with a small part of her mind, but they had no immediate or cohesive impact on her and she registered no external reaction. She waited for someone to tell her about Matt, and when no one did she repeated her question:

"How did Matt die?"

"Come and sit down," Ann said again.

"I don't want to sit down, will you stop asking me to sit down and please please tell me what happened to my husband?"

Awkward silence. Rebecca sensed dimly that their hesitancy was not solely the result of a desire to spare her the specifics of Matt's death, that there was something else they were reluctant to reveal and which they wanted to spare her. What? she thought—and then she guessed what it must be, but this also had little distinct impact on her. Like an anesthetic, the numbness had begun spreading through her mind again.

She said in a barren tone, "Where was he killed?"

Lew Coopersmith, slowly and resignedly: "At the lake."

"Last night?"

"Yes."

"They shot him, is that it? Was he shot?"

"Yes."

"Was he alone?"

The awkward silence.

"Was he alone?" Rebecca repeated.

"No one else was shot last night."

"That isn't what I asked. Was Matt alone?"

Pleadingly Ann said, "Becky, Becky. . . ."

"He wasn't alone, was he? He was with another woman, together with another woman. Isn't that right?"

Silence.

"Yes of course," she said, "of course he was. Who was it? No, it doesn't matter, I don't want to know, it doesn't matter."

Shuffling movement around her, toward her, away from her. Faces averted, faces staring. Pity touching her like fat, soft, unwelcome hands. She did want to sit down then and found a place without assistance. Head bowed, she thought dully: Well, that makes it all very simple, doesn't it? No need for a decision now, no need for anything now. Matt was dead, and the truth was out; they all knew the truth at last: Matt Hughes a philanderer, Matt Hughes consorting with a local woman and doing it right here in Hidden Valley (even she would never quite have expected him to be that brash, that foolhardy; even she did not really know all of what had been concealed beneath his generous, boyish, pious exterior). How surprised they must have been—and how fitting that they should have learned it in this of all places. And what would they say if she were to tell them of the long, long line of other women, all the past deceits?

Oh yes, there had been quite a bit of goodness in him,

and his death was violent and premature, and she had lived with him and slept with him for seven years; but she could not now or ever grieve for him. The well of Matt-directed emotions had run dry. She had given him everything she knew how to give, and he had left her with nothing whatsoever of value. How could she possibly mourn an unfaithful husband who had even *died* in the company of another woman?

Ann sat down beside her and covered one of her mittened hands, not speaking. Rebecca was grateful for that; she did not want dialogue of any kind. She sat without moving or thinking for several moments. Then, gradually, some of the numbness began to recede, and she became aware of the heavy tumescence that was Ann's unborn child, of her surroundings, of why she and all the others were here in the church, of the things the three men outside had already done: the full horror of the situation penetrating for the first time. Fear surged consumingly in her stomach again: her fingers closed tightly around Ann's and clung to them. Matt was dead, murdered—and what of Ann and her baby and everyone else in the valley? What of Rebecca Hughes?

What was to become of *them?*

Eight

Cain sat on the far edge of the pulpit, spine curved to the outer organ casing, forearms resting on his pulled-up knees. It was warm enough inside the church, but his skin crawled with cold—the kind of cold that has nothing to do with temperature.

The dark gunman's clearly homicidal dementia had prepared him for most any contingency on the ride down from the cabin, yet the magnitude of what was actually taking place in Hidden Valley—recounted to Rebecca Hughes while he had stood listening and ignored on the periphery—had stunned and repulsed him. The concept was monstrous; you could not immediately reconcile your mind to it. Things like this can't happen, you thought; they can't happen to *you.* And then you remembered men like Hitler and Richard Speck and Charles Manson, and that all their victims must have at first experienced the same staggering disbelief, and you understood that such things could and did happen at any time, at any place, to anyone.

Anything can happen, Cain thought now; madness doesn't have to have a thing to do with it. A man can get drunk to celebrate some great good fortune and run over a child while driving home. A man can send his wife out for a package of cigarettes, and she can be raped and murdered on the way to the corner gorcery. Yes, and a man can repair a home appliance and make an unconscious error that causes the death of his entire family. . . .

He raised his head and looked toward the rear, to where Rebecca Hughes sat. Compassion moved through him, as it had minutes earlier. It was bad enough for himself and each of the others, but she had taken a vicious triple blow: the nightmare itself, the death of her husband, the fact that he had been killed during a blatant affair with another woman. Or maybe she had already known about his infidelity, and that was the underlying source of her confessed loneliness; she had almost instantly guessed what they were holding back from her.

Cain's eyes roamed over the other women, the men, the children. They were strangers to him; none of them seemed even to be aware of his presence at this moment, except for Frank McNeil, who stood but gave the impression of crouching against the near wall, mutely hating him with eyes like water-shiny pebbles. And yet Cain's involvement with all of them—even McNeil, he could no longer seem to feel animosity toward the man—was the same as if they had been relatives or friends of long standing. He *cared* whether they lived or died, as he had realized at last that he cared intrinsically whether *he* lived or died.

At the upper edge of his vision he saw one of the stained-glass windows, and centered his gaze on it, and thought then of God. A full year since he had been inside a church, last Christmas with his family; six months since he had denied to himself the existence of a benign Deity. If there was a God, would He allow a gentle wife and mother and two small innocent children to die so cruelly and unnecessarily? Would He allow wars and poverty and racial hatred and the kind of wanton terrorism which had exploded here in Hidden Valley? Rhetorical questions. You believed or you didn't believe: simple as that. Once

Cain had believed; and now, here, he was not sure he had ever really stopped believing.

On impulse he got to his feet and crossed slowly to the altar; looked at the open Bible on the prayer cloth, at the melting votive candles in their silver holders. And standing there, he grew conscious of low but discernible voices coming from inside the vestry, the door to which stood ajar a few feet distant. He recognized them as belonging to John Tribucci and Lew Coopersmith, recalled that he had seen Tribucci say something to the old man a minute or two earlier and then both of them step up onto the pulpit.

". . . got to do something, Lew," Tribucci was saying. "We *can't* accept the word of a lunatic that nothing will happen to us; he's psycho enough to have carried out this whole fantastic scheme and committed one brutal murder already, and that makes him psycho enough to slaughter us all. He could do it in a rage when he finds out just how little of value there is in the valley or because he knows we can identify him or even because he gets some kind of warped thrill out of killing. And I can't believe those two partners of his would be able to stop him; for all we know he may be planning to kill them, too, he may have done it already." Beat. "Mass murder isn't the only threat, either; there's a good possibility he intends to take hostages anyway when he leaves, to make sure we don't sound the alarm right away. Kids, women—Ellen, or Judy, or Rebecca . . . or for God's sake, even Ann. He wouldn't hesitate to shoot them when he had no more use for them, you know he wouldn't."

Coopersmith said, "Don't you think all of that's been preying on my mind, same as yours? But what can we *do,* Johnny, trapped like we are?"

"There's one thing we can do," Tribucci said, "one thing he overlooked: a way out of here."

"What? What way?"

"Through the belfry up there. Go up the ladder and

break out one of the windows; then cut the bell rope—I managed to hold out my penknife when they were collecting our belongings—and tie the rope around a bell support and climb out and down the rear wall."

"And you're thinking of going after help, is that it? Johnny, even if you could get away from the church without being seen, how would you get out of the valley? Snowmobile, the way they're planning to? What are the odds of you reaching one undetected? Of getting it out of the village undetected? Of making it clear to Coldville in the middle of a stormy night with the temperature at zero or below? And suppose you *did* manage all that—the county couldn't get men back here before morning, except by helicopter, and if the storm holds, a chopper wouldn't be able to get off the ground at all."

"Lew, listen to me—"

"Suppose you didn't make it out of the village in the first place? Or suppose you did and the psycho discovered one of the mobiles missing? What do you think he'd do then?"

With deceptive calm Tribucci said, "I'm not talking about trying to go for help, Lew."

Nothing from Coopersmith.

"That was the first thing I thought of when I remembered the belfry," Tribucci said, "and I rejected the idea for the same reasons you just gave. The idea I didn't reject involves me and one or two others, and we don't leave the valley once we get out of here."

Cain, listening, knew all at once what Tribucci was getting at; he realized he was breathing heavily, if silently, through parted lips.

Coopersmith knew it too, now. He said, "Go after weapons and try to take them head to head."

"That's it, Lew."

"You realize what that would mean?"

"It's kill or be killed, and you can't argue with that morally or otherwise—not with all the lives at stake. I'm not a killer, any more than an eighteen-year-old soldier forced to fight in an alien jungle is a killer, but I can do what that kid has to do for some of the same reasons and for some that are a lot better."

"Maybe you can," Coopersmith said. "And I can too, because I've spent my life in the kind of job that requires a man to be ready to kill other men if he has to; but I'm sixty-six years old, I'm an old man—it's taken me a long time to admit that to myself but I'm admitting it now; I'm an old man with slow reflexes and brittle bones and if I tried climbing out of the belfry I'd probably break a leg, if not my neck. Who else is there, Johnny? Vince, maybe, only I don't have to tell you how poor his eyesight is. Joe Garvey? He's been hurt already, and while he's got the courage, he hasn't got the caution or the patience; he'd be a bull in a china shop. Martin Donnelly? He can't kill a fly without flinching. Dave Nedlick? Greg Novak? Walt Halliday? Doc Edwards? There's nobody but you and me, and that means there's nobody but you."

"Then I'll go alone."

"Against three professional hard cases, against a madman? What chance do you think you'd really have?"

"A better chance than we've got sitting in here waiting to be slaughtered." Thick, desperate rage surrounded Tribucci's words. "I've got to try it, Lew, don't you see that? *Somebody* has to do something, and that somebody is me."

"What about all the others? Some of them—McNeil, for instance—would vote to do nothing, wait it out, take the psycho's word. Have you got the right to make a decision for seventy-five people? Because if you do go, you're going to have to do it without telling anybody else; you're going to have to make that decision."

"You know the answer to that as well as I do, Lew: if my going can mean saving the lives of everyone in the valley—my family's lives—then yes, *yes,* I've got the right. . . ."

Cain had heard enough. He moved away from the altar and stopped by the organ. Tribucci's right, he thought, one look at that dark one's eyes is enough to tell anybody he's right; it has to be done, one way or another. Anger stirred inside him again, began to burn with increasing candescence. His eyes wandered the oppressively silent room, located Rebecca Hughes again, rested on her bloodless face—and she reminded him of Angie; she did not resemble Angie in any way, but she might have been Angie. The children, too, the huddling children were little boys who might have been Steve and little girls who might have been Lindy. And what if it *was* them sitting out there? What if they were alive and they were here now, the way Tribucci's family was here now?

Sweat formed a thin beaded mosaic on Cain's forehead, trickled down along his cheeks. No, he thought then. No, no.

Yes, the other half of him said.

No I'd freeze up, I'd panic, I'd—

We'd do what has to be done.

Before he quite realized what he was doing, he had turned and taken two steps in the direction of the vestry door. And when his foot lifted for the third step, the back of his neck prickled and a tingling sensation washed down through his groin. His mind opened, like a blossom, in epiphany.

Forward, he thought, walking forward. I've been walking backward for six months, and I've just taken my first forward steps in all that time.

Yes! the other half of him said again, and the two halves remerged spiritually at last and made a bonded whole. Without hesitation, he kept on walking forward.

Nine

Tribucci and Coopersmith, still debating in low, taut voices, lapsed into immediate silence when Zachary Cain came into the vestry. He stood in front of them, arms slack at his sides, bearded face and gray eyes animate with not quite definable emotions.

He said, "Can I talk to both of you for a minute?"

Tribucci frowned, the cords in his neck bulging like elongated ribs. Coopersmith had to be on his side, to handle things here in the church once he set out on the recon, to help him plan out a course of action, and he was close to convincing the old man now; Cain's surprising instrusion—the man had never spoken directly to anyone, except to make a purchase, in all the time he'd been in the valley—could not have been more ill-timed.

And Cain said to him, "I overheard you talking a couple of minutes ago—about the belfry, about what you want to try to do. No one else heard it; I was alone by the altar."

Tribucci exchanged a quick look with Coopersmith. He said then, "Well?"

Cain held a breath, released it slowly. "I want to go with you."

They stared at him—and a kind of low-key electrical tension developed among the three men. None of them moved for a long moment.

"I mean it," Cain said finally. "I want to go with you."

Unlike some of his neighbors, Tribucci had never resented or disliked or mistrusted Cain; although he was an odd sort in a lot of ways, there had always seemed to be a gentleness and a basic decency beneath his eccentric taciturnity. But now he was immediately suspicious. How could Cain possibly care enough about the people of Hidden Valley to want to risk his life for them? Did he have some idea of pretending to join forces just so he could get out of the church and save himself? And yet—that didn't make sense either. If he wanted to escape in order to run away, coming to them as he had just done was pointless; all he would have had to do, now that he knew about the belfry, was to wait until he, Tribucci, was gone and then sneak in here and leave in the same fashion. . . .

Coopersmith, studying Cain probingly, said, "Why? Why do you want to go?"

"Because I think Tribucci's right, I think that madman wouldn't hesitate to commit mass butchery, I think the only alternative is to go after him and the other two. Tribucci might be able to pull it off alone, but his chances are twice as good if there are two of us."

"That doesn't exactly explain why you're volunteering."

"You said it yourself: there isn't anybody else."

"Not what I meant. Look Cain, we don't know a thing about you. Since you came to the valley, you've taken pains to keep to yourself. I respect a man's right to live his life the way he sees fit, as long as he doesn't hurt anybody else, but in a crisis like this, where the lives of so many people are in jeopardy, we've got to *know* you before we can put any trust in you."

"That's right," Tribucci agreed grimly. "Who are you, Cain? Why do you want to put your life on the line for people you hardly know, people you've shunned?"

A long, still hesitation. Then, staring at the wall to one side of them, Cain said very softly, "The reason I came to Hidden Valley, the reason I've lived here as I have, is that I was responsible for the deaths of my wife and two children this past June."

Tribucci winced faintly; Coopersmith's hand lifted, as if to rumple his dusty hair, and then fell across and down his shirt front. But there was nothing for either of them to say just yet.

Still talking to the wall, Cain went on, "I was one of these do-it-yourself people, don't waste money on plumbers and electricians and repairmen when I could take care of what needed to be done with my own hands and enjoyed the work besides. We had a fairly old house with a fairly new gas stove in the kitchen, and it developed a minor gas leak and I fixed it one night—thought I'd fixed it okay, there didn't seem to be any more problems. The following Saturday I went bowling in a tournament, and when I got home there were . . . there . . . ."

His voice had grown heavy and liquid, and he broke off and swallowed audibly. When he was able to go on with it: "I came back and there were fire trucks and police cars and an ambulance and a hundred or more people on the street, and the house . . . it was burning, there had been an explosion, one wall was blown out. My wife and son and daughter were . . . they were inside when it happened and there was nothing anyone could do, they never even knew what hit them, and their bodies . . . I saw their bodies. . . ."

A shudder went through him; he shook his head a single time as though to erase the mental picture of that scene. "When I'd fixed the stove leak," he said, "I unknowingly twisted or bent the gas line fitting at the baseboard somehow and caused another leak, one of those slow ones that you can't smell because it all builds in the walls; that was the official verdict, and that's the way it had to have been. It was my fault, my carelessness, that caused the deaths of the only three people in the world I loved. I didn't want to go on living either, not then. Committing suicide was . . . impossible, and yet I thought staying in San Francisco was impossible, too. So I quit my job, I'm an architect, and made arrangements with our bank to send me a small allotment every month—we'd saved more than twenty thousand dollars toward a new home—and I came here because it was a place I knew, I'd done some fishing and hunting in this area.

"For six months I've been in a kind of coma, drinking too much to numb the pain and guilt, never really numbing it at all. I didn't care about anything, I didn't want contact with you people, I thought I could exist in that coma forever because I thought it was what I wanted. But it wasn't and it isn't, I've come to realize that now; I'm lonely, I'm terribly lonely, I need to start living again. If I got out there to face those men, I might die, but if I do nothing in here I might die too; and if I'm killed out there, it will be in a cause worth dying for. I want you people to live too, caring for myself has made me start caring for others again and I don't want to see women and children die as helplessly as my family died. There was nothing I could do to save them, but maybe I *can* help to save your wives and your children. That's why I want to go, that's why I need to go. . . ."

Cain fell silent but continued to stare unseeingly at the wall. Tribucci moved his head slightly and once more looked at Coopersmith.

Do you believe him? Coopersmith's eyes asked.

I believe him, Tribucci's eyes answered, and Coopersmith dipped his head almost imperceptibly. They had just witnessed the laying bare of a man's heart and soul, and the sincerity of his confession was to both of them unquestionable.

Turning, Cain met their gazes again. "I've been in the Army," he said, "so I know the principles of seek-and-destroy and I know how to use a handgun. I'm not in the best of shape, but I think I can climb down a rope all right. I'm also afraid, I can't lie to you about that, but I'm as sure now as any man can be without having been tested that when the time comes, I'll be able to stand my ground and pull the trigger on any of those three men."

Tribucci believed him about that, too. All doubt had vanished now; his instincts told him what type of man Cain was, and he had always implicitly trusted his instincts. The two of them, he thought insightfully, were of the same basic nature: they felt things deeply, they loved and hated deeply, and when a crisis arose they could not be passive or indecisive, they were compelled to act. And these character traits, for better or worse, were of course the reason why (he understood this for the first time) he had taken on the two cyclists thirteen years ago. If Cain had been with Charlene that night on the beach, he might have done the same thing; and if Tribucci had lost his family as Cain had lost his, he might have reacted in much the same fashion as Cain—when it happened and right now.

"Do I go with you?" Cain asked him.

Tribucci had made his decision. "Yes," he said simply. And then pivoted to Coopersmith.

Eyes steady and penetrating, features set in hard, perceptive lines, the old man was not old at all; except for the flesh-and-bone shell in which the essence of him was trapped, he was young and strong and sagacious. But it was that shell which meant so much now, that shell which prevented him from leading the kind of assault he had been trained for, that shell which had forced him into an admission a few minutes ago that his pride and his spirit had never previously allowed. But he was not old; he had never been old, and he would never be old.

"All right," he said, as Tribucci had known he would, "I'm in it anyway, so I might as well be in it all the way. With both of you."

Cain said, "When do we go?"

"As soon as possible. But there's some talking out to be done first. You don't rush into a situation like this without planning strategy; too many things can go wrong as it is. First consideration is the two of you getting out of the belfry and away without being spotted."

"Well if there's still a guard," Tribucci said, "it figures he'll be in front in one of the cars. With the storm that's up and howling out there, he's not going to be walking around. And the storm itself is all in our favor; it'll cover any noise we make breaking out the belfry window, fill in our tracks before too long, keep visibility down to a minimum."

"It's not going to cover the sound of breaking glass here in the church."

"There's the organ," Cain said. "If you could get somebody to play a few hymns, the music should be loud enough to drown splintering glass."

"Okay—good. I'll talk to Maude, and if she won't do it, Ellen will. I'll try to get as many people singing as I can, too; that'll keep them all together out front, so no one wanders in here at the wrong time."

Tribucci said, "Second consideration is weapons. We can't take the chance of going to the Sport Shop, but we can circle through the trees on the west slope, to the houses along Shasta. Joe Garvey's got a Walther automatic that he brought back from Europe a few years ago and uses for hunting small game. And Vince keeps a pair of target revolvers."

"That leaves the big question," Cain said. "How do we deploy once we're armed?"

"Only one way to handle it," Coopersmith told them. "Come back here, so you're in a position to protect the church; don't try to do any stalking, that'd be like playing Russian roulette. If there's a guard, take him first—as quietly as possible, maybe with a knife if you can get close enough to do it that way." He studied the impassive faces of the two younger men. "Shooting a man is one thing, stabbing him with a knife is another—you know that, don't you?"

"We know it," Tribucci said thinly.

"All right. Next thing you do is set up in ambush and wait, and keep on waiting no matter how long it takes. But not both of you in the same place, and I don't have to tell you the reason for that. You'll have to figure your exact positions once you get to that point."

Cain nodded, and Tribucci said, "Agreed on all of it. Anything else?"

"One thought," Cain said. "If we're going to be waiting in that snowstorm, we'd better put on hats and mufflers and as much extra clothing as we can handle while we're at Garvey's place."

"Right." Tribucci's mouth quirked. "Lew—Ann and Vince are going to miss me pretty fast, even if nobody else does. I'd tell them beforehand, but I'm afraid there'd be a scene. . . ."

"There's liable to be a scene anyway, sooner or later, but that's my problem; I'll tell them once you're gone. You just leave this end of things to me; you're going to have enough to worry about outside."

Tribucci exhaled heavily through his nostrils, looked down at his watch. "Five oh five. It's dark now, but it'll be darker still in another half hour. Go at five thirty-five?"

"Five thirty-five," Cain said.

Coopersmith said, "That covers just about everything, then. We'd all better wait out front until it's time; leave now one by one. The two of you come back in here, separately, between half past and twenty-five to. I'll have Maude or Ellen playing the organ as soon afterward as I can manage it."

The three men stood for several silent pulsebeats. Tribucci wanted to say something to Cain, to tell him he was sorry about the tragic loss of his family, to thank him for the choice he had made; but he had no words, it was not the time for words like that. Later, he thought, when it's over. Later. . . .

He moved first to the closed vestry door.

Ten

There was $3,247 in the Mercantile's safe.

Brodie had taken too much time getting the box open, and Kubion's patience had ebbed away finally and he'd told him to quit diddling around, quit diddling *around* you queer bastard, and Brodie said he was doing it as fast as he could, and Kubion just looked at him over the raised muzzle of the automatic. Six minutes later Brodie had the combination dial punched out with hammer and chisel and the safe door open wide. Inside were sheafs of papers and some ledger books and a key-type strongbox. With Kubion watching him closely, Brodie snapped the lock on the strongbox and counted out the money it contained onto the desk's glass top.

$3,247.

Kubion stared at the thin piles of currency. Three thousand lousy goddamn lousy dollars! He had figured ten grand at least, maybe fifteen or twenty, some banker Hughes had been some hick banker son of a bitch. If he wasn't dead already he'd be dead right now, just like all the hicks were going to be dead pretty soon, pretty soon.

He centered his gaze on Brodie standing by the desk in

a litter of tools and bits and pieces of safe metal. Brodie's face was stoic, but those purple eyes of his were like windows and you could see what he was thinking, you could hear we-told-you-so-didn't-we running around inside his head as plainly as if he were saying it aloud. Kubion shouted, "Shut up, shut the fucking hell up!"

"I didn't say anything, Earl."

"This is only the beginning, you hear, there'll be more in the other stores and in the houses, plenty more."

"Sure there will."

"Plenty more," Kubion said again. The impulse, the need, had begun whispering to him; the ball of his index finger moved tightly back and forth across the automatic's curved trigger.

Brodie said quickly, "I'd better gather up the tools before we leave here. We might need them again."

Kubion's temples throbbed. His finger continued to slide across the trigger, increasing pressure.

"Did you hear what I said, Earl?"

"I heard you."

"There's probably other safes in the valley: the inn, the Sport Shop, the café, the Hughes' house or one of the other houses. I can't open them without tools."

"There won't be any other safes."

"We can't know that for sure, not yet."

"If there are I'll get combinations or keys from whoever they belong to, I don't need you for that."

"Suppose whoever it is gives you trouble and you have to kill him before you find out a combination? Suppose there's a safe at the Hughes' house and the wife doesn't know that combination either? Could be Hughes kept a spare bundle at home, some of these guys don't like to keep it all in one place, right?"

Kubion's finger became still. The impulse was still whispering to him, but it was saying now: Don't kill him yet . . . he's right, you might need him . . . don't kill him yet, soon but not yet. . . .

He said, "Put the tools back in the box, hurry it up, shag your ass."

Brodie let breath spray inaudibly between his teeth. Immediately, carefully, he knelt and put on his coat and gloves and then began feeding the scattered tools back into the cardboard carton. When he was finished, Kubion ordered him to lace his hands behind him again; stepped forward and scooped the bills off the desk top left-handed and wadded them into his trousers. He went back to the doorway, told Brodie to pick up the carton and come out. A moment later, following him down the aisle between the counter and the wall shelves of liquor and bottled goods, Kubion felt the chill breath of the wind that came stabbing through the glassless door half. Snow whipped in the darkness outside, eddied into the store; the cry of the storm was like that of something alive and in pain.

Kubion's mouth twisted into a vicious grimace. Snow, wind, cold, goddamn Eskimo village with wooden igloos, and three thousand in the safe and have to keep Brodie alive and Brodie's back like a target in front of him, urge saying don't kill him but then saying smash something else, smash something! He stopped moving, smash something do it *now*, and transferred the automatic to his left hand and swept his right through the bottles of liquor on the nearest of the shelves, driving a dozen or more to the floor. Glass shattered, dark liquid splashed and flowed. Brodie whirled and stared at him, carton held up at chest level, and Kubion yelled, "Don't say a word, don't move I'll kill you if you move," and picked a bottle off the shelf and threw it into the grocery section, toppling a pyramid of canned goods in another banging, clattering counterpoint to the shriek of the wind. He caught up a second bottle and pitched it at the gated Post Office window, missing low, this one not breaking, and a third bottle was in his hand and he flung that across the store at the left front window. The heavy bottom struck the cardboard replica of Santa Claus at the base of the spine and drove it and exploding fragments of glass outward to the sidewalk. One of the torn reindeer clung to a jagged piece of window, flapping in a sudden gust that hurled more flurries of snow through the opening.

The impulse grew silent then, momentarily satisfied, and he leaned panting against the counter. After several moments the smile reappeared on his mouth, and he straightened up again and returned the automatic to his right hand.

"We'll hit the Sport Shop now," he said. "Then the inn and the café and the rest of the buildings along here. Then the Hughes' house."

"However you want to do it," Brodie said carefully.

"That's right, Vic, however I want to do it."

They went out into the sharp white wind.

Eleven

The interior of the church had grown progressively duskier with the coming of night. The votive candles on the altar had melted down, and the filtered daylight shining through the stained-glass windows had faded and then disappeared altogether. Spaced at intervals along the side walls, brass-armed electric candles burned palely, cheerlessly, and did little to dispel the pockets of grayish shadow forming on the pulpit and along the front wall.

In one of those pockets, by the peg-hung garments at the south front corner, Rebecca stood alone and wished that she could cry. Crying was a purge, in the same way vomiting was a purge, and it would get rid of some of the nauseating dread that persisted malignantly inside her. But there was no emetic for tears. You could cry or you couldn't, and even as a child she had rarely wept. Once she had considered this a sign of inner efficacy; in truth, however, it was nothing more than a simple incapacity, like not being able to sing on key or stand on your head or perform backflips.

A voice beside her said softly, "Mrs. Hughes?"

She had not heard anyone approach, and she blinked and half turned. Zachary Cain was standing there. She searched his bearded face briefly and found no pity; empathy, yes, but mercifully, no pity. She thought then that he seemed *different* somehow. She hadn't noticed it at the cabin earlier or on the ride down, she had been too frightened to notice anything; but there was a definite strength in him only hinted at previously, and the haunted irresolution which had ravaged his features last night had been effaced. It was as if he had undergone some sort of tangible metamorphosis; and today's ordeal had had no apparent effect, or possibly some esoteric fortifying rather than weakening effect, on that change.

She said, "Don't say you're sorry. Please don't."

"All right. I . . . know how you must feel."

"Do you?"

"I think I do."

"Nobody can know how I feel right now, Mr. Cain."

"I can, because I've been through it—some of it."

"What do you mean?"

He said slowly, "I lost my wife and two children six months ago, in San Francisco. My carelessness caused the deaths of all three of them."

Rebecca stared at him.

"That's why I came to Hidden Valley," Cain said, and told her briefly what had occurred and the way it had been for him since.

The only words which came to her when he stopped talking were the same emptily condolent ones she had just asked him not to say to her. She moved her head slightly from side to side, right thumb and index finger worrying one of the buttons on her open parka.

At length she found other words and her voice. "Why did you tell me all that? Why now?"

"I'm not sure. Maybe . . . well maybe because of what you're going through and will keep on going through for a while, the similarities of the things that have hurt both of us."

"Keep my chin up, roll with the punches, don't let happen to me what happened to you—is that it?"

"I didn't mean it exactly that way."

Rebecca looked away from him. "No, of course you didn't," she said, and then, in an undertone: "It's just that everything seems so hopeless now. What's the use of thinking about the future when there might not *be* any tomorrow for any of us? We might all be killed today, just as my husband was killed."

"We're not going to die," Cain said.

"I wish I could really believe that."

"You can. You have to."

He extended a hand, as if to touch her and transmit by osmosis some of his own conviction; but he did not make contact, and his arm lowered and dropped again to his side. He held her eyes for a long moment, and Rebecca once more felt the new strength in him, felt some of the same intimacy they had shared the night before.

He said finally, "You're going to be okay, all of us are going to be okay," and one corner of his mouth spasmed upward in what might have been half of an ethereal smile. He moved past her and away along the front wall.

Rebecca watched him stop in front of the entrance doors and stand there staring straight ahead; watched him for a full thirty seconds. Then she thought that she wanted to sit down again and took a place in the nearest pew. She looked at the round whiteness of her joined knees, saw them mistily—and realized that the eyes which never cried were suddenly brimming with tears.

Cain waited gravely, leaning against the locked doors, for it to be time to go into the vestry.

His nerves jangled now and then, as if in reaction to a silent alarm bell, and a clot of fear existed parasitically just under his breastbone. But his earlier self-composure and the sharp anger remained forcefully dominant. He had only to look deep within himself again to know that he would be able to do whatever had to be done.

He thought of the unburdening of himself to Tribucci and Coopersmith. He had known, of course, that he would have to tell them, and he'd been both reluctant and willing. Like the words which had piled up inside him and finally spilled over to Rebecca last night, the entire tragedy had reached the limit of containment—she had been perfectly right in her comments about bottled-up emotions needing an outlet, too, sooner or later—and with self-perception there had come the need to relieve some of that pent-up pressure. The telling had been much easier than he might have thought, and even easier still when he'd related some of the facts to Rebecca minutes ago, and would be progressively easier each subsequent time he did it—if there were to be any subsequent times. The onus became so much more bearable when you confided to somebody, he knew that now: not because you wanted their pity or reassurances, but because it was like lancing a festering boil and letting some of the hurt drain away with the pus.

He had come to Rebecca with at least a half-formed intention of doing exactly as he had done—and he was not quite sure why. There were surface reasons, but there was also an underlying motivation that was elusive and amorphous. Perhaps it had something to do with Rebecca herself rather than Rebecca as just another person, something to do with empathy and mental concord and the way she had huddled against him in the pickup. . . .

Abruptly he told himself: You're doing too much thinking, there's just no point in it now. Remember what the military taught you about survival in combat: concentration on fundamentals, on the external and not the internal; instinct, training, death as an abstract, doing the job at hand. The military was wrong about a great many things, but not about that.

Cain glanced down at his watch, and it was five thirty-two. He located Tribucci with his eyes. alternately pacing and standing along the northern wall. Coopersmith had been sitting by his wife, but now Cain saw him stand up and come toward the front, stop by the woman who worked in the Mercantile—the church organist.

Time, he thought. And walked with careful, though apparently aimless, strides to the opposite aisle and past Tribucci and up onto the pulpit.

Coopersmith bent at the waist, resting his left hand on the pew back, and said *sotto voce* to Maude Fredericks, "Maude, I think it would be a good idea if you played some hymns for us."

Pouched in red, tear-puffed hollows, her eyes moved dully over his face. Ordinarily she was a strong-willed woman, but the day's life-and-death crisis, coupled with the twin shocks of Matt Hughes' death and unfaithfulness —Coopersmith knew she'd maternally worshiped her employer—had clearly corroded that inherent strength.

"You mean now?" she said.

"Yes."

"Why?"

"It would give us all a little comfort," he told her, and it was at least part of the truth. "A hymn is a prayer, you know that, Maude."

"Is He listening? If our prayers reach Him, why has He allowed us to suffer like this?"

"I don't know, Maude. But I haven't lost hope or faith, and I don't believe you have either."

Faint color came into the crêpy whiteness of her cheeks. "No," she said, "no, I suppose I haven't."

"Will you play some hymns then?"

She nodded and rose, and they went together to the pulpit. Sitting at the organ, Maude reached out to touch the open hymnal with the tips of her fingers, then she began to flip the pages slowly toward the rear of the book. Coopersmith did not see Cain, and Tribucci had just entered the vestry. He turned and announced quietly what he had requested of Maude. A few nods or murmurs of acceptance followed his words, though most of the drawn faces registered a kind of benumbed apathy. There was a single vocal objection.

"What for?" Frank McNeil demanded in shrill tones. "What's the sense of it? We don't need any damned hymns."

The Reverend Mr. Keyes, conscious for some time now, struggled onto his feet. Pain-narrowed eyes sought out McNeil and pinned him with a look of uncharacteristic vehemence. "We are prisoners here, yes, but this is nonetheless a house of *God.* I won't have further blasphemy, I won't have it!" His voice was surprisingly strong and galvanic.

"The Reverend's right," Verne Mullins said. "Watch that mouth of yours, McNeil."

More softly, Keyes said to Coppersmith, "Thank you, Lew. The playing of hymns, the singing of hymns—conjoining ourselves in prayer—is exactly what is needed now. Only Almighty God can put a swift and righteous end to this siege of wickedness."

God and two men named John Tribucci and Zachary Cain, Coopersmith thought. He saw McNeil's pinched mouth form words without voice, could read them plainly: "Hymns, prayers, religious mumbojumbo—ah *Christ!*" Pursing his own lips, he went to sit once more beside Ellen; took one of her large, rough-soft hands in both his own, and gazed over at the vestry door.

"They'll do it," he thought, and then realized that he had spoken it aloud.

Ellen said, "What, Lew?"

He did not have to fabricate an answer; in that moment, Maude Fredericks began to play.

As he came into the vestry, Tribucci saw that Cain was

standing like a sentry beside the ladder which led up into the belfry. He went over next to him, taking the penknife from his trouser pocket and thumbing it against his palm while he buttoned his coat. They did not speak.

Long minutes dragged away, with the only sound that of the wind hammering beyond the outer wall. Tribucci was a simple, if intelligent, man who did not think in terms of metaphysical or Biblical symbolism, but standing there, waiting, he was struck with a wholly chilling perception: In its snowbound isolation, invaded by godless forces, this tiny valley had been transformed into a battleground; All Faiths Church was the focal point, its ultimate sanctity to be preserved or irrevocably destroyed along with the lives of seventy-five individuals; the conflict being waged and about to be waged here seemed in an apocalyptic sense to transcend the human element and become a battle between random representatives of Good and Evil.

Hidden Valley, California—on a Sunday two days before Christmas—was a kind of miniature Armageddon. . . .

Raised voices came suddenly from inside the church proper. Tribucci tensed, listening. Another minute passed, and then the organ burst into swelling sound out on the pulpit; the Reverend Mr. Keyes commenced to sing in a shaky contralto, and Lew Coopersmith's voice and a few others joined in. The chill deepened within Tribucci as he turned ahead of Cain to start up the ladder.

The hymn was "Onward, Christian Soldiers."

Twelve

When Cain emerged into the belfry behind Tribucci, he saw that there were four obelisk-shaped windows: two set side by side in the western and eastern walls. They were a foot and a half wide, of plain glass puttied into wooden frames. The church bell itself was not visible, exposed high above, but its four heavy redwood supports slanting outward to the walls beneath the windows filled most of the enclosure. The bell rope hung down between the supports.

He stepped from the ladder onto the narrow catwalk which hugged all four walls, and peered through one of the frosted panes, westward. There was nothing to see except snow-embroidered darkness, the vague shapes of the cottage at the rear and the rising line of red fir well beyond.

Opposite him, Tribucci was looking through an eastern window. Cain asked, "Can you see the church front?"

"No. Too much roof. Lights in half a dozen buildings on Sierra and in a few of the houses, but the house lights have probably been burning since the roundup. It figures at least the psycho is still somewhere along Sierra."

Cain gloved his hands. "We'd better break the windo
first."

"Right."

"I'll punch a hole low center, so most of the glass stay
in the frame. Then we can work it loose and set th
shards in here on the catwalk."

"Good," Tribucci said. He had come around the ca
walk and was drawing on his own gloves. "We don't wan
to be dropping down onto jagged glass in the snow."

Standing in close to the window, Cain started to dra
his arm back. Tribucci caught it and said, "No, wait, th
hymn," and Cain realized the organ was crescendoin
through the last few bars of "Onward, Christian Soldiers.
He nodded and sleeved sweat from his forehead, think
ing: Close—go slow, no mistakes, no mistakes.

There was silence for a full fifteen seconds, and the
the organ began playing "Cross of Jesus," and the singin
voices lifted once more. Cain waited another ten second
held a breath, and jabbed his fist against the pane. Th
single, measured blow was enough; he had had just th
right amount of force behind it. In the narrow confines c
the belfry, the sound of the glass breaking seemed overl
loud—but there was no cessation of the organ or th
singing. The hole in the pane was jagged but clean, web
bing the remaining glass into fragments that held th
frame.

Carefully, Cain slipped fingers into the hole and wig
gled one of the shards until the old, stiff putty yielded an
the splinter came loose; he set it to one side. Tribucci fo
lowed suit with another fragment, and together they man
aged to clear the opening in something less than two min
utes. The last section of glass that Cain jerked free wa
razor sharp, and in the darkness he gripped it wrong; th
spine sliced through his glove, cut deeply into his righ
palm. He felt blood gush warmly and set his teeth agains
the lancing pain.

Wind-driven snow pelted through the aperture—ic

inpoints against their faces—and fluttered down into the estry below. But there was nothing to be done about hat. Tribucci leaned out of the window, checking both vays along the rear of the church; then he put his head ack inside, dipped his chin to Cain, and began pulling up he bell rope, coiling it around his left arm. When he had ll of it, he used his knife to saw through it as high up as ie could reach.

The organ now, after another brief pause, was playing "Faith of Our Fathers."

Tribucci looped the cut end of the rope over one of the hick supports at its juncture with the wall, tied it secure-y, and tested the strength of the knot. He dipped his chin igain, to indicate that he was satisfied it would hold their veight, and played the coiled length out and down the uter wall.

"Doesn't reach all the way to the ground," he said. "There'll be a drop of six or seven feet, but the snow'll ielp cushion our landing."

"You'd better go first," Cain said. "I cut my right palm on a piece of glass, sliced a tear in the glove, and blood eaking through will make the rope slippery."

"Can you hold onto it? Is the cut deep?"

"I'll manage somehow. Go ahead."

Tribucci climbed onto the windowsill, facing into the belfry, and gathered up slack in the rope and made a loop around his right wrist, then he leaned back and swung out against the steeple wall. Shoes sliding on the snow-slick boards, body stretched back into an almost horizontal plane, he went down with quick agility. When he reached the last foot of rope, he hung for an instant and then let go. His feet disappeared ankle-deep into the surface snow, and he went to one knee; but he was up again im-mediately, thrusting his right thumb upward, moving in close to the wall and toward the north corner.

Cain ran his right gloved palm gingerly along one trou-ser leg, to clear away some of the blood. The organ stopped again as he stood up into the frame, and he wai ed tense-bodied until it resumed with "God of Mercy. He wiped his right glove a second time, took up the rop and looped it around his left wrist. And went out the wa Tribucci had.

The pressure of the rope against his palm made th glass cut burn hellishly; long-unused muscles strained wrenched, in his armpits and across his shoulders. He fel his grip begin slipping before he had gone halfway, hel on desperately until he was ten or twelve feet above th ground. The instant he felt the rope slide irreclaimabl through his knotted fingers, he willed his body to relax There was a moment of giddying free fall, then solid im pact that stabbed pain upward through both legs to hi groin and hips. He toppled forward, sprawling. Snow clogged his nose and mouth, and he spat it out soundless ly as he pulled himself up onto hands and knees. The pai in his legs had begun to decrease; he had not broken o sprained anything.

Tribucci caught his arm and helped him upright. H asked urgently, "Okay?"

"Okay," Cain said.

A short exhalation of breath plumed like smoke fror between Tribucci's lips. He said, "North and south wall are clear. So far, so good."

"I'll follow your lead."

As he trailed Tribucci along the side of the cottage, it attached garage, Cain flexed his arms and shoulders t loosen the taut-stretched musculature; his right glov seemed filled with flowing, sticky-cold blood. The line o trees began a hundred yards beyond, and they crossed th sloping open space at a shuffle-stepped run. The storn lashed at them, surrounded them with dancing skeins o whiteness as nearly impenetrable as the curtain of nigh itself. Cain's face started to numb, and his feet were we and chilled inside his boots; his ears ached, his eye burned.

They reached the wood finally, and its density cut off some of the storm's tumult. There was no movement along their backtrail—or at least none visible through the flurries. Tribucci set a lateral course a few short yards inside the timber, so that the church and the village buildings remained dimly perceptible on their right. Minutes later they reached a point from which they could look down the two-block length of Shasta Street. Most of the houses were dark, but two showed lights; the illumination there and on Sierra was blurred by the fluxing snow. They went farther north, until they were on a line with the side wall of the nearest, completely dark house, and then followed the line down and across a bare yard to a rose trellis at the house's front corner.

The neighboring dwelling was one of those that showed light in some of its windows. Tribucci said against Cain's ear, "That's Joe Garvey's place."

"Doesn't seem to be any tracks out front."

"The Garveys were among those picked up in the canvass. It should be empty."

"We've got to make sure before we try going in."

"Yeah. Best if we come up to it from the rear."

They went along the side of the dark house, into its back yard. A waist-high wooden fence separated the two adjoining properties, and they crossed to it in a humpbacked run, passed over it one leg at a time in a low profile. A check of the two lighted windows in the western wall revealed an empty kitchen and an empty bedroom; they looped around past the back stairs and along the eastern wall and looked into an empty living room through the only illumined window on that side.

When they saw no activity on Shasta to the immediate east, they edged around to the front and past another living-room window and came up to the roofed porch. The entrance door was standing wide open, rattling in the wind; thickly undisturbed snow overlaid the inside hallway floor. Cain said, "Empty," and Tribucci repeated the word in accord. They climbed the steps quickly and entered the hallways, the living-room.

"Garvey keeps his gun in a cabinet in the washroom," Tribucci said. "I know that because I've gone fishing with him a couple of times, and he stores all his sporting equipment there."

The washroom was located off the kitchen, and the cabinet—four by six feet, made of metal, door unlocked—took up half of an end wall. The Walther automatic, a .380 PPK, lay wrapped in chamois cloth on an interior shelf, clean and well cared for. Its butt magazine was empty, but on the same shelf Tribucci found two full clips in a cigar box containing gun oil and other cleaning accessories.

He said, "You want to take this one?"

Cain nodded, accepted the weapon and the two clips, fitted one into the butt, and put the other into his left coat pocket. The gun was light for an automatic of that caliber, compact; its plastic grips felt cold and rough. He dropped it into his right coat pocket, and they moved back into the lighted kitchen.

A utensil drawer under the drainboard yielded a pair of narrow-bladed, eight-inch carving knives. Another drawer held a ball of string, and Tribucci cut off three pieces and tied the blade of one of the knives to his right thigh beneath his coat, leaving the handle free: a makeshift sheath. Cain did the same with the second knife.

In the front hallway again, Cain said, "Next step is to find extra clothing. I need another pair of gloves, too; my right one is full of blood from that glass cut."

"You won't have any trouble using the gun?"

"No. Cut seems to've stopped bleeding now, and it's in the fleshy part of the palm."

There was a closet in the hall, and inside was an old gray overcoat with a pair of cracked-leather gloves stuffed into one of the pockets. But that was all: no mufers or hats of any kind. Tribucci said, "I'll see what I an find in their bedroom," and hurried away.

The gray overcoat was knee-length, heavier than the horter one Cain wore; he made the exchange and found iat it fit him well enough. Once he had it on, he peeled ff Coopersmith's gloves, wiped his dark-stained right and—the blood, coagulating, felt as viscous as liquid dhesive—and tried the new pair. They were a size too mall, but not so tight that they would hamper free finger iovement.

At the open front door, he looked out and down Shasta gain. All that moved was the wind-hurled snow. Cain ırned as Tribucci reentered the hall wearing a thick iuffler and a woman's fox-pelt cap pulled down over his ars; his own light-colored overcoat was heavy enough so hat he hadn't needed to replace it with another, but he'd ut on a wool sweater beneath it. In one hand he carried a econd muffler, a second sweater, and a man's lamb-wool ossack-style hat.

He gave those items to Cain, watched as he put them n. "Best way to do it now, I think, would be for the two f us to split up: you back to the church and me after the ther guns at my brother's. One of us has got to get into a rotective position as quickly as possible."

Cain weighed the proposal for several seconds. 'Agreed," he said then. "If there is a guard out front, I'll ee if I can locate his whereabouts. But I won't make a nove until you come—unless there's a definite threat and don't have any choice."

"I'll make it back as fast as I can." Tribucci held his vristwatch up to his eyes. "Six twenty. Figure less than ıalf an hour. You'll be along the church's south wall?"

"Right," Cain said. "We'd better have a signal, though. Ve won't be able to recognize each other from a distance, nd things are going to be tense enough as it is."

"Suppose I stop in front of the cottage door and give a eft-handed wave over my head."

"Good. I'll make the same gesture in return."

"Split up in the wood; it'll be safe if I go that way."

They moved out of the hallway and down off the porch, climbed the wooden boundary fence, and retraced their original route into the trees. Once there, Tribucci put a hand on Cain's arm, squeezed it, and then slipped away quickly and was swallowed by the heavy fir shadows. Cain turned in the opposite direction—and he was immediately conscious of being alone. When two or more men were working together, interacting, in a crucial situation, the unit they formed became an entity unto itself—stronger than each individual because it fused their strengths into the whole. You thought as part of the unit, and as a result, you were able to maintain rigid control over your own personality. But when the unit was temporarily disbanded, and you became a man alone, a little of that control began to slip; you tried to continue blocking out emotions, to keep your mind functioning as calculatingly as it had been, but a few inevitably, if dimly, seeped through: fear, anger and hatred, enormity of purpose.

And for Cain, too, a repulsion of—a reassurance from—the weapon that seemed to have become a sudden immense weight in his right coat pocket. . . .

Thirteen

Brodie came out through the broken mouth of the Valley Café, braced his body against the force of the storm, and then stepped beyond the perimeter of the fluorescent light spill and started across Sierra Street. Behind him, Kubion trailed like a sentient and menacing shadow.

They had ripped off the Sport Shop and the Valley Inn and now the café, and the total take had been slightly more than four bills. Counting the fifteen hundreed Kubion had taken from the people at Mule Deer Lake, he now had a little more than five thousand on him. At the outside there would be another grand in the flour sack of purses and wallets Loxner had collected in the church, and no more than a couple of thousand in all the village homes combined.

All of this, the whole puking business, for maybe eight thousand—*eight thousand dollars!*

Kubion had worked himself up into another destructive rage, the way he had in the Mercantile, and had made a broken shambles of the café: smashing glasses and crockery and two wall mirrors. Watching him, Brodie had had to struggle to maintain a grip on his ragged control. Kubion was far over the edge now; all you had to do was look at him to see how much he wanted to start killing people. There just wasn't any way Brodie was going to buy himself any more time than he'd already been allotted. The café hadn't had a safe, and neither had the Sport Shop or the Valley Inn; he'd said there was still the Hughes' house and the filling station and the other buildings in the village, and Kubion said, "There's only the Hughes' place and that's it, that's our next stop. We're going up there now and there'd better be a safe, Vic, there'd better be a safe for you to open with those tools in the pickup, you hear me Vick there'd better be a safe."

It didn't make any difference whether there was a safe or not; the Hughes' house was intended to be Brodie's execution chamber.

But Kubion still hadn't given him even the smallest of possible openings, and in the two hours since they had started looting the village there hadn't been any sign of big stupid gutless Loxner, eliminating the last faint hope of help from that quarter. Kubion's freaked-out head had forgotten all about Loxner—they hadn't gone anywhere near the church in those two hours—and that was the closest he'd come to any sort of mistake. Brodie kept telling himself that Kubion getting crazier and crazier would work both ways, that it would make him careless as well as more dangerous; he kept telling himself the opening would come, don't take a last desperate gamble because the opening would come.

He reached the window on the eastern side of Sierra, started along it toward the pickup in the next block. The surface snow there was freezing and slick; he walked it with slow, cautious steps, risked a glance over his shoulder. Kubion's dark face stared back at him: no smile now, lips moving as if in silent monologue. Brodie told himself again that an opening would come.

And one came.

Just like that, with startlingly coeval suddenness, Kubion made the kind of mistake Brodie had been waiting for.

Thoughts and eyes focused elsewhere, he had not been paying any attention to his footing; his right shoe came down on one of the patches of glassy snow, found no traction and slipped, and the leg kicked up rigidly like a football placekicker following through. His left arm flailed at the air and his body jerked into a horizontal plane and he fell bellowing, landing heavily on his buttocks, left leg twisted slightly as he skidded sideways into the snowpack at the curbing.

Brodie's reaction was almost instantaneous. Instinct obliterated surprise and fatigue, and when he saw that Kubion had managed to hold onto the gun, it rejected any effort of trying to jump him across the ten icy steps which separated them. He spun and ran, diagonally back the way they had come because Kubion's body was bent toward the south and because Lassen Drive to the west was the nearest release street, the nearest shielded path of escape. He fled in a headlong, weaving crouch through the less treacherous snow which blanketed the middle of the street, coming on the far windrow near the corner of the inn. Another bellow sounded behind him, and then the flat wind-muffled explosion of a shot. Nothing touched him but the flakes of obscuring snow.

He leaped over the windrow, muscles hunched and rippling along his back, head tucked down against his chest. Sliding on the ice-quilted sidewalk, he lunged against the building wall, caught the corner, and heaved himself around it as a second shot echoed dimly and a bullet slapped into the boarding a foot or two to his left. He vaulted the ragged snowpack on Lassen Drive, to evade more sidewalk ice—lost his balance this time and sprawled out prone on the street and planed forward half a dozen yards like a man on an invisible sled before he was able to drag his feet under him again.

There were no more shots, but he did not look back; he stretched his body forward into the wind, summoning reserves of stamina, and kept on running.

Fourteen

Coopersmith was standing at the foot of the vestry ladder, looking up into the belfry, when the door swung open and Frank McNeil came inside.

Pivoting abruptly, he saw the café owner bump the door closed with one hip and press back against it. McNeil gaped with frightened, furtive eyes at the wetness on the floor directly under the belfry, at the flakes of snow which sprinkled down and liquefied on Coopersmith's head and shoulders. Sweat beaded his upper lip like a thinly glistening silver mustache.

Face void of expression, Coopersmith crossed to him and said evenly, "What are you doing in here, Frank?"

"I knew it," McNeil said, "I knew something was going on. You and John Tribucci and that Cain alone in here before, had to have your heads together about something, and then you with the organ music and hymn singing and neither one of them is out front now, I looked when I saw you slip in here a minute ago and they're not there and not in here either. They got out, didn't they? They broke out through one of the belfry windows, didn't they?"

A tic made Coopersmith's left eyelid flutter in arhythmic tempo, so that he seemed incongruously to be winking. "Keep your voice down," he snapped.

"For Christ's sake, why did they do it, why did you help them do it, what's the matter with you, they'll be killed out there, they'll be killed and we'll be killed too, we're all going to be *killed*—"

Coopersmith slapped him across the face. "Shut up, McNeil, shut up!"

McNeil's eyes bulged exophthalmically, and his fingertips trembled over the reddened surface of his cheek. He made a soft, choking sound that might have been a sob and turned to fumble the door open. Coopersmith reached for him, caught his shirt sleeve, but the rough material slipped from his grasp; McNeil went through the door, onto the pulpit beyond.

He backed away to the left and leaned up against the curved outer edge of the organ, still touching his cheek. Coopersmith came out grimly and shut the door. The silence in the dim room was funereal now. Maude Fredericks had played eight hymns and said then that she could not do any more; the Reverend Mr. Keyes had stood up immediately, shakily, and offered a long prayer to which Coopersmith only half listened because he was not sure Cain and Tribucci had had enough time to get out. When the minister finally subsided, he had gone instantly into the vestry to make sure. He knew now that he should have gone first to Ann and Vince; knew as well that the open-handed slap he had just given McNeil was a second misjudgment, that he should have hit him with a closed fist instead, knocked him unconscious. McNeil was half out of his head with fear—a coward, something less than a man at this moment—and his eyes and the quivering white slash of his moth made it plain he was going to tell everyone Tribucci and Cain were gone.

Coopersmith said, "Frank," sharply, aware that some of the others were looking at the two of them now and sensing the tension between them. He took three quick steps toward the café owner, said his name a second time.

And McNeil told them: loudly, running his words together, putting it all in the worst possible perspective.

The immediate reaction was just as Coopersmith had known it would be. There were spontaneous articulations of alarm, a half-panicked stirring as men and women got to their feet—some turning to their neighbors, some pushing forward onto the pulpit. Ellen came up beside him, took his arm, but Coopersmith's eyes were on Ann Tribucci. She was standing between Vince and Rebecca Hughes in a rear pew, face milk-white, and her lips moved with the words "Johnny, Johnny, oh Johnny!" Vince caught her by the shoulders, steadied her; his features were set in hard lines of concern, but they betrayed little surprise.

Questions, remarks pounded at Coopersmith from several directions. He waved his arms for quiet, shouting, "Listen to me, all of you listen to me!"

The voices ebbed. He faced his friends and neighbors steadily, let them see nothing but assurance and authority and self-control. Then, keeping his voice calm, low-keyed, talking over interruptions, he explained the situation to them: why the decision had been made, why the secrecy, how it was being handled by Tribucci and Cain, exactly what they were now attempting to do.

More apprehensive vocalization; a soft cry from Ann that cut knifelike into Coopersmith and made him wince. The Reverend Mr. Keyes stepped forward, supporting his bloodied scarf-bandaged right hand in the palm of his left. " 'Give them according to their deeds, and according to the wickedness of their endeavors: give them after the work of their hands; render to them their desert.' " Then: " 'The righteous shall rejoice when he seeth vengeance; he shall wash his feet in the blood of the wicked.' " No longer benign, no longer clement, he spoke harshly the passages from Psalms in the Old Testament; his spirit now, seemed to seek communion not with the God of Love and Charity, but with the God of swift and merciless Wrath.

McNeil pointed a spasmodic, accusatory finger at Coopersmith. His face was lacquered with sweat. "You had no right, you had no *right* to make a decision that might cost me my life!"

"The decision was the Lord's," the Reverend Mr. Keyes said. "The Lord granted them the wisdom and the courage to do what must be done, and the Lord will grant them the strength to carry it through."

"The Lord, the Lord, I've heard enough about your Lord—"

The Reverend Mr. Keyes started toward McNeil angrily. Webb Edwards restrained him. Eyes touched the minister, touched McNeil, returned to Coopersmith; the preponderence of expressions revealed a vacillation between hope and deepening terror.

Joe Garvey, his nose puffed into a discolored blob from the pistol whipping he had taken earlier, said thickly, "Lew, I can understand why Johnny would risk his life for us, and I can trust him and believe in him. But what about this Cain? He's an outsider, a man who's made it plain all along he wanted nothing to do with any of us. How could you and Johnny be sure of what *he'll* do out there?"

"That's right," McNeil cried, "that's right, that's right! A bird like that, a lousy vandal, he'll run away and try to save himself the first chance he gets. Oh you crazy old man, you crazy old fool!"

Blood surged hotly in Coopersmith's temples. "What right have you got to judge and condemn a man you don't know anything about—a man with guts enough to fight for your miserable life and everybody else's life here? Cain won't run away, any more than Johnny will. And he isn't the one who broke into the café; whoever it was, it wasn't Zachary Cain."

"The hell it wasn't, he's the one all right—"

"That's enough!" a voice shouted suddenly. "I won't listen to any more against Mr. Cain, I'm the one who broke into the café, *I'm* the one."

The voice belonged to McNeil's son, Larry.

Coopersmith stared down at the youth; of all the Hidden Valley residents who might have been responsible for the breaking and entering, Larry was one of the last he—or any of the others—would have suspected. Sandy McNeil said something to her son in a hushed voice, but he shook his head and pushed out into the center aisle. She came after him, one arm extended as if beseeching, as he stepped up onto the pulpit and approached his father.

McNeil was looking at him incredulously. "You, boy—*you?*"

"Me, Pa." To Coopersmith, Larry's thin face seemed for the first time to contain maturity, a kind of determined manliness. "I slipped out of the house around 3 A.M. both mornings, when everyone in the village was asleep, and used an old tire iron you had in the garage to jimmy the door. Then I propped it wide with the orange crates so the snow could blow in and ruin as much stock as possible. I'd have owned up to it sooner or later anyway, with you threatening to have Mr. Cain arrested; but now that I know he's gone out there to try to save us, I just can't hold it inside me anymore."

McNeil's lips worked soundlessly for a moment. Then, in a low voice that cracked as brittly as thin ice: "My own son, Jesus, my own son."

"Always talking about Ma," Larry said, "always talking about her in front of other people, putting her down, saying dirty things. And the way you treated her, both of us, like we were nothing to you and we're not, all you care about is yourself. That's why I did it. I thought it would be a way to hurt you. I'm sorry for it now, I wish I hadn't done it—not only because it was wrong but because I was thinking and acting the way *you* do, I was being just like you. And I don't ever want to be like you, Pa, not ever. . . ."

His voice trailed off, and the silence which followed was thick and uneasy. Sandy McNeil looked at her husband, at her son, and then she moved closer to Larry and took his hand; the gesture, the stolidity of her expression told Coopersmith she had made a decision for the future, if there was to be one for the two of them, which she would not compromise.

McNeil's cheeks were gray and damp and hollow. He watched his wife and son walk away from him; searched the eyes of the others and found no sympathy, found nothing at all for him. He seemed to fold in on himself, to shrivel and age perceptibly until he became like a gnome whose eyes glistened wetly with the cancer of cowardice and self-pity. He groped his way to the organ bench and sat on it and put his head in his hands.

The collective gazes turned from him and settled again on Coopersmith. Quietly, he told them about Cain—who the man was, why he had come to the valley, why he had volunteered to join Tribucci. And when he was finished, he saw a grudging acceptance of the situation on the majority of faces. The palpable, fear-heavy tenseness was more acute than ever, but there would be no panic, no chaotic infighting. Things in here, at least, appeared to again be under control. . . .

"Webb!"

The cry came from Vince Tribucci, jerked heads around once more, brought Dr. Edwards running down the center aisle in immediate response. Vince was leaning anxiously over his sister-in-law, helping her into a supine position on the pew bench; Rebecca held her head, pillowed it gently on one thigh. Ann's swollen abdomen heaved, convulsed, and her face was contorted with pain

She had her lower lip clenched deeply between her teeth, as though to keep herself from screaming.

Ellen clutched at Coopersmith's jacket. "She's gone into labor; the shock put her into labor. Dear heaven, Lew, she's going to have her baby. . . ."

Fifteen

At the approximate point where he and Tribucci had first entered the wind-combed trees, Cain stopped against the bole of one fir and studied the area. The tracks they had made coming across the sloping snowfield had been partially obliterated by the storm; through the flurries he could make out nothing except the dark outlines of cottage and church, the vague illumination of the church's stained-glass side windows.

With his gloved fingers opening and closing steadily, agitatedly, around the butt of the Walther PPK, he started down and across the open area. The wind shoved harshly at his back, bending him forward from the waist, and the tails of his coat flapped against his legs like the wings of a fettered bird. Firn crackled and crunched beneath his boot soles. He kept his head up, watching the cottage looming ahead, breathing shallowly.

Long moments later he reached the rear of the attached garage, took the gun out of his pocket, and went along the building's southern, front wall. Icicles hung from its eaves like pointed giant's teeth; shutters closed across one of the facing windows rattled loudly above the storm's querulous skirling. Cain stopped at the forward corner, and from there he could see the gray-black opening of the glassless belfry window and the ice-coated rope hanging down out of it; but neither was discernible from any distance.

Crossing to the church, he edged slowly and carefully toward the front. When he had come midway, he could see all of the near third of the parking lot. Three cars, each of them shrouded in white, were parked nose up against log brakes set on a line with the church's southern wall. Snow had built little ledges on the sills of their windshields and near passenger windows, and was frozen to the glass itself in streaks and spatters.

Cain went another dozen steps, and two more cars came within range of his vision—both parked with their front bumpers extending to the edge of the church walk, one in the center of the lot and the other down near Sierra Street. Their windows, too, were like blind white eyes. Within a foot of the corner, he squatted and leaned his left shoulder on the icy boarding and stretched out just enough so that he was able to see the area immediately fronting the church. One last car, as frozen and abandoned-looking as the other five.

A muscle in his left leg began to cramp with cold, and Cain straightened up again. A guard in one of those cars would logically keep at least one window facing the church clear of snow and ice, so he could watch the entrance doors; too, it was likely he'd have the engine running and the heater and defroster on, with a wing open or window rolled partway down to circumvent the threat of carbon monoxide poisoning. There were no puffs of exhaust smoke, no sounds above the wind, no car windows open or clear. No other sheltered place in the vicinity. No tracks anywhere.

No guard.

Okay, Cain thought. Okay.

He craned his head forward a second time and swept his gaze over the parking lot, Sierra Street and the wind-shaped drifts in the meadow beyond. The lights shining farther into the village were all there was for him to see; the snow flurries continued to place visibility in a constant flux. Pulling back, he tugged the fur hat down tighter over his ears and rubbed at his cold-deadened face. The wiry beard hairs were like brittle threads of ice, and he imagined that in the rubbing he had depilitated part of the growth. He swallowed a nervously humorless laugh, shook himself mentally to keep his thoughts in tight check.

How do we deploy when Tribucci gets back? he asked himself. One of us here, one of us by that car nearest the entrance? That seemed the best way to do it, all right. They would be separated, but not so far apart that one would be unable to offer protection for the other or to minimize the potential advantage of a crossfire. And they would be positioned at the closest possible points to the doors, so as to guard the entrance fully and effectively. They'd have to figure a way to cover the tracks from here to the car, though; they couldn't afford to wait for the storm to do it. Maybe there was something they could use in the cottage—a whisk broom, a trowel, something.

The wind began to gust, whistling mournfully, sweeping snow in misty sheets down close to the ground. Cain bunched the collar of his coat tighter against his throat with his left hand, repocketed the gun with his right. Minutes passed. Again he checked the area fronting the church; again he saw nothing. His feet were so achingly chilled now that he had almost no feeling in his toes; he lifted first one leg and then the other, like a man doing calisthenics in slow motion, to keep the blood circulating. The movement of time seemed to have slowed down to an inert crawl, as if the bitterly cold night had managed to wrap it, too, in a cloak of ice—

Time, Cain thought.

Abruptly he pushed back the left sleeve of his coat and squinted at the luminous numerals of his watch. It was seven five. Tribucci had said it would take him less than half an hour to get the guns from his brother's house and return here, but it was nearly forty-five minutes since they had parted in the wood. If nothing had happened, he should have been here by now. If nothing had happened. . . .

The clot of anxiety under Cain's breastbone expanded. He made one last quick and fruitless reconnaissance of Sierra Street and then hurried back to the rear corner and across to the cottage and along its façade again to the garage corner. He stared beyond the snowfield at the trees: black-and-white emptiness everywhere.

Where *was* he?

Where was Tribucci?

Sixteen

Moving through the familiar darkness inside his brother's home, John Tribucci went from the rear porch into the downstairs study. At an antique sideboard along one wall, he bent and opened the facing doors and rummaged through the interior until his fingers located the cowhide case he knew Vince kept there. He took the case out, set it on top of the sideboard, and worked the catches to lift the lid.

Inside was a matched set of .22 caliber, nine-shot Harrington & Richardson revolvers—a gift from Vince's father-in-law some three years earlier. One of Vince's favorite all-weather pastimes was target shooting, and he preferred Western-style pistols such as these to automatic target weapons like the Colt Woodsman. Tribucci had done some shooting with his brother, with these guns, and knew the feel and action of the model. Both were loaded, safeties on; he put one into the left pocket of his coat, clutched the second firmly, and went out of the study and started back through the house.

As he came into the kitchen, he grew aware for the first time of the subtle, homely fragrances which lingered in the warm black: his wife's Lanvin perfume, Vince's after-breakfast cigar, the batch of Christmas *pfeffernüsse* cookies Judy had baked just before the four of them left for church. A vivid image of Ann entered his mind then, and his throat closed and his stomach twisted with a rush of emotion that was almost vertiginous. He leaned against the refrigerator for a moment, holding onto the image, trying to think of her laughing and happy instead of the way he had left her in church, the way she would be now that Coopersmith had surely hold her what he and Cain were doing. Then, deliberately, he forced his mind blank of everything but his immediate purpose and stepped out onto the wide back porch.

He pushed through the door there—it had been customarily unlocked, and he'd come in that way initially—and hurried around to the front yard, into the deep shadows beneath one of the twin fir trees flanking the walk. The house was located on Eldorado Street, slightly more than half a block off Sierra; he peered eastward, then down the length of Shasta Street. The falling snow was like a huge, wind-billowed lace curtain that combined with the darkness to obscure anything more than fifty yards distant. A thin haze of light from the buildings on Sierra tinged the sky in that direction.

Tribucci moved out from beneath the fir and ran in long, light strides across Eldorado, coming up against the broad entrance doors of the building which fronted Placer on the east; owned by Joe Garvey, it served as a garage for extensive automobile and truck repairs and also as a storage shed for the village snowplow. On the opposite side of the street was a wide, bare hummock of ground, deep-drifted, that extended south to Lassen Drive and north to the beginnings of the pass cliffs—a shorter path into the wood higher up, but a slow and precarious one because of the snow depth. He would follow the longer but quicker route by which he had come: first down to the corner, to make sure Lassen was clear, and then traverse Placer and traverse Lassen and go up slantingly into the trees.

He was three steps from the corner when the dark figure came running at fly speed out of Lassen Drive.

Startled, Tribucci stood immobile for an instant; then, instinctively, he took a step back hard against the building, embracing the heavy darkness there. The running man crossed Placer—not looking back, not looking anywhere except straight ahead of him. When he reached the low picket fence enclosing the front yard of Webb Edward's house, he jumped it without slowing and disappeared around the screened-in porch.

It all happened so quickly that Tribucci had been able to distinguish nothing of the fleeing man's physical characteristics; but he had been hatless, and that meant it couldn't have been Cain, wasn't Cain. One of the looters . . . running from the psycho? You ran that way when somebody was after you, and maybe the maniac had tried to kill him—already killed the third one?—and he had broken away somehow. Was the psycho in close pursuit then? Was he just around the corner on Lassen? Tribucci worked saliva through his dry mouth, momentarily indecisive. Retreat or stay where he was? He might be seen either way, and this wasn't the place for a fight; he had to get back to Cain and the church—

A new movement caught his eye through the storm, kept him hugging the garage wall: in indistinct shape running through the yard of the Beckman property adjacent to Edwards'; cutting back across Placer at an angle, obscured white face turned to the north but with the screening snow and the ebon shadows, not seeing him, Tribucci, from that distance; vanishing once again into the Modoc Street corner lot belonging to the Chiltons.

Urgency tugged commandingly at Tribucci's mind, vanquishing the indecision. Get away from here, he thought. Get away from here now.

And the second figure appeared in the middle of Lassen fifteen feet away, oblong pointing finger of an automatic darkly defined in one hand, stalking—limping—in the runner's snowtracks.

Tribucci stiffened again; his ears seemed suddenly filled with the thrumming of his pulse. The second one stopped, looked across at Edwards' house—and then, as if with sixth sense, turned and stared north along Placer, stared right at him, could not miss seeing him across that short a span of ground. Tribucci recognized the charred, savage face immediately, confirmation of what he already knew, and a mixture of fear and hatred and fury constricted his anus and opened his jaws in a wolflike rictus. He had waited too long, it was too late to run, and he had no place to run to; he had to fight *now*.

Kubion took two steps toward him, gun arm leveled. Tribucci fired from in close to his chest, missed in his haste, saw the other jerk to a halt as if in surprise and then lunge to one side, onto his right knee with his favored left leg dragging. Moving sideways, Tribucci snapped his arm out and locked the elbow and braced his body; fired again—missed again, snow kicking up like a puff of white dust near the trailing leg. Damn you to hell damn you damn you! and started to squeeze off a third time, but the automatic in Kubion's hand flashed then and

stab! in his chest,

and flashed again and

stab! in his chest.

the stock of the bullets' impact driving away his breath —no no I blew it—and his legs buckled, the nerves in his gloved right hand were like filaments of ice. The revolver fell free, he felt his body slumping and heard the wind and the vague echoes of the shots as he toppled loosely into the half-frozen snow. I blew it good but oh *please* God don't let me have blown it completely—and a congealing red-black haze formed and thickened inside his head, spinning him, spinning him, obliterating all sound and all feeling and the sudden bright image of Ann that clung to his last shred of consciousness. . . .

Seventeen

Kubion stared down at the snow-spattered form of the man he had shot, recognized him as the one brother from the Sport Shop. Savagely he said, "You fucking hick Eskimo son of a bitch!" and drove the point of his shoe into yielding flesh just below the ribs, did it a second time. Then he backed up against the wall of the garage and probed the night around him with slitted, restless eyes.

Despite the direction of the snow tracks, he'd thought at first it was Brodie there in the building shadows and then the bastard had plugged away at him with that horse gun and Brodie hadn't had time to locate a weapon but Christ on a crutch he'd almost walked into it, the first bullet had missed him by a foot but the second had almost gotten him but he was ten feet tall and nobody could kill him least of all a lousy hick, but still it had been close. *Goddamn* it he'd been positive none of them would try to get out of the church and here this one was stupid stupid, not through the locked front doors not that stupid but maybe some other exit he'd overlooked when he'd examined the interior on Thursday or by breaking out the glass in one of the windows, and how many others were there? Oh, there'd be at least one more that was certain because one alone was too much of a risk even for stupid Eskimo hicks but now Tribucci was a dead hero and he'd make the other one or two dead heroes too. And Brodie, he'd kill Brodie slow and painful when he found him the fag shit, all that crap about safes but the urge telling him no and he'd thought he had everything nailed down and then that lousy ice and not watching his footing and falling and twisting his ankle, sprained and hurting and swelling up and hobbling him, and Brodie getting away and things all of a sudden screwing up just like the Greenfront job, things you couldn't figure ahead of time. But there was no way things were going to screw him out of this score no way because there'd be a fruit jar somewhere with the big money he *knew* it, and it was only a matter of time before he was back on top and killed Brodie and killed them all. . . .

The urge moaned and trembled inside him, softly, softly. He opened his mouth and pulled freezing air and flakes of snow into his lungs. Things screwing up sure but Tribucci was dead, and it was a good thing he'd had the shoot-out because now he knew some of them were free; coming after Brodie with the idea he could spot him on the run had been smart then but not now, no point in trying to trail him like a goddamn Indian and maybe walking into an ambush. Maybe Brodie'd try for the Sport Shop, he'd be after a weapon first thing all right, but it was too obvious and maybe he'd go somewhere else; still, the thing to do was check it out quick and careful and even if he couldn't flush him he knew what Brodie would do after he was armed no question about that. He knew what the other hick heroes would be doing too, they'd want to protect those in the church and too many men running around in the village would increase chances of discovery and they'd be smart enough to understand that so they'd be waiting by or near the church for Tribucci to come with the guns that he wouldn't be bringing. The churc was the lay okay, all the way all the way.

Not looking at the motionless figure in the snow, Ku bion sidestepped to the corner and went around it and ra limpingly back along Lassen Drive to Sierra Street.

Eighteen

As soon as he was sure the immediate area was clear, Brodie climbed over a five-foot boundary fence into the north-south alley bisecting the block between Modoc and Lassen and kicked open the back door of the Valley Inn. The wind muffled the sounds of splintering wood and snapping metal, sent swirls of snow into the heavily shadowed storeroom ahead of him. Directly opposite and to one side, he could make out a narrow corridor leading into the front of the building. He ran down there, came out in the restaurant kitchen, and crossed to a swing door in the far wall. When he had pushed through, he was in the inn's darkened dining room.

Lights burned a pale amber in the lounge area beyond the center partitions. On the wall behind the far end of the bar, Brodie could see the glass-fronted guncase he had noticed earlier—and the twin, ornately scrolled shotguns shining dully within. Spread across the bottom of the interior shelf, just as he remembered, were boxes of shells.

He ran around into the lounge and swung his body up onto the bar, over behind it. With a heavy decanter from the backbar display, he broke the glass out of the guncase door and cleared clinging shards from the opening. The shotguns were .12 gauge pumps with 26-inch barrels, three-shot Savages. Brodie pulled one of them loose from its clip fastenings, pawed open a box of cartridges, fed three into the magazine, and worked the slide to jack the first into firing position.

Despite the deadliness of the piece, it was cumbersome—and the storm would retard accurate shooting at any range over twenty yards. There were plenty of handguns in the Sport Shop, but once Brodie was certain he'd made good his escape and could think calculatingly again, he had decided against that objective. Kubion had to know that his first consideration would be to get himself a weapon and that the Sport Shop was the one place to pick up on guns and ammunition. Maybe Kubion would be following snow tracks, the way you'd expect, but then again, since Brodie hadn't seen any sign of him when he'd looped around and doubled back across Placer Street, it could be he had gone to the Sport Shop instead. Christ, he could be anywhere, doing anything.

Brodie dropped a handful of extra shells into his coat pocket, went over the bar again, and ran through the dining room and kitchen. He slowed there and entered cautiously into the dark corridor, bringing the shotgun up so that the stock butted hard against his shoulder, moving to where he could see the open rear door. Snow still churned inside, blanketing a section of floor in an unbroken swath. He edged into the storeroom, circled silently around to the wall beside the door. Then, swiftly, he stepped over in front of the opening, still three paces inside, and fanned the pump across the fence. Nothing showed, nothing moved. He saw that the only tracks in the alley snow were his own, hesitated for a moment, and then ran out through the doorway to the left; pulled back to the building wall, sweeping the shotgun's muzzle from the fence northward along the alley and back again. The narrow expanse was empty in both directions.

With the pump sighted once more on the fence, Brodie waded sideways through the snow to the south. Just prior to Modoc Street, the fence ended against a low line of shrubbery, and he could see a portion of the adjoining house's front yard: smooth-swept whiteness. He went over there, fanned the area behind the fence, and then swung the weapon outward in an arc to Modoc. Clear. Carefully, he backed farther into the yard at an angle that allowed him to see down Modoc to Sierra in one direction, and back deeper along the fence in the other. He was completely alone.

His moves so far had been the right ones; he'd been inside the inn less than five minutes—not long enough to have trapped himself if Kubion was following his tracks, just long enough to have balanced the odds a little. There was no question what his next move had to be: the church. Loxner figured to be long gone, hiding out somewhere, but there was still an off-chance he'd remained in the car and even a mush-belly was better than no help at all. And doing the cat-and-mouse bit in the village was pure stupidity; you didn't play games with a maniac. If he could get to the church before Kubion, and Loxner *was* gone, he could burrow in somewhere and try to pick Kubion off when he showed—and he would show all right, he could already be on his way there because he'd remember Loxner now. But that didn't change matters. Any way you looked at it, the church was where Brodie had to go.

He hurried through the facing yards of two houses, watching his flank as well as what lay ahead. Then he cut across Modoc and went into another yard and along the side of a dark frame house. There was no fence separating that property from the one which fronted on Shasta; he passed beneath a row of bare-branched fruit trees, paralleled a second dark house, and came to a stop beside a wooden pony cart the owners had put in for landscaping decoration.

He squatted there to catch his breath, to momentarily relieve the sharp ache of fatigued muscles. The shotgun seemed to have grown heavier, more unwieldy. Opening the bottom two buttons of his coat, he used the lining on one of the flaps to wipe his wind- and snow-stung eyes.

As far as he could see, then, Shasta Street was clear both east and west. He levered up again and ran at an angle across the roadway, plowed through thick drifts to a fir tree at the edge of the church acreage. Kubion's car was discernible from there; like all the others on the lot, it was draped in white, windshield and windows ice-veiled. It looked as if Loxner were gone, all right, but he was still going to have to make sure.

Brodie slogged forward through the surface pack with his body humped over and the pump gun up against his shoulder, covering both front and rear corners. When he had reached the near wall, he went to the corner and stared out into the lot. The snow everywhere was unmarred. If Kubion had managed to get there before him, he hadn't come across the lot and he wasn't in the lot.

Stepping out, Brodie moved to the front stairs and sat on his haunches next to them, fanning the shotgun from south to east to north. Then he looked down at Kubion's car again, came up, and scurried crablike across the walk to the nearest vehicle; went around behind it, half turned back toward the church. Once he got to the car, he raised his left hand and rapped hard against the cold metal of the door. No response from within. He knew that the dome light in the car didn't work, and he reached up and caught the handle and jerked outward. Ice seals crackled, breaking away from the metal; the door opened wide.

Brodie said "Jesus!" between suddenly clenched teeth, because Loxner hadn't gone anywhere, because Loxner was still sitting there behind the wheel—with his mouth hanging open and both hands wrapped around the blood-coated haft of Kubion's pocketknife embedded just under his breastbone.

Nineteen

Cain was not startled when he put his head out to look around the church's southern front corner and the looter was less than twenty yards away, armed with a shotgun, moving across the front walk and into the parking lot.

He had been expecting one or more of them for several minutes, ever since he'd stood at the cottage's far end and waited for Tribucci to appear out of the trees. There was only one possible explanation for Tribucci's continued absence: something had gone wrong, he had been seen and killed or wounded and pinned down somewhere. And that meant the psycho was now aware at least one man had gotten out of the church, that he would want to find out as quickly as possible if there were others, that the element of surprise had at best been neutralized and at worst been transferred in part to the opposition.

He had forced down the stirring of a strong mixture of emotions, forced himself to remain calm and to think strategically. Deliberation had been brief. The only thing he could do was to situate himself at the south church wall, alternating between front and rear corners; that way he could cover all immediate approaches without leaving any more telltale tracks than he already had. He'd spent the past ten minutes moving back and forth along the wall, watching and waiting for something to happen, and now the waiting was over—part of it, or all of it.

The man in the parking lot was not the psycho; Cain was able, through the flurries, to determine that by size, coloring, and clothing before pulling back rigidly against the boarding. His fingers tightened convulsively around the butt of the Walther, and he brought it up against his chest, thinking: Why the parking lot, why not around on this side? He can't think I'm out there, there isn't any spoor. . . . All right, it doesn't matter; what matters is what he does not, where he goes—what I do and where I go. One mistake and it's all over: remember that, don't forget that for a second.

Cain inched his head out again. The looter had reached the vehicle parked by itself at the forward end of the lot, was pulling open the driver's door. He reacted to something inside the car; but the dome light did not go on, and because of distance and angle and the storm, Cain couldn't tell what it was. With taut movements, the man straightened and backed off two steps; swept the shotgun south to north across the front of the church, not seeing Cain—not yet.

But he's going to come back here now, Cain thought, and when he does it'll be in this direction; he came from the north, and he can't know what there is on this side. Retreat to the back? No—retreating won't accomplish anything positive, there isn't going to be any more retreating. Too late to go after him, and that would be a fool's move anyway with that shotgun he's got and across open ground. Stay here, then, right here. Don't take eyes off him, don't make any unnecessary moves because movement is the thing that'll give me away; he's not going to be able to penetrate stationary shadows until he gets closer—believe that. Wait, wait until the last possible second, play for one shot at dead aim and don't even think about missing. . . .

The looter was moving now, shuffle-stepping toward the church and diagonally to the south. He held the shotgun centered on the building, ready to swing either way, but his head turned in a slow, intent ambit, coming out of profile. He seemed to be facing Cain squarely then, to hesitate—

don't move, don't breathe.

—and finally he swiveled his gaze slowly to the north again.

Sweat trickled down from Cain's armpits, froze along his sides; the brassiness was back in his mouth, sharp and raw. When the looter's attention was focused fully away from him, he lifted his left arm cautiously to eye level and anchored it against the corner edge of the church; brought the Walther up in the same motion and rested the barrel on his forearm. He released the held breath into his left coat sleeve, drew another. Squinting, he peered along the iron muzzle sight.

The looter took another step, and another.

Aim for the head or body? What did the Army tell you about something like this? Can't remember, can't think—make a decision! Body then, larger target, center on the chest, the heart.

Another step.

All right, steady now, steady. Slow, even pressure on the trigger. Squeeze it, don't pull it, when the time comes.

The looter came to a standstill.

Not yet! He doesn't see me, he's not looking here. Wait. Last possible moment, one shot. Come on, you, come on, come on.

Moving again—one step, two.

Steady.

Twenty yards now, any second now.

Steady steady steady.

And the looter stopped again, jerkily this time. His

body started to dip into a crouch, the pump gun swinging hard across in front of him.

He's seen me, Cain thought—and let his finger compress the trigger.

The recoil jumped the automatic's barrel off his forearm, the roar seemed to hammer deafeningly in his ears. He snapped the muzzle down again, trying to re-brace it—but the man was falling, Cain realized this with a kind of fascination and watched him fall as though in cinematic slow motion, one foot coming up, leg bending, body turning and then arching backward, falling with the shotgun still held in his hands, striking the yielding snow on his back, the pump jarring loose finally and rolling up over his head and away; the body settling, becoming still, lying there in twisted repose.

Cain leaned heavily against his left arm, weakness in his legs, weakness in the pit of his stomach. The illusion of slow motion vanished, and he thought: *My God, my God,* dully. He did not move from his position, staring at the sprawled figure in the snow beyond. Breath shuddered and rattled in his throat. The chill of it, the numbing wind against his face, sharpened his thoughts again: you did it, okay you did it, and now you've got to do it again. His eyes probed the parking lot, the church's façade, the area behind him to the west. Empty darkness.

He rubbed harshly at his face, stepped out bent-bodied, and went quickly, gun extended, toward the motionless body. The looter lay on his back, and when Cain came up to him he could see the sightlessly open eyes, the grimaced mouth, blood on the mouth, blood on the coat front. Dead—yes. Heart-shot. He backed around the body, swallowing a faint ascendance of nausea, and approached the car at which the looter had crouched.

The door still stood partially open. Nausea surged again when Cain squatted and looked inside and saw what the looter had reacted to: the body of the third man behind the wheel, the blood, the haft of the pocketknife—dead in there all this time. The psycho had done it, no doubt of that, and that was all the explanation he needed; details were meaningless. All that had meaning now was not one but *two* of the terrorists were dead, and in all probability Tribucci as well, and it was only the psycho and himself who were left. Just the two of them, one against one.

Sure—one against one.

Well suppose he sought help, suppose with the way things were now he went up to the church doors and tried to break them open or shouted for some of the men inside to break them open, told them what the situation was. . . . No, that was foolish thinking. He didn't know where the psycho was, and he would make a fine target up there on the steps. And the threat of a stampede was a real one, you couldn't predict the actions of each and every one of seventy-five trapped people once the doors to freedom were open to them.

He'd have to do it alone, then; nothing had changed, nothing could change. Remain here at the church, guard the entrance, and begin the waiting all over again. Back around the south corner? Or right here in the lot? The lot—behind the car nearest the front doors. The surface snow was full of tracks now, and without that problem to worry about, the lot was the more tactical location. From here he could see both front corners, and Sierra Street, and most of the village to the north, and all of the lot, and the open incline leading up into the trees beyond the lake roads' fork.

Rising up, Cain ran in a low stiff crouch to that nearest car, an old finned Mercury. The flurries were less heavy now, and the force of the wind seemed to have abated somewhat; the darkness harbored nothing that he could see. He knelt in the snow at the right rear fin—and almost immediately he could feel the chill penetrating his trousers and the heavy skirt of his overcoat. He could feel, too, the aching cold-tightness of muscles and joints throughout his body and the beginnings of enervation in his limbs. It was as if the freezing night were sucking strength out of him like sweat through the pores of his skin.

Make it soon, damn you, he thought. Make it *soon.*

Twenty

Crouched beside an evergreen shrub on Shasta Street, a half block off Sierra, Kubion watched skull-grinning as Brodie died in the church parking lot.

He had come across Sierra and made a rapid, though guarded, check of the Sport Shop, front and rear; then he'd recrossed the street at Modoc and gone up to Shasta, into it laterally through thickly concealing darkness. When he reached the shrub, he paused to reconnoiter the church and the short length of Shasta to the west. It was while he had been doing that that Brodie came out of one of the yards in the next block and ran across to the fir tree at the edge of the church property.

Going to the church all right, Kubion had thought. Got him a shotgun or a rifle, some piece in a snowstorm but he's running scared, and the first thing he'll do when he gets over there is go to the car looking for Loxner. Fifty yards closer and you wouldn't go anywhere you fairy son of a bitch, but maybe it was better this way maybe he'd flush any other stupid hero hicks hiding in the area. Big black blowfly, that's what Brodie was, big black blowfly circling around and when he landed he was going to get squashed flat, spill his guts all over the goddamn snow.

Brodie had stepped out from under the tree, and through the gusting snowfall Kubion's slitted eyes had followed his progress to the church and to the car. Surprise! Surprise, Vic! Oh, Jesus his face must have been something to see right then, trying to figure out when and how it happened well I did it just after we took over the church, I put the knife in him while you were walking away with your back turned, the whispering told me it was time; one stroke clean when Duff was leaning over the seat to get the flour sack and he never made a sound and you thought all along he was alive, you could see him sitting behind the wheel all the while and you thought he was alive and he was just another dead lump of shit. . . .

The grin had stretched Kubion's cold-cracked lips as Brodie turned and started back toward the church. Now what, blowfly? Now what? And that was when he saw the brief muzzle flash from the church corner; Brodie falling, staying down without moving. Kubion stood up against the shrub, head craned forward; nothing changed in his face, the skull grin remained fixed. Seconds later the shadows at the corner separated, and he watched the figure of the man materialize.

Mothering bastard! Hick got him hick killed him; where did he get the gun? Well fuck that, he had it and he'd picked Brodie off with it, one shot lucky shot and Brodie was dead, he'd wanted Brodie for himself but it was okay this way too—okay, okay. Kubion kept staring over at the lot, saw the hick check the car and then come back and take a position behind another car and now show himself again. So—digging in out there this time, where he could cover all approaches and the church doors. No way to slip up on him but that was okay too because he knew exactly where the hick was and that the hick was armed and that there probably weren't any others or they would've come into the lot, or else he'd have gone to them to report if they were too far away to know what had happened with Brodie. Right on, he was right on top again ten feet tall; no more screwing up from here on in no more screwing up.

The impulse was talking to him again, telling him exactly what he had to do because it was time now to finish everything.

Fire-bomb the church, it murmured. Fire-bomb the church!

Get material for Molotov cocktails from one of the houses and cross to the church from where the sharp-shooting hick couldn't see him and toss a couple through one of the stained-glass windows on the far side and the front. When the hick heard and saw what was happening, his instant reaction would be to try to help the ones inside, forgetting everything else because that was the way these silly Eskimos always reacted and always would react, and he'd run up to the doors and Kubion would stand out and pick him off and then dump another cocktail on the entrance to make sure nobody broke down the doors and nobody got out alive.

He could imagine vividly the way it would be, he could see the bright burning flames and he could hear the screams; and when he backed away through the shadows to Sierra, he felt a sharp hurting in his groin and realized that the urge's excitement had given him a stone-hard erection.

Twenty-One

Within the church, balanced precariously on the edge of panic, the people of Hidden Valley waited for some indication of what was taking place in the storm and darkness outside—and for the bitter incongruity of the birth of a child.

At Webb Edwards' direction, the pews forward and rear of the one where Ann Tribucci lay had been cleared immediately after he'd satisfied himself that her labor was not false. With the exception of Lew Coopersmith, who had taken up a listening post at the front doors, all the men and all the children had grouped on or near the pulpit; most of the women were spaced in the pews between or along the walls. Edwards had taken the prayer cloth from the altar and draped it across the pew backs above Ann, to form a kind of awning that would offer a measure of privacy. Some of the heavier winter coats helped anchor the cloth. Sally Chilton had taken Rebecca's place, holding Ann's head in her lap, mopping perspiration from her paper-white cheeks, talking to her softly, soothingly. Once Edwards had removed some of Ann's garments, he had placed his own soft fur-lined coat beneath her hips;

then he'd gotten two heavy shawls from Judy Tribucci and Ellen Coopersmith, had unfastened the string tie he was wearing and divested it of its thin, metal, caduceus-shaped slip ring—swaddling clothes and umbilical binding and surgical cutting tool, all poor unsterile substitutes that would have to do because there was nothing else, there was not even any water for cleansing. Kneeling at the edge of the prayer cloth, he massaged her heaving abdomen gently and timed the frequency of her pains.

Rebecca stood against the south wall, hugging herself, not wanting to watch this grim enactment of what must ordinarily be the moving spectacle of childbirth, watching anyway because Ann was her friend and because it was as momentarily inescapable as their prison itself. Would there be complications? It was a wretched possibility. And if there were, would Webb Edwards' simple medical knowledge be enough?

Would it matter to Ann and the baby even if there were no complications at all?

Minutes ticked away—empty, barren. Rebecca listened to the softly vocal praying of the Reverend Mr. Keyes, Ann's muffled cries, the monotonous droning of Sally Chilton's voice and that of Agnes Tyler crooning to her unresponsive daughter—and her nerves grew tighter, until they seemed on the verge of snapping like rubber bands stretched to the limit of their elasticity. She wanted to scream, to fling herself at someone, to run in circles until she collapsed: something, anything, to relieve the inexorably mounting pressure. She could not stand it much longer, she thought; none of them could stand it much longer. When she looked around at the others, she could see some of what she felt in their groping movements, in the way their eyes shifted from Ann to the front doors to one another, in the hollowness of their faces. It was like watching, being a part of, the beginnings of a collective nervous breakdown.

She swallowed thickly, thinking: I've got to get a grip on

myself, I can't let go now, there's still hope—there is still hope. Cling to that, to faith in Johnny and in Zachary Cain, to *faith*. We're not going to die. We're not going to die. . . .

And she remembered that Cain had spoken those same words to her earlier, remembered again the conviction in his voice and the new strength of him. Curiously, she had not been surprised when she'd learned he had gone out there with Johnny and what the two of them intended to do; her only surprise had been that they'd found a way to get out in the first place. Like Johnny, Cain—and this was something she now understood she'd seen in him from the first, dormant but perceptible—was a basically forceful, selflessly compassionate man: the kind of man who acted and reacted strongly to any given situation. The hell he had put himself through because of the death of his family was testimony to that, just as what he was doing now, for them, was testimony to it.

I wonder what Matt would have done if he'd been spared, she thought. For all his benevolence and professed love for the people of the valley, would he have volunteered to go out there and try to kill three men to save all our lives? She did not think so; no, she did not think so.

The entire nature of her relationship with Matt seemed to have become quite clear now. There hadn't been anything left of their marriage or of her love for him; the last binding threads had unraveled a long time ago, and she had been living a foolish lie, hiding the debilitating ugliness of that lie behind the guise of weakness and self-pity—not fully understanding what it was doing to her as a woman, as a human being. And yet she *had*, slowly, been coming to an understanding of the truth, would have reached that understanding sooner or later. And when she had, the strength so long repressed in her would have manifested itself and she'd have left him and gotten a divorce. It was a simple matter of self-preservation: if she had stayed with Matt, she would have died spirituall died inside, and for all her weakness and timidity and in decisiveness she would never have allowed it to happen Knowing that, she knew herself: she had at last rediscov ered her own identity.

Only now, bitterly, it might have come too late.

There you go again, she told herself; stop it now, sto it. It's not too late, think about something else, thin about anything else. Think about Zachary Cain; yes, thin about him, and what he said, and the way he looked, an the way he was and is and will be when you see hir again. . . .

Fifty minutes after she had gone into labor, and merci fully without complications, Ann Tribucci gave birth.

From his position at the doors, Coopersmith saw Ed wards lift the newborn infant by the ankles—long finger-thick umbilical cord trailing down beneath th prayer cloth like a wet white rope, seeming to puls faintly—and use a clean handkerchief to sponge away ac cumulated blood and mucus from mouth and nose; sla tiny buttocks sharply to begin normal respiration. Th child's cries echoed piercingly through the grim silence.

Ann said weakly, tearfully, "Webb . . . oh Webb. . . ."

"It's a girl, honey," Edwards said. His voice was thick "Normal in every way and you can hear how healthy sh is."

He laid the baby down on one of the shawls, took u his string tie and bound off the umbilical cord, used th tie's metal caduceus clip to saw through it. Then he wipe her dry and wrapped her in the other shawl and hande her across to Sally. His hands and clothing were spattere with reddish fluid as he knelt again to minister to Ann.

Coopersmith, as some of the others had already done looked away; he had fathered two sons but had seen nei ther of them born, and he'd never realized that childbirt could be quite so messy—a messiness that only adde fuel to the sick terror in the room. Facing the side wall, he heard Ann say, "I want to hold her, please let me hold her," and he thought: Life and death, in the midst of one you have the other, and you can't separate them; one Tribucci born and one ready to die, the Lord giveth and the Lord taketh away. . . .

The tightness had returned to his chest, the sourness like trapped gas to his stomach. He passed a hand over his face. And standing there that way, with his ear close to the joining of the two doors, he heard something else, something outside—a faint cracking sound thinned by the storm. He knew immediately that it was a shot, strained to pick up further sounds; there were none. He turned his head to see if anyone else had heard the report. Each of their attentions, he saw, was centered on Ann and Edwards and the cries of the baby, or turned within.

Let it be Cain or Johnny who fired that shot, he thought fervently. Let them stay alive and do what they have to do—so all these people can live, so Johnny's baby can live. You've given, but don't take away; let Cain and Tribucci live. . . .

Twenty-Two

John Tribucci was still alive.

He was alive because the bullets which had entered his chest had both missed vital organs—one chipping the left collarbone and one lodging against a right upper rib—and because of the two vicious kicks in the side Kubion had delivered just after the shooting. Shock had been responsible for the red-black haze, the initial unconsciousness but if it had not been for the kicks, the freezing wind and snow would have prevented him from coming to and eventually have done the job the bullets failed to do.

The sudden pain in his side brought him out of it gradually, into a vague awareness of where he was and what had happened, and he did not move perceptibly or make any sound. He lay there at first feeling only the cold and the pain in his side where he had been kicked and a bitter hollow helplessness, half expecting a final bullet, the *coup de grâce,* that he would never really feel or hear. Instead there was the audible crunching of steps going away from him—not far, it seemed, just up to the garage wall a few yards distant, but far enough for Trubucci to begin to taste faint hope. His thoughts cleared somewhat then, and h clung with silent desperation to the threads of consciousness, giving thanks that he had fallen with his face turned downward against one arm, so that each thin expulsion of breath went into the snow and did not dilate upward in a telltale white vapor.

In his wounded and cold-stiffened condition, he knew it would be suicidal to go after the second .22 revolver in his left coat pocket or the knife strapped to his leg, or to make any sort of movement at all, while the psycho remained in the vicinity. He waited, playing dead—and kept on waiting. Pain began to seep through the numbness in his chest, muted at first but gathering a pulsing intensity; he was aware of the faint cold stickiness of blood on his upper torso.

And then, above the cry of the wind, he thought he heard steps crackling again, retreating to the south. But he was not completely sure, and still he kept his body immobile. One or five or ten more minutes ebbed away. He began to feel a kind of torpid warmth, lying there in the snow, and that was a certain sign you were on your way to freezing to death; he could not wait any longer, if he didn't move very soon now he would never move at all.

Tribucci forced his eyes open into slits, blinking the lids free of ice flakes, and then turned his head slowly up and around. He could see all right; the haziness was gone. It was snowing less heavily now, giving him greater visibility than he had had earlier, and there was no one at the garage wall and appeared to be no one to the south along Placer. When he had worked his head around to look to the north, he saw nothing in that direction either.

He got his hands under him and lifted himself slowly, weakly, into a kneeling position, setting his teeth against the rising agony in his chest. The depression in the snow where he had lain was spotted darkly with blood, but most of the fluid had been contained inside his clothing, taking his undershirt to his body. Trembling with cold and enervation, he lifted one leg and planted his shoe firmly and heaved upward onto his feet; staggered, fell t one knee again; pushed upward a second time and grope his way to the garage wall. He leaned against it heavily panting.

How much time had passed? Tribucci dragged his lef arm up and looked at his watch, and it was seven thirty seven. More than an hour since he had left Cain, three quarters of an hour since he had come out of Vince' house across Eldorado. He swallowed into a constricte throat and tried to collect his thoughts into coheren order.

The psycho knew now that at least one person had go out of the church, and he had to be thinking that mayb there were more as well. He would head there, then, h wouldn't keep on reconning the partner who'd been running away from him—and maybe that one would make fo the church as well. Cain would have realized by now tha something had happened, too much time had elapsed fo him to think otherwise, and he would be extra-cautiou but so would the runner and so would the psycho, particularly the psycho.

Tribucci sleeved snow and chilled sweat from his face breathing rackingly. I've got to get to the church, h thought, and I've got to get there fast: warn Cain, joi him in a stand. There might still be a little time, but n enough for him to attempt the trek on foot; too dangerou with the psycho's whereabouts unknown, the runner' whereabouts unknown, and the frigid wind and sno would sap too much of his remaining strength. He had t do something overt, then; there just wasn't any othe choice.

Take a car; a car was fast and direct, and it would giv him some protection as well. Vince's Buick? It was in th garage across Eldorado—but God he didn't have a ke for it, and he wasn't enough of a mechanic to be able t jump the ignition wires. His own car was at the churc he and Ann and Vince and Judy had gone in that th morning. Was there another vehicle in the village somewhere that might have the keys in it? He could not think of one, there might not *be* any, and he would waste precious time, too much time, if he—

Snowmobile, he thought.

Vince's snowmobile.

It, too, was in his brother's garage, and the key for it was kept in a storage compartment under the cowl; friends were always borrowing the machine with Vince's carte blanche permission and he felt it was simpler to keep the key there than on his person. It was as good as a car in that it could travel just as quickly, better than a car because it was smaller and more maneuverable in the snow and would not be noticed as soon from a distance. He would be fully exposed driving it, a moving target, but there was nothing to be done about that; he had to get to the church, he had to get to Cain.

Tribucci pushed away from the wall, located the dropped .22, and bent for it. The motion made his head spin dizzily and sickness funnel into his throat, but when he straightened again the nausea receded. He shoved the gun into his free pocket, went back toward Eldorado Street with his left arm pressed hard across his chest, running drunkenly on legs which felt as if they had been rubberized. He fell once, dragged himself up; he could not seem to get enough of the biting cold air into his lungs. The pain in his chest was a fiery, pulsing counterpoint to the hammerlike tempo of his heart.

He went down twice more crossing to Vince's front yard, willed his body up again both times. Fresh blood welled from the two bullet wounds, and it was like a coating of viscid oil on his skin. He wondered dimly if he were bleeding to death. No. He wouldn't bleed to death and he wouldn't freeze to death, remember Ann, remember the baby, remember Vince and Judy and seventy of his friends and neighbors locked inside the church—and Cain, remember Cain.

He flung himself across the last few feet to the garage doors, banging hard against them with one shoulder. Gasping, he fumbled at the latch and got the doors open and shoved them wide against the powdery snow. He lurched inside. The odors of grease and winter dampness permeated the thick ebon interior, and Vince's old Roadmaster gleamed dully in front of him. To the rear, Tribucci could make out the familiar shapes of tool-littered workbench and power saw and drill press, the chain-supported wooden storage platform which protruded from the upper back wall. He leaned against the car, used it to uphold the weight of his body as he shuffled around it toward the area beneath the suspended platform.

The snowmobile, beneath a dun-colored canvas tarp, sat parallel to the wall. With numb fingers he pulled the tarp off, thinking: Let there be gas in the tank. He caught hold of the plexiglass windshield with both hands, turned and dragged the machine out from under the platform. It moved easily across the smooth cement floor on its waxed skis and heavy roller treads. Tribucci laid his shoulder against the windshield, his hip against the edge of the cowl, and pushed the mobile past the Buick and out into the snow in front of the garage.

His vision now was obscured with sweat and shimmering black pain shadows. He pawed urgently at his eyes. When he could see again, he swung one leg over the Etha-foam seat, sat down, and braced his feet, knees up, on the narrow metal running boards on each side of the frame. Then he pressed his forehead against the top of the windshield and fumbled under the cowl, located the storage compartment, found the key in its magnetized metal case.

It seemed to take him minutes to get the key threaded into the ignition slot. He turned it finally, hit the electric starter button, and the engine coughed and didn't catch and he thought, Oh, Christ, please! and pressed the but ton again—and this time the motor came to life in a low, throbbing whine.

Breath whistled through his nostrils. He took one of the Harrington & Richardson .22s from his coat, the one which had not lain in the snow, and wedged it between his crotch and the padded seat, butt outward, where he could get at it instantly; but he left the safety on to guard against accidental discharge. Then he caught the handlebars, shifted into Forward, worked the hand throttle, and sent the snowmobile skimming at an angle across the yard and out onto Eldorado Street.

The jouncing, accelerated motion made razorlike lancinations slice through his chest, and his thoughts were sluggish, his reactions were sluggish. The wind hurled snow back against his face, distorting his vision again. He fought desperately to keep the machine on a steady course, to hold away the congealing red-black mist which had begun again to form inside his head.

Hang on, give me the strength to hang on. . . .

And Tribucci swings the snowmobile around the corner onto Sierra Street, weaving erratically, straightening out again. His arms have taken on the weight of stone. Down the center of the street, beneath the darkened Christmas decorations mocked and made ludicrous by the bleak savagery of a nightmare, between wedges of light that reach out dully through broken doors and shattered and ice-frosted windows. Warm reddish black within, cold whitish black without; ominous shadows, the valley of shadows, *Yea, though I go through the valley of the shadow of death, I will fear no evil. . . .*

He comes past the Sport Shop then, and the church looms ahead of him through the now thinly sifting snowfall. He ducks his head against his left arm, to clear his vision again, as the snowmobile planes across Shasta Street. Cars in the parking lot all dark and icebound, nothing moving—take a chance. He bounces up over the sidewalk curbing—sharp cut of pain, pain and Cain, find Cain, get to Cain—and veers toward the southern front corner.

He sees something, something dark against the snow between Shasta Street and the north wall: man-figure, stopped, poised, not Cain, carrying something that looks like a sack.

The psycho, Tribucci knows instantly it is the psycho.

He makes an unconscious screaming-sobbing sound in his throat, wrenches the snowmobile back to the right. The psycho is running now, limpingly, toward the rear of the church, sack like an obscene caricature of Santa Claus's toybag bouncing against one leg. His right arm crosses his body; the gun which is in his hand flashes: wild shot, missing both Tribucci and the snowmobile.

Leaden fingers fumble at the dashboard, locate the headlight knob, pull it out and twist it to high beam. Bright yellow cones jab glitteringly through the snowy darkness. Tribucci swerves left too abruptly and then overcorrects; the snowmobile begins to yaw. Get him, get him, run him down! and he tries to center the psycho in the headlights but seems to have no more control over the machine, no more control over his own bodily movements. Breath heaves out in out in through his open mouth, pain boils in his chest, weakness spreads tangibly and the red-black mist grows and twists through his mind like a helix, no hold on, and his left hand slips off the handlebar throttle, his right undergoes a paroxysm and jerks forward and sends the smowmobile sliding sideways toward the church, the helix widens blackly and he can't hold on any longer, he can't hold on any

Twenty-Three

When Cain first saw the blob of motive darkness coming unevenly along the center of Sierra Street, he did not know what to think. He stared at it through the thinning flurries: not quite distinguishable, the fuzzy patches of light from the buildings on either side failed to reach it. Stiffened joints protested painfully as he pulled his feet under him and flattened his upper torso across the layer of freezing snow which covered the Mercury's deck.

Drawing nearer, the blob began to take on shape and substance—and when it passed the Sport Shop, Cain recognized it as a snowmobile. But the driver, crouched low behind the snow-speckled windshield, was just another heavy shadow. The psycho? It didn't make sense that he would be coming so openly, coming on a *snowmobile*. . . . Weaving, the machine angled toward the parking lot on a direct line to where Cain was hidden; the whining sound of its engine reached his ears. He still could not make out the driver, but he was thinking then: Tribucci? Whoever was piloting the snowmobile either knew nothing at all about handling one or else was hurt, badly hurt—Tribucci?

Cain saw the mobile lurch again, due west; instead of coming into the lot, it was going parallel to the north wall. When it was fifty feet away, abreast of the Mercury, he was finally able to make out the driver in dark profile: wearing a cap, wearing what appeared to be a woman's cap, wearing a light-colored overcoat. Tribucci! Relief, and a sense of sharp exigency welled inside him—and moving spontaneously, he pushed out from behind the car, ran along its side with his left hand upraised in frenetic signal.

The snowmobile's dual headlights snapped on.

What's he doing, what's he doing? Cain thought, and ran another five steps; but Tribucci did not see him. The machine wobbled left, wobbled right, made a sudden right-angle turn toward the church, swirling a quadrant of light, and tilted up on its near side. Trubicci spilled off the seat, the howl of the motor cut off as it stalled. The snowmobile shuddered to a halt, full on its side, in a thin cumulus of dislodged snow.

Cain saw all this running, cutting toward the corner, coming out into the open—saw then the dark figure forty yards away, twenty yards from the rear corner, and knew why Tribucci had put on the headlights and realized with the abrupt taste of ashes in his mouth just how foolish his own actions had been. But it was too late now to reverse direction, the psycho could see him just as plainly, and without hesitation he threw himself forward and down in a flat running dive. He landed on his belly and left forearm, keeping the Walther up—heard a buzzing slap in the snow to one side of him, the muted sound of a shot. Frantically he propelled himself toward the snowmobile on elbows and knees, putting the machine between himself and the other man. A hole appeared in the plexiglass windshield, spurting ice crystals, making a loud cracking noise; a third bullet spanged somewhere into the undercarriage. He came up against the cowl, arched his body round the curved line of the windshield, and braced his ight forearm in his left palm.

Kubion was running again—hobbled steps—toward the ear corner.

Cain fired after him, missed badly both times and saw im disappear into the shadows at the end wall. He ulled back, trembling slightly, dragging his left arm cross his eyes, and crawled toward the motionless figure f Tribucci lying face down five feet away. Kneeling low eside him, Cain rolled him gently onto his back. Frozen lood and two charred holes in the upper front of his oat; shot twice, unconscious but still clinging to life: nouth open, breathing liquidly. Blood in his throat. Turn is head to one side so he doesn't strangle on it. Nothing lse he could do for Tribucci, not now if at all. He had to oncentrate on the psycho—but he couldn't stay where he vas, he couldn't wait, he had to make some kind of ofensive move. . . .

And he knew then just exactly what it would have to e.

Half dragging his left leg, Kubion ran the length of the hurch's rear wall and came up hard against it at the outh corner. Immediately, black eyes staring back to the north, he set down the gunny sack—four quart mason ars of gasoline siphoned from a car in one of the house arages on Shasta Street; a half dozen oily rags he'd ound, along with the jars, in that same garage—and ipped the empty clip out of the automatic. He heaved it away furiously, located the extra clip buried beneath a vad of currency in his trouser pocket, bills spilling out nnoticed, and jammed that one into the butt.

The impulse, now, had reached a vertex of shrieking nside his head, making it pound thunderously, jumbling and interfusing his thoughts: No pursuit but let him come et him try cat-and-mousing blow his head off Christ!

screwing up screwing up things keep screwing up snow
mobile coming catching me in the open like that just tw
more minutes fucking *snowmobile* so sure only one othe
hick out and killed Tribucci so who was driving had to b
Tribucci killed him but he wasn't dead and got to snow
mobile oh these Eskimo bastards one in the lot alerte
running out fat target but lousy snow cold darknes
throwing off aim and clip empty had to run because hin
with the gun he'd shot Brodie with well all right nothin
really changed and nothing *more* going to screw up te
feet tall can't stop me can't stop *me* come on hick give i
to you burn all of you up watch you burn. . . .

Kubion bent and caught up the sack again; turned hi
body with his weight on his good right leg and backe
away from the building at an angle. When he could see al
of the south church wall and that it too was clear, he ra
along it and stopped beneath the nearest of the stained
glass windows. He lowered the sack a second time, looke
up at the pale light in the window—looked back at th
sack and reached into it and brought out one of th
mason jars, one of the oily rags.

Wedging the jar between his right arm and body, so h
would not have to release the gun, he unscrewed the ca
and fed one end of the rag inside; worked the cap back o
to hold the cloth in place. His body shielded both from th
falling snow, kept the rag dry. He glanced both way
along the wall—nothing stupid hick wasn't going to com
but he would come later bet your ass he'd come late
when he heard them yelling in there when the fire bom
exploded in there when they started dying in there—an
then glanced up again at the stained-glass window. Th
need shouted, shouted, and his breathing grew heavier
the skull grin reformed on his mouth.

All right all *right*.

Kubion brought his left hand up and fumbled for th
box of wooden matches in his shirt pocket.

Cain, leaving Tribucci, crawled back against the padded seat of the snowmobile. He peered closely at the dashboard, ran gloved fingers over both handlebars and located clutch, throttle, gearshift, brake. He had driven a snowmobile only once in his life, two winters before when he and Angie and the Collinses had spent a weekend at Mammoth Mountain; but they were simpler to operate than a car, and it had taken him, that time, no more than a minute to get the knack of it.

He leaned his shoulder hard against the seat, gripped the windshield in his left hand, and shoved upward. The machine rose, tilted, dropped with a flat heavy thud on its skis and roller treads. Cain waited for half a dozen heartbeats, but the shadows at the rear corner remained substantially solid. He opened the top three buttons of his coat, tucked the Walther into his belt, and then wrapped his left hand around the near handlebar and engaged the clutch lever; his right moved along the dash to the starter button, pressed it. The headlights dimmed slightly as the engine coughed stuttering to life, brightened again as the stuttering smoothed into a stabilized rumble.

Still nothing at the corner.

Cain lifted a leg over the seat, maintaining his grip on the clutch lever, and pulled himself into a hunched sitting position. He caught hold of the right handlebar, shifted into forward, opened quarter throttle, and let the clutch out slowly. Tht machine began to move forward. He spun a sharp turn to the northwest, spraying snow, and made sure he had full control before opening the throttle wider. Nearly abreast of the rear corner, he made another looping turn to the south; straightened out. The headlights were like probing yellow blades slicing into the night's dark fabric, and he could see all the area between church and cottage. No sign of the psycho. He'd gone around on the south side then, maybe all the way around to the front; whatever he'd been carrying in that sack was bound

to be lethal, and God, if he had time to open the locke
front door. . . .

Grimly, Cain give the snowmobile full-bore throttl
and sent it skimming to the south equidistant between th
two buildings, leaning his head out to the left becaus
frozen snow and the webbed bullet hole made the wind
shield inpenetrable. When he came on the south corner
he circled out and made another hard skidding left.

And the sweeping beams found Kubion in close to th
wall, halfway toward the front.

Having heard the engine, having seen the headlamp
glow before the gleaming shafts cut around to him, h
was backing away rapidly: sooty face nakedly hideous
right arm locked, gun leveled, left arm cradling a quart ja
with a rag hanging down out of it like a brown-spottec
tongue. Fire bomb, Cain thought, oh Jesus—and Kubion
dipped his face along his upper right arm, to shield hi
eyes from the blinding light, and squeezed off a wild shot
Cain snapped his head back partway, hunching his body
lower, gripping the handlebars with such pressure that hi
wrists ached and he could feel, vaguely, pain surge again
through the glass cut in his right palm.

Kubion fired again, there was a screeching fingernails-
on-a-blackboard sound as the bullet scraped a furrow
across the right front edge of the cowl, and then Cain saw
him glance feverishly over his shoulder and come to the
realization that he was not going to be able to beat the
onrushing machine to the front corner. He jerked to a
stop, limned against the wall like a spotlighted deer, and
triggered a third shot that sang high over Cain's head.
The snowmobile was almost on top of him now.

Dropping the jar, twisting his body, he flung himself
out of the way.

Cain tried to turn into him, missed by a foot and went
by. He braked immediately, frenziedly, and swung the
snowmobile in a tight turn, saw that Kubion had landed
on both knees and was struggling up. The moment the

head lights repinned him, Cain opened the throttle wide again. Kubion staggered sideways in the deep snow, lifted the automatic and fired a fourth time; glass shattered and the left beam winked out. But Cain sustained control, the snowmobile bore down relentlessly.

Kubion slowed and tensed for another leap.

This time Cain was ready.

Almost upsetting the machine, he veered in the same direction—toward the church—at the instant Kubion made his jump. Kubion's right foot came down, left leg trailing aslant; the upthrust, rounded metal guard on the right ski hit flesh, snapped bone, just below the knee and sent him spinning and rolling violently through the snow.

Pain lanced white-hot in Kubion's leg and groin and lower belly, and ice granules filled his open mouth and pricked like slivers in his lungs. He came up finally on his buttocks, coughing, sucking breath, clawing at his eyes. The snowmobile, ten yards away, was swinging around once more and he heard the shrill howl of its engine as the single high-beam light struck him, again half blinded him.

Inside his head the impulse screamed and screamed and screamed—snowmobile hick son of a bitch with snowmobile Jesus Christ why won't things stop screwing up ten feet tall you *can't* do this to me kill you kill your snowmobile kill you all kill—and he twisted over onto his right knee, left leg useless, bones broken and grating, pain pulsing, and brought his right arm up

and he didn't have the automatic,

he had lost the frigging *gun,*

and the screaming was a rage of sound, the snowmobile's engine was a rage of sound, glaring yellow eye hurtling down on him and he pitched his body flat and rolled and rolled but then the screaming in his head and the screaming of the machine blended into one and a new, supreme agony exploded in the small of his back, surging metal hurled him broken-doll-like toward the church wall. His head struck the icy wood jarringly, more agon bursting like shrapnel through his brain. He lifted onto hi right hand and tried to stand up, tried to just kneel, but hi body was all searing pain, paralyzed by pain.

Six feet away the snowmobile had come to a stop, it one headlight shining over his head, and dimly he saw Cain rise up out of it, saw the gun in his gloved fingers a he came slowly forward. Spittle drooled from the corner of Kubion's mouth, freezing there, and he thought You won't shoot Eskimo snowmobile shit not face to face began screaming aloud then, screaming, "Won't shoo hick bastard won't do it oh you fucking—"

Cain shot him three times in the head at point-blank range.

Twenty-Four

They heard inside the church the initial exchange ›f shots, and they heard the accelerated whine of the nowmobile's engine, and they heard those final three, lose-spaced reports beyond the south wall. A kind of ›reathless paralysis succeeded the first and carried them hrough the second, but when the last came and was fol-owed by silence from without, the thin edge of panic fi-ıally crumbled away.

Bodies massed confusedly toward the front; there was a ising torrent of sounds and cries. Ann's newborn daugh-er began to wail. Gibbering, Frank McNeil stumbled ›nto the pulput and tried to force his way into the vestry ›ast Joe Garvey; Garvey threw him against the wall, hit ıim in the stomach in a release of pent-up emotion, and ⁄IcNeil went down gasping and moaning and lay with his ıands over his head. Coopersmith stood back hard ıgainst the entrance doors, arms spread, and shouted, 'Stay calm, for God's sake stay calm, we don't know vhat's happening, we've got enough people hurt as it is!"

They didn't listen to him; they did not even hear him. Chey had lived in fear of the worst for all the long, long

hours, and they expected the worst now. Have to get ou
their faces said. Going to be killed anyway, have to g
out. . . .

Heavy footfalls on the stairs outside—and the a voic
a voice wearily raised no more than a few decibels abo
normal but still loud enough so that almost everyo
could hear it and recognize it. That voice did what n
other but one could have: it froze them all in place agai
it stilled them, it transformed terror into incipient relief.

"This is Cain," the voice said. "This is Cain, I've g
the key and I'm going to open the doors, give me room."

Key scraping the lock as Coopersmith swept the
back, clearing space; doors opening.

Cain stood there with his feet braced apart and th
limp form of John Tribucci cradled close to his ches
"They're dead, all three of them," he said. "You'r
free now, they're dead."

And the people of Hidden Valley surged around hi
like waves around a pinnacle of rock.

Twenty-Five

For the first few seconds after consciousness re-
urned fuzzy and disjointed, Tribucci did not know where
: was. Someone was holding his hand, chafing it briskly,
ıd there were faint garbled voices, and there was soft-
ːss beneath him and warmth over and around him. He
ıd no pain, only a tingling seminumbness everywhere
ccept in his face and in the hand that was being rubbed.
ain! he thought immediately, and made a noise far down
his throat, and wanted to sit up. Gentle hands held him
ill.

He fluttered his eyes open. Bright shimmering grayness,
ıt then dissolving and images beginning to take shape—
ale blue walls, fluorescent ceiling lights, face hovering
ver him as if disembodied and saying words that now he
ould comprehend: "Johnny, it's all right. You're in my
nergency room, son, it's all right."

He squeezed his eyes shut, opened them again, and this
me he could see more clearly. His throat worked.
Webb?"

"Yes, it's Webb."

"You . . . you're out of the church. . . ."

"All of us, Johnny—we're all safe. Cain too."

"Thank God. But how? How did Cain . . .?"

"There's no time for explanations now. Sally and I a going to put you under anesthesia; you've got two bulle in you, and we've got to get them out. But we wanted y awake first, there's something you have to know."

Ann, he thought suddenly. "Oh, God, Ann, what abo Ann, she—"

"She's fine, she's upstairs in my room; I gave h something to make her sleep. Johnny, listen carefull Ann is fine. When she found out in the church what y and Cain had gone to do, she went into labor. And s gave birth; she gave birth there in the church to a healt little girl. Do you understand, Johnny? Ann's fine and t baby's fine, you've got a daughter."

The fuzziness would not release his thoughts, but understood, yes, and he tried to smile, lips cracking a stretching faintly. "A daughter," he said. "Ann's fine a we have a daughter."

"That's right, that's good. You've got everything to li for now. You're badly hurt, but you're going to liv you're going to keep on fighting; you're not going to st fighting for a second, Johnny, do you hear me?"

"Not for a second," he said.

Edwards sighed softly and his face retreated, and Sal Chilton's wavered into Tribucci's vision. He felt the sti of a needle in the crook of his left arm.

"She looks like Ann, doesn't she?" he asked.

"Just like Ann," Sally said. "Wait until you see her."

Tribucci felt himself beginning to drift. "Marika," said, "we're going to name her Marika." Drifting, drifti —and his last thought before the anesthesia took hi under was that if it had been a boy, they would sure have called him Zachary. . . .

The Reverend Peter Keyes waited in the adjacent ant room, his now professionally, if hurriedly, bandaged rig and resting in his lap, left hand clutching his Bible. The hot of morphine Sally had given him minutes ago, to ease he pain, had also made him drowsy; but he would not leep yet—not yet.

After a time, eyes tightly closed, he raised the Bible nd held it against his breast. "Oh Lord my rock," he said aloud, softly, "thank you for not forsaking us all. . . ."

In the parlor at the front of the house, Coopersmith sat n silent vigil with Ellen and with Vince and Judy.

As soon as Edwards came in to tell them Johnny was oing to live—and he *would* tell them that, a man who ad been through what Tribucci had would not be allowed to die now—Coopersmith thought he would find Cain and try to put into words some of what he felt in his heart. He had never had a feeling of love for a man before, other than his two sons; but now, tonight, he loved both Cain and John Tribucci. All the hate and all the pressure and all the terror were gone; tomorrow there would be pain and sorrow when he woke and remembered nd saw the ravaged face of a Hidden Valley that would never be quite the same again—yet for what was left of his day, he would have nothing except love inside him.

Sitting there with Ellen's head against his shoulder, he was very tired—a physical weariness, nothing more. When the hate and terror drained away, they had carried with them the inner tiredness and the last remnants of hose earlier feelings of uselessness and incompetence and emptiness. And he would not let them come back, any of hem. He was sixty-six years of age, that was true, but he had lived a long and rich and fruitful life, and he was *still* iving it, and he had his health and all his faculties, and he had the capacity to love, and he had the reciprocal love of an unselfish woman who had shared his bed and his dreams and his rewards for more than forty years. He hadn't realized it before, but that was so much more than some men had. So much more.

He smiled wanly across at Vince and Judy, gave them an encouraging nod, and they returned both in kind. Like him, they seemed to know that death and tragedy would not touch any of them again for some time to come.

And within the semidarkened church, sitting slumped and thinking about many things and about nothing at all, Cain did not hear the doors open or the soft steps come forward to the pew. But after a time he sensed that he was not alone and turned his head, and Rebecca was standing there watching him.

"Hello, Zachary," she said. She was drawn and grave but there was a kind of self-assurance, a kind of pride, in her eyes and in her carriage. "I thought you might still be here."

"Yeah," he said. "I was going to leave pretty soon, I want to find out how Tribucci is."

"I just came from Dr. Edwards' house. He's operating now to remove the bullets. He wants Johnny in a hospital as soon as possible because of the threat of pneumonia. Greg Novak is taking one of the snowmobiles to Coldville at dawn, so there'll be helicopters in some time tomorrow."

"He'll live," Cain said positively. "He'll live."

"I know he will; we all do."

"He's a fine man. They don't come any finer."

Rebecca sat down beside him, turning her body so that she was facing him directly. "You look exhausted, Zachary."

"I killed two men tonight," he said. There was nothing, no expression, in his voice.

"And saved seventy-five other lives. That's the only really important thing, isn't it?"

"Yes—it has to be."

"I don't suppose any of us will ever really forget what happened today," she said. "But I've got to believe that things do stop hurting after a while."

"They do," Cain told her. "After a while."

"Will you . . . keep on living here in the valley?"

"No," he said. "No."

"Where will you go?"

"Back to San Francisco."

"And then what?"

"See if I can get my old job back, or one like it. Start ebuilding my life."

"I'm not so sure I can keep on living here either. Too uch has happened, too many things have changed." She aused. "What's San Francisco like?"

"It can be a beautiful city—the most beautiful city in e world."

"Would I like it if I came there?"

He looked at her for a long moment. "I think so," he aid finally. "I think you might."

"I'll be staying at the Tribucci house for a few days," he said, "with Judy and Ann and the baby. Vince will go ith Johnny. Now especially it's a time none of us should e alone."

He waited, not speaking.

"Will you come for dinner tomorrow?"

"Yes," he said, "I'd like that."

"Will you walk me there now?"

Cain nodded, and they stood together and strode slowy out of the church. It was still snowing lightly, but there vas very little wind; the clouds overhead had begun diiding, and you could see patches of deep velvet sky hrough the fissures. The storm was nearly over.

In a few short hours it would be the day before Christas.